Martin Stanley was born in Middlesbrough in 1972. He was educated in Teesside and later in Bristol, where he studied graphic design.

In addition to *A Funny Thing Happened...*, he is also the author of: *The Curious Case of the Missing Moolah, The Green-eyed Monster, Bone Breakers, The Hunters* and *The Glasgow Grin*. In addition to the Stanton brothers books he has authored *The Gamblers*, a violent noir tale set in Bristol, and *The Greatest Show in Town*, a collection of crime and noir stories.

He lives, works and socialises in London.

You can find him hanging around online at his blog *www.thegamblersnovel.wordpress.com*, where he reviews books, talks crime fiction, and occasionally posts up short stories.

If you wish to contact him personally (to boost his fragile ego and congratulate him on writing something you enjoyed, to ask him stuff, tell him stuff, or just to join his subscriber's list) please email *thegamblersnovel@gmail.com*.

Get *The Greatest Show in Town (and other shorts)* for FREE when you sign up to Martin's mailing list at *www.martinstanleyauthor.com*, along with future access to other exclusive, never-before-published Stanton brothers' short stories.

A FUNNY THING HAPPENED ON THE WAY TO BILLINGHAM FORUM

(A STANTON BROTHERS THRILLER)

MARTIN STANLEY

The author would like to thank Dan Sollis for his invaluable assistance in editing this novel into something readable. He devoted a lot of hours to the cause, and evidence of his work can be found on every page. *A Funny Thing...* didn't come together easily, but Dan's efforts made the grunt work of editing and polishing a lot easier than it would have been if I was doing the work myself.

The basic geography contained in this book is more or less accurate, but the locations, buildings and businesses are either used fictitiously or are products of the author's imagination.

Cover photo, cover design & book layout: Martin Stanley

Author's note:

Teesside locals may very well recognise some of the street names and areas used in this book, but the businesses and residences are either fictional or they exist in a form that has been twisted by the writer's imagination. Locals with a keen sense of recent history will be able to place this particular Stanton brothers' adventure in a fixed year, because Billingham Forum was fixed up a few years ago. Some of the other areas mentioned in this novel are entirely fictional. Liberties have also been taken with the geography.

1.

Kevin Nicholson awoke in agonising pain, but his eyes remained closed.

He didn't want anybody to know he was awake. The thought of going through all that pain and humiliation again was too much to bear. It took everything he had not to let his body succumb to shock. His bottom lip trembled occasionally, but he just about managed to hold it together.

Blood seeped from the folds of his buttocks, leaving sticky trails as it ran down the inside of his thighs. Its copper scent was in the air, beneath the earthier smells of shit and piss.

He was too afraid to move. It even hurt to breathe.

The slightest twitch sent spasms of pain through his bowels. Just the thought of moving made him want to vomit.

For a moment, he drifted, letting his mind float free, and tried to forget that he was lying on a cold concrete floor with his pants around his ankles and his hands tied behind his back. He ignored the blood and faeces that leaked from his torn rectum and disregarded the mocking laughter from the other side of the garage.

A cool breeze swept through the room. Somebody must have opened the door.

Kevin wanted to watch, but he was still far too terrified to open his eyes. Rubber-soled feet scraped the concrete as men shuffled away from the building. The sounds of laughter drifted outside and began to fade.

Kevin opened his eyes slightly so that they appeared closed from a distance. Two silhouettes – one tall and slim, the other much fatter – stood by the doorway of a prefab office at the rear of the building. When Kevin realised they weren't paying him any attention, he risked opening his eyes a little more.

The tall, slim figure was Jonno Fielding. He wore dark blue jeans, a grey shirt folded at the sleeves, and a blood-spattered white apron tied tightly around the neck and waist. In his gloved right hand was a long broom handle, the tip still glistening with blood. Kevin's blood.

The fat man in a vintage military jacket and baggy blue jeans was Harry

Sparks. He pointed in Kevin's direction. "He's in a bad way."

"Am I supposed to fuckin' care?"

"I'm serious, boss."

"So am I."

"You went too far."

Jonno scoffed. "Too far? I'm trying to make a fuckin' point here, *Harold.*"

"Yeah, but…"

"What *should* I have done? Held his fuckin' hand through the ordeal? Given him a peck on the cheek and some comforting words afterwards?"

"I'm not saying that…"

"The moment I look weak in front of these men is the moment I lose everything. One of these pricks, mebbe even you, might decide I'm a bit of a sister and move in on my action. I've got too much riding on this to care about your delicate fuckin' sensibilities."

"I don't wanna move in on your…"

Jonno waved the broom handle in Kevin's direction.

"This mong lost two grand's worth of shit. Am I supposed to let that slide?"

"No, I'm not saying…"

"Then what are you saying?"

Harry's gaze drifted in Kevin's direction. The junky narrowed his eyes.

"He would've paid eventually, boss."

"Not seen much fuckin' evidence of that. In fact, I've not seen much of this prick at all in the last few weeks. The fact I had to pay somebody to find him suggests he was doing his best to avoid me."

"If we don't do owt, he's gonna die."

"So what? When he's gone, we'll chop him up and bury the bits. Who's gonna miss this junky piece of shit?"

Kevin's heart thumped against his ribcage. Everything now depended on the goodwill of Harry Sparks, which meant he was fucked. He fought the urge to shiver, kept his breathing slow and quiet, and maintained the pretence of being unconscious. Regrets tumbled through his mind like falling confetti. His life flashed before his eyes. It was a dreadful life littered with bad decisions. And now it was about to end.

Harry stepped closer to Jonno. "Billy Chin," he said. "He's gonna miss this particular piece of shit."

Kevin almost opened his eyes wide with alarm – this was an unexpected development.

"Are you serious? This fuckin' loser?"

Harry nodded. "They're tight."

Which Kevin knew was a lie. And Harry damn well knew it too.

"How tight?"

"Like a fuckin' drum skin."

Billy and Kevin were friendly, but they weren't tight. They shared conversations and the occasional dose in one of Billy's squats. Sometimes they did each other favours and exchanged useful gossip. Billy might spare him a thought if he died, but he wouldn't really care. Of course, he'd pretend to care if there was something in it for him, and would use his death to leverage money or favours out of Jonno.

"Billy hates everybody," Jonno replied.

"True, yet he still has a soft spot for this gadgie."

"Why?"

Harry shrugged. "Who knows how Billy's mind works? All I know is that they're tight, and Billy's gonna be pissed if this gadgie ends up missing. Christ, Billy's gonna be radged, anyway – raping one of his boys with a splintered broom handle isn't gonna put him in the best of moods."

"Fuck Billy."

Harry snorted. "You gonna say that to his face, then?"

Jonno shuffled uncomfortably and dropped the handle on the ground. Harry let out a quiet humourless chuckle.

"The last person who told Billy to fuck himself was Bob Bracha. Remember him?"

Jonno shrugged his shoulders and looked away.

"Although nobody calls the poor cunt Bob anymore, do they? Nowadays, he's got the catchier name of Snake Plissken on account of the patch he wears because Billy carved his left eyeball out of his fuckin' head. Mind you; he could just as well have been called Ironside given how his fuckin' legs don't work too good nowadays."

"Oh, so I'm s'posed to let that piece of shit get away with it," Jonno replied, pointing at Kevin.

Harry shook his head. "Does he look like he's got away with owt?"

Jonno glanced at Kevin and kicked the broom handle away. "Mebbe not."

"He's wearing his arsehole on the outside," added Harry. "He's living fuckin' proof of what happens when somebody messes with you."

"Still…"

"Still nothing, boss. We really don't wanna get on Billy's bad side. It's not worth it. If his people stop buying our shit, we stand to lose a lotta custom – considering they're all junkies. But if his people stop *selling* our stuff, too, then we're gonna find it much harder to shift. And they will stop selling if they think they're gonna get killed every time summat goes wrong.

"But we can still salvage this. Get him to a hospital. Turn him into an example. Let him become an urban legend the junkies tell each other over a bubbling spoon. *'Oh, shit, you remember Kev Nicholson? I heard he got impaled on a fuckin' broom handle for losing two grand of Jonno's money.' 'Oh, really? I heard it were only two hundred.'* Use it as a means of keeping the others in line."

Jonno nodded absentmindedly, kneading his bottom lip like putty. Then he turned in Kevin's direction again and craned forward slightly. Kevin's eyes became narrow slits. The garage returned to shadows.

"You reckon he can hear us?"

Kevin's heart kicked up another gear.

Harry shook his head. "He passed out after a few minutes of Bedknobs and Broomsticks. He's fucked up. He's not gonna come round anytime soon. And if we don't do summat sharpish he's not gonna come round at all."

"Okay, then. Go get Jim. Then gimme five minutes."

"Why?"

"'Cause I'm telling you, that's why," Jonno replied.

Harry moved past Jonno and into the office.

"Oh, and Harry?"

The fat man stopped, turned and looked through the office window. "What?"

"If you ever stop me again when I'm in the middle of punishing somebody then I'll turn my fuckin' anger on you. Got it?"

Harry nodded once. "Loud and clear."

"Now go get Jim."

Harry exited through the back door.

Jonno looked over at Kevin, who remained still and silent, and then turned away and walked over to an untidy pile of discarded car parts, boxes, and pallets. He leant forward and rummaged through the detritus until he found a retractable ladder. Opening it to full length, Jonno placed the ladder against the painted concrete wall beside the office.

He climbed to the top of the ladder, took a knife from his apron pocket and carefully pushed the blade around the edge of a block. He prised it out from the surrounding bricks and held the hollow, painted cast against his chest. Jonno rummaged in the cavity, removed something, and put it in his back pocket.

He pushed the cast back into position until it sat flush with the other blocks. Then he smeared something around the edges of it with his fingers and clambered back down. He retracted the ladder and placed it back where he found it. Jonno dropped what looked like a small tube of paint in the apron pocket, wiped his fingers, and pulled a bundle of cash from the back of his jeans

Shouting the names of Harry and Jim repeatedly, Jonno counted off two sums of money from the main bundle before he put it back in his jeans.

Jim Hanway came into the room first. He wore a yellow hooded tracksuit so big and shiny it looked like a Hazmat suit on his short, skinny frame. His face was all prominent teeth and cheekbones. And these rodent features were made more unpleasant by pale, heavily pockmarked skin and a thin neck adorned with crude tattoos.

Jonno pushed some cash into Jim's right hand. He looked at the money with a confused expression. His nose twitched a few times. His mouth opened as if he had something interesting to say.

"Don't bother asking what I think you're gonna ask," Jonno said. "Just put this tit in the back of your car and take him to hospital. Then take the car over to Feldman so he can get rid of it."

Jim's face twitched again as he studied Kevin. "Right to the hospital entrance?" he said with a hint of fear in his voice. "There's cameras all over it. Some fucker'll recognise us, like."

"Then use your initiative, for fucksakes. Dump him nearby, where there's no cameras. Then call an ambulance to come get him."

Harry emerged from the office. Jonno fanned several fifties in front of the fat man's face. "Take these to Ben Moody and thank him kindly."

Harry counted the notes. "Didn't you promise him five hundred?"

"So?"

"I only count three-fifty here."

"And?"

"He's gonna kick up a fuss."

"The day I start caring about the upsetting the feelings of the junky community is the day I retire from this fuckin' business. Moody can consider himself lucky he's getting owt from me. Besides, considering he's just snitched out Billy's BFF he's not gonna kick up too much fuckin' fuss, is he? Not if he wants to keep his eyes in his head."

Harry pocketed the money and started walking away. Jonno clicked his fingers repeatedly and called him back. "Where the fuck're you going?"

Harry's nose wrinkled and his eyebrows lowered into a confused scowl. "To pay Ben."

"That fuckwit can wait," Jonno said, pointing at the junky. "Help Jim carry this piece of shite."

Kevin closed his eyes. He took inhaled slowly and braced himself for pain. Two pairs of feet scraped and scuffed the nearby concrete. Clumsy hands grabbed his damp wrists and ankles and struggled to maintain a decent grip.

Kevin tried to swallow but couldn't. His mouth was desert dry, and terror made his mind buzz. The anticipation was almost unbearable. He didn't want to move. Even the simple act of breathing sent twinges of pain through his body.

Harry counted it down.

Three…

Kevin's face tightened.

Two…

His legs tensed.

One…

He let the air out of his lungs.

Lift.

Harry and Jim grunted as they heaved him off the ground.

Shards of pain sliced Kevin from bowels to guts. He tried not to scream, but the discomfort was too great, and he let out a piercing shriek.

This sudden outburst made Jim yelp with surprise and let go of his ankles. When Kevin's feet hit the ground, another wave of agony tore through him, and he howled again.

Jonno guffawed. "Aw, did the nasty man scare you, Jimmy?"

Jim tried to argue his case, but his boss wasn't interested and waved a disinterested hand in their direction. "Don't care, Jim. Just pick him up properly. If you drop him a second time, I'm gonna fuck you up."

They lifted Kevin off the ground again and staggered towards the entrance. Every step and stumble sent fresh spasms through him: each one worse than the last. And as pain built to a crescendo, the room wobbled and blurred. Spots danced and multiplied before Kevin's eyes until everything disappeared and finally, mercifully, his world faded to black.

2.

Bobby Manning cast suspicious glances at the inhabitants of the pub, hamming it up with narrowed eyes and fast jerks of the head. So it didn't take the elderly regulars long to mark him out as odd. They huddled together, warming their pints with body heat and too much breathy conversation, and made more than a few wary glimpses of their own. They studied his gaunt face, the scruffy clothes, and the track marks on the inside of both arms. Almost without thinking, many of them pulled coats and bags a little closer, and some moved their wallets to pockets that weren't as easy to pick.

A barman with a lumpy face and greasy thinning hair attempted to wipe down the wooden surface of the bar, but he was so busy watching Bobby that he rubbed the same spot like he was in a loop. His jaw flexed repeatedly, betraying his anger.

Eric Stanton noticed all the eyes on his drinking partner and leant in close, whispering: "Stop acting like you're in some kinda spy film. All your bullshit's drawing attention. You might think you resemble James Bond, but you don't. At best you're Cunt, Junky Cunt."

Bobby curled his lips in disgust and gathered together his belongings.

"Not having that. That's well outta order, mate," he said, putting on his jacket. He tried working the zipper, but his hands were shaking too much. After a few moments of struggle he gave up and left the coat unzipped. Like the rest of his clothes, it was far too big. It would have fit perfectly a year ago before the drugs whittled him down to skin and bone.

Eric knocked back his pint and looked up at him. "Then I'll be seeing you. The door's that way."

Bobby wouldn't leave until he had his money. He was shaking and twitching and desperate. It looked like it had been some time since his last fix.

"We're in the middle of nowhere," Eric hissed, glancing around. "None of these people know who you are. And if you actually paid attention you'd realise they don't wanna know you, either.

"*You're* the one who suggested this fuckin' place, not me. I didn't even know Mickleby existed until I found it on the map."

Bobby shuffled on the spot. "Can't help being paranoid."

"Jonno might be well connected, but he's not *that* well connected, so relax."

Bobby stayed on his feet and continued playing with his zip.

Eric rolled his eyes. "Well, if you're not gonna relax then do me a favour and go someplace else. I quite fancy drinking my next pint in peace."

He nodded at the barman and tapped the empty glass with his forefinger. The barman didn't return the nod, but he did start pouring another lager.

Bobby saw foam bubbling on the fresh pint and licked his lips. He turned back towards Eric with a faint smile on his face and slowly sat down. Eric held up two fingers, and the barman worked on a second glass.

Bobby pulled the slider up and down the length of the zip without thinking and stared into space. Eric tried getting his companion's attention by clicking his fingers in front of his face, but the junky was too far into his trance to notice. Eric sighed, got up from his seat, paid the taciturn barman and slammed the drinks down in front of Bobby. Beer sloshed out of one of the glasses and made a puddle on the table.

The sound made Bobby jump. He stopped playing with the zipper and reached towards the perfect pint. Eric tutted and shook his head.

"Yours is the other one."

Bobby grabbed the other glass and took a large swig. "I'm taking a real risk doing this," he said. "Gotta know me back's being covered."

"Fine," Eric said. "Consider yourself covered."

"If Jonno finds out I'm involved he's gonna shag me fuckin' arse with a broom handle. I'm not even kidding about that. He put Kev Nicholson in hospital 'cause of it. The poor bastard still needs to shit in a bag over six months later. Kinda like me bowel movements regular mate, if you know what I mean?"

Eric thought about how far his companion had fallen in the space of a few months. Various addictions were destroying his ability to think rationally. It was obvious that Bobby had more to worry about than broom handle rape. If Jonno found out who was setting him up, it was more likely to end in death.

Still, if Bobby was happy to practice self-deception, Eric wasn't about to convince him otherwise. Instead, he nodded and said: "Yeah. I get you. All you gotta do is point out the main players and give us a breakdown of how it works."

Bobby scoffed. "Like it's that easy."

"Easy as you want it to be. If you explain the set-up, we'll sort the rest."

"Well, it's a three-man job," Bobby said, dropping the volume. "And it's pretty exposed."

"How exposed?"

"Billingham Forum, during the daytime."

"Hiding in plain sight?"

Bobby nodded. "Pretty much."

"Sounds like it could get messy?"

"Not if youse do it right."

"Go on."

"This thing's now so slick it's a two-man operation," Bobby replied. "Way back when we first set it up nobody trusted anybody and there was goons all over the shop. Everywhere you turned there was another meathead in a zipped up jacket with a gun near his armpit. But now… well, like I sez, both sides trust each other, and they've got pretty fuckin' complacent."

"Just two men?"

Bobby nodded again. "You've got Harry Sparks delivering cash for Jonno and A N Other delivering aitch for Ramon."

"Carrasco?"

"That's right."

"I've heard of him."

"What've you heard?"

Eric shrugged. "That he's a big thing down in Leeds."

"Pretty much."

"Will there be trouble?"

"Not if youse are careful."

"Okay."

"Careful means you hit the money *after* the exchange. Careful means you do it quick and make it look like a fluke."

"So we're not touching the drugs?"

Bobby shook his head and sipped his pint. "If you hit both at the same time then they're gonna know it were a set-up. And once they've worked that shit out it won't be too fuckin' long before they realise it were me what's behind it."

Eric smiled. "That's fine with me. I'm not interested in Heroin," he said. "Who's working for Ramon?"

"There's two I know of," Bobby replied. "One's a white boy who wants to wake up one morning and find he's turned black. Dresses like he's in a bad gangsta rap video with a shitload of gold round his neck and his trousers around his fuckin' ankles. Talks like he's from the ghetto, calls hisself ToJo, but he's actually a rich boy named Toby from deepest darkest Yorkshire. His Dad owns the Jones Brewery."

"Sounds like a fuckin' idiot."

"He is, but he's always packing blades, and he's got a gun in the glove compartment. It'd be dangerous to underestimate him."

"And the other?"

"The second gadgie's an old fella called Leo. He's about sixty, but don't let that fool you. Underneath that wrinkly fuckin' skull of his is a sharp brain. He always carries a gun. And if push comes to shove he'll use it too. He looks like that baldie outta *The Shield* but a lot meaner."

"How d'you know all this?"

Bobby shrugged. "I used to do the exchange for Jonno before it became a two-man job. I spoke with ToJo and Leo a few times, back in the day. I kept me ears open, listened and learned, and fixated on the details. You know how it is, right?"

"And since Harry took over the drop, I've followed 'em a few times. Watched at a discreet distance. I've seen ToJo three times and Leo once."

"When's the next exchange?"

"Couple of weeks. It's always on the same date."

"That doesn't gimme much time to get a crew together."

"True, but if you don't hit 'em now, it'll probably be too late."

"Why?"

"The Forum's closing."

Eric frowned. "Since when?"

"Since they decided to fix it up," Bobby said. "Gonna be closed for a couple of years. You not read the local papers?"

Eric shook his head.

"Well, trust me, it's closing. Once that happens there'll be no way of knowing when and where the next deal's going down without following them around again."

"Then I guess we better do it sooner rather than later."

Bobby grinned.

Eric drained his pint. "So whaddaya want for the info?"

"Half."

Eric laughed humourlessly. "Forget it. We're the ones taking all the risk."

"Then gimme an equal split?"

"That's not gonna happen either."

"But I'm the one providing the info."

"You're not getting a quarter share."

Bobby's mouth turned down. He looked like he was about to cry. "Then I'm prepared to accept ten grand."

"That's a shame because I'm only prepared to offer five."

The junky's eyes glistened. "That's a bit cheap, innit?"

"Take it or leave it."

Bobby bit his fingernails, mulled it over, and spat the pieces on the table. Then he smiled without showing teeth, leant in slightly, trying to be friendly, and patted Eric's shoulder gently. "Fine, I'll take it. But I wannit up front."

Eric shook his head. "No fuckin' way."

Bobby pulled away and sighed like an angry teenager. "I've got expenses."

"You mean smack?"

"Nah, legitimate business expenses, like."

"You mean needles for smack?"

Bobby let out a disgusted tut. "Fuck off," he said in a voice that was somewhere between a whisper and a sigh, soft enough to be carried away by a light breeze. Despite the attempt to keep his voice down, Eric heard Bobby.

"If we're in a partnership then you've gotta shoulder *some* of the risks. If I give you five grand up front, there's no incentive for you to tell the truth. You can fuck us over good-style, safe in the knowledge that you've got your dough. You get three hundred now and the rest once the job's done."

"Half?"

Eric shook his head. "It's non-negotiable."

"It's shit."

He pointed at the exit. "Don't like it then leave, and feel free to peddle it to somebody else."

Bobby tapped the table with a bony finger. "How'd I know you'll even pay us. For all I know you could fuck us over and skedaddle with the proceeds. You won't hafta pay owt if Jonno grabs me."

Eric leant in, his expression serious, eyes cold. "Listen up, 'cause I'll only say it once. I'm not in the business of fuckin' over my partners. When we shake hands – that's it – we're partners. That means while the job's on if you're in trouble then I'm gonna fight your corner. Nowt else matters.

You getting me?"

He extended his hand. Bobby stared at the palm for a few moments, his expression pensive, almost like he was studying the life and fate lines before he sighed and shook the hand limply. "Yeah, I hear," he replied.

Eric stood up and put on his leather jacket. He hitched his thumb towards the exit. "I'll drive you back," he said. "And you can start filling me in on all the details."

Bobby followed him to the door. "Whaddaya wanna know?"

They exited into the rainswept courtyard and walked into the wind. The cold rain stung their faces. Eric pushed forward and walked across the road to where his car was parked. He opened the door and climbed into the driver's seat, and then he opened the passenger side door. Bobby got in beside him.

"So whaddaya wanna know?" Bobby asked again.

Eric turned the key in the ignition and revved the car. "We've got about twenty-five miles till we get to Middlesbrough. So why don't you pass the time by telling me *everything?*"

3.

Eric followed the directions that Bobby supplied and came to a stop outside a surprisingly attractive, modern flat block not too far from Grove Hill. A tall sign declared that it was the work of Owden Construction, which no doubt meant that it had been built using stolen bricks and mortar, assembled by the finest illegal immigrant labour that the slave wages could buy.

"Nice place. Who lives here?"

"Me girlfriend."

Eric couldn't help but be surprised. "You have a girlfriend?"

Bobby gave him a fish-eyed stare. "Drugs aren't me only hobby, you know."

"Since when did taking poison intravenously constitute a hobby?"

"Pastime, then."

"How does your lady friend feel about the drug use?"

Bobby sniffed and turned his face towards the flat block. "She's into it. And a lotta other things besides."

"Then how the fuck can she afford a place like this?"

Bobby sneered. "Daddy pays the bills. Thinks the sun shines outta his little girl's backside," he said. "It's a perfect set-up."

Eric laughed. "You do realise he'll wise up sooner or later?"

"By the time that happens, we'll be long gone."

Bobby ran his fingers along the top of the glove box, pressing them into the craters of melted plastic that somebody had made by stubbing out cigarettes on the surface. "Why don'tcha come on in and say hello?"

"Thought you didn't wanna be seen in public with me? Thought you wanted to be *low key?* Otherwise, what was the point of going out to Mickleby?"

"Nobody knows I'm here," he said. "Come on in and enjoy yourself."

Eric snorted. "Enjoy myself? Are you offering me smack?"

Bobby lifted his hands high to shoulder height with the palms facing Eric. "Whoa, calm down: you got the shitty end of the stick there, mate. It's not smack I'm offering."

Eric's eyes narrowed in suspicion. "Then what?"

Bobby gave a slight shoulder shrug. "An hour with me girlfriend."

Eric grinned. "Are you for real?"

"Mebbe if you and her hit it off, you might wanna increase me cut of the take?"

Eric laughed out loud. "I'll give you points for blind fuckin' cheek."

"Mebbe if she does a good job you might wanna go as high as seven and a half?"

"That'd need to be a spectacular fuckin' hour."

"The best of your life."

"That's a bold claim."

"She's so good in the sack you'll renounce all other women. In fact, you'll probably go gay."

Eric shook his head sadly. "Pimping your girlfriend, man. That's fuckin' weak."

"In't like that, mate," Bobby replied with a shrug. "We have an… *arrangement.*"

"Touching."

"You don't understand."

Eric smiled again. "And I don't wanna understand."

"Don't tell me you're a prude?"

"I'm not a prude," Eric replied. "There's just some shit you shouldn't do."

"Well, the offer still stands. You won't regret it. No holes barred."

Eric tapped his fingers along the steering wheel. "I'll pass, thanks."

"Your loss."

"And next time you try to pimp your girlfriend to me," he said, "I'll drop your cut from five grand to two."

The junky raised his hands again and gave him a nervous smile. "Didn't mean nowt by it, mate. Just thought…"

"I know what you thought."

"We're good, though, right?"

"If you get out in the next ten seconds…"

The junky tore at the door handle in his eagerness to exit the vehicle, and then he shuffled towards the entrance of a ground floor flat. He knocked for a long time before the door finally opened.

An attractive blonde girl in a tight pink tracksuit smiled at Bobby. She wore a vacant, dreamy expression like she was still feeling the effects of a recent fix. There were dark rings under her eyes, and her shoulder-length hair was messy through lack of care. Even though she was barely out of her teens, the life she was leading had already hardened her features.

She lurched forward and wrapped her arms listlessly around Bobby's neck. Then the girl pressed her lips against his right ear and whispered something. He responded by putting his hand down the front of her tracksuit bottoms.

She looked around momentarily, afraid of what the neighbours might see, and tapped Bobby on the shoulder when she noticed Eric watching them from the car. Bobby was too busy fondling her to care about an audience and started to pull her pants down.

Eric observed the girl carefully. Even with a fix running through her veins she was the kind of person who didn't like her private business aired in public. Her expression was one of distaste rather than desire. There were still a few traces of innocence that her boyfriend hadn't yet destroyed. She shuffled uncomfortably at the touch of Bobby's fingers and tapped on his shoulder a few times, but he was too consumed by lust to notice. Eric wound down his window and shouted Bobby's name twice.

The junky turned around; his face was red, and he was breathing heavily. An erection bulged the front of his jeans.

"Take it inside," Eric said.

The girl gave a brief, relieved smile.

Bobby nodded and pushed her roughly through the open door, which he then slammed shut. Eric stared at it it for a moment, his thoughts on the girl. She deserved better than Bobby Manning, but experience told him this was probably as good as it was going to get. From here it was downhill all the way.

Eric started the car and pulled away from the kerb.

Now he needed to find the third member of the crew.

4.

Eric remembered something a friend once said: *When a man is tired of London he is tired of life. But when a man is tired of living, he moves to Lingdale.* This phrase crossed his mind as he parked his car in front of a row of small, pastel-coloured terraces and walked across the road to The Lingdale social club.

It was an ugly brown bungalow with large frosted windows and graffiti-laden walls. Eric went up the steps, through the open double doors, into an entrance hall covered with fading posters announcing bands that no longer existed. The thumping bass of an old Motown track Eric vaguely recognised shook the ground beneath his feet. He went through the first door on his right and into the lounge.

Despite the large windows and the loud music, the room was dark and lifeless. Years of cigarette smoke had turned its low ceiling a toxic shade of yellow and the place still reeked of tobacco despite the smoking ban. Eric's shoes stuck to the beer-slicked green vinyl as he made his way across the dance floor. He wiped his feet on the carpet and walked past tables of sad-faced drinkers working their way through happy hour pints. One particular drinker looked up from his almost empty glass and caught Eric's eye. He drained the final mouthful and tapped the glass with a forefinger.

Eric ignored him as he approached the bar. A tall elderly man with a shiny, cue-ball-shaped head and low-hanging jowls smiled at Eric and waved his hand at the broad selection of ales and bitters on display. The smile disappeared when his new customer asked for two pints of the cheapest lager.

He poured the drinks carelessly and huffed with suppressed rage when Eric asked him to top them up. Eric picked up the wet glasses and carried them back to his friend's table. He took the chair opposite and pushed one of the drinks towards the thin, red-faced, grey-haired man.

The man lifted the glass in the air, slurring: "You're a lifesaver… Stanners, m-me lad."

"And you're drunk, Mickey."

Mickey Dunn dribbled his first sip down the front of his hastily buttoned check shirt, then wiped his mouth with the back of his hand before taking another swig. He slammed the glass down on the table and wagged a finger in Eric's direction. "I'm not drunk, sir. J-Just pickling my brain with p-preservatives for... a longer shelf life."

"Keep going like you are and you won't have a shelf life."

"If God wills it..."

"You don't believe in imaginary friends any more than I do."

When Mickey Dunn was sober, he was one of the finest villains around. Military training meant his hand-to-hand combat skills were exceptional, and he was an outstanding shot with either a pistol or rifle. Past military traumas had eroded his sense of fear. Occasionally, Eric wished his friend did suffer moments of terror because then he might be afraid of the damage he was doing to himself.

"Don't tell me what... I-I believe in."

"Okay, I'll tell you what I believe. You're gonna kill yourself if you keep basting your liver in that shite."

"So sayeth... the man..."

"I haven't fuckin' finished, Mick," he snapped. "I believe you're gonna need a miracle if you keep going. And tell you what, mate; if God comes down and takes away your cirrhosis and thirst right here and now, I'll fall to my knees, clasp my hands together, and repent my criminal life right here and fuckin' now."

"He works in myst... mysterious ways."

Eric shook his head and snorted. "At least your imaginary friend is working. What the fuck are you doing?"

Mickey waggled the glass in the air, spilling some of his drink. "Working on me... hangover, Stanners."

Eric had hoped his friend might have been at the beginning or end of a major bender, during the period when he might be open to reason, but this was the breathless peak; when excessive alcohol trumped even the most reasoned arguments.

"I have some real work for you."

Mickey shrugged. "Don't wannit."

"It pays well."

Mickey's bloodshot eyes turned mean as they angled in Eric's direction. "You not hear me... first time around?"

"Was hoping you might reconsider."

"Nope."

He necked the rest of his drink and looked at Eric in the hope of more alcohol.

Eric sipped the flavourless pint briefly and then pushed it away in disgust. Mickey snatched up the glass, spilling some of the drink on the table, in his eagerness to drown his sorrows. Eric left a folded tenner in a puddle of spilt beer and watched the liquid soak slowly into the note.

Then he got to his feet and brushed himself down. Mickey didn't bother looking at him. Instead, he kept his eyes angled down as he finished his pint. Then Mickey pushed the glass away and noticed the money. He grabbed the damp note, looked at it for a moment, and then stared up at the ceiling in confusion as if for a brief moment he believed that this money had fallen from the sky.

Eric walked away. He turned briefly to watch his friend for some indication that he might have changed his mind, but Mickey was already at the bar, pressing the wet note into the barman's hand and jabbing his finger at the spirit bottles. Grimacing, the old man fingertipped the money into the till and gave Mickey his change. Then he poured a pint and triple whisky chaser.

Eric couldn't stand to watch anymore; his friend was too far-gone to ask for help, and he didn't want to hang around and fund further visits to the bar. Nor did he want to listen to slurred stories and incoherent rants.

Besides, Eric had work to do – he needed replacement muscle for his plan to work.

5.

Eric stood with hands in jeans pockets and watched Joey Judd shovel Chicken Szechuan into his mouth. Sauce, grease, and grains of egg-fried rice coated his dark beard; although he was too busy eating to notice the mess he'd made. When he finally looked up from the oily carton, Joey eyeballed Eric with suspicion. "You want one of me men?"

"That's right."

Joey wiped the back of a hand across his beard and studied the grease spot before turning his attention back to the matter at hand. "What if I say no?"

Eric smiled. "Didn't realise this was multiple choice?"

Joey pushed the half-eaten meal away, folded his tattooed arms, and sat back in the booth seat. Despite the fact that it was Friday night, and the Trinity Tavern was heaving, the big man had the cubicle all to himself. Stood to reason, as he owned the place, plus it would be physically difficult to get anybody else on the seat because he took up so much of it with his bulk. He was six-two, twenty-five stone, and his body was a seething mass of bulges and folds crammed inside skin-tight Jacamo chinos and polo shirt.

Pale green eyes studied Eric's expression for signs that this was a joke. When he realised it wasn't, Joey ran a hand across the black stubble that flecked his otherwise bald scalp and let out a sigh. Turning his head left and right, he scanned the room until his gaze lingered on a couple of muscle-bound heavies by the bar. They read his expression and barged through the crowd towards the cubicle.

Eric knew he'd be thrown out of the pub if he didn't think fast, so he took a mobile phone from his jacket pocket and let his finger linger over the send button. The pre-prepared message contained just one word: *trouble*.

"Well, here's a multiple fuckin' choice I think you might like. What will my brother do when he gets this message?" Eric said. "Will he: A) Tear this fuckin' bar apart? B) Break your men into tiny fuckin' pieces? C) Wipe the blood off the floor with your baldy fuckin' head? Or D) Do *all* of the above?"

The muscles beneath Joey's eyes twitched and tightened. "Derek's outside?"

"*Please?* You think I'd come in here without some kinda backup plan? D'you really think I'm that much of a cunt?"

Joey's right hand came up from the table and waved frantically at the onrushing heavies. They stopped a few feet away, lingered for a moment, then drifted back into the throng. Eric watched until they were gone. Then he approached the table and leant towards the bar owner. "You owe us."

Joey exhaled. "Some fuckin' debt."

"You negotiated the terms."

Joey had owed Eric's former boss a lot of money but fell behind with the payments due to bad financial planning. Tired of waiting for his cash, he decided to kneecap Joey as a warning to others. Eric knew things would get very dangerous if that happened – months of tit-for-tat kneecappings and killings – so arranged for Joey to repay his debt in a way that didn't involve money.

For an ugly fat boy, Joey had snagged himself a remarkably attractive partner and Eric's boss often talked about what he would give to spend the weekend with her. Sensing opportunity, Eric arranged for them to meet face-to-face and work out their differences in exchange for a favour. He gave his boss a 'tip' that Joey was looking to use his wife as collateral, and gave Joey a 'tip' that the boss quite fancied making an indecent proposal. In exchange for a dirty weekend with Joey's wife, the boss wrote off the thirty grand he owed.

"Me missus couldn't sit properly for a week. She didn't shit right for a fortnight."

"*You* negotiated the terms."

"She said Piper practically turned her arsehole inside out."

Eric raised his hands. "You know the boss. His tastes tend towards the exotic."

"That's not fuckin' exotic, like. That's just fuckin' perverse."

"It paid your debt, didn't it?"

Joey shrugged. "Aye. You got us there, like. But I still didn't agree to anal."

"Take it up with Alan, not me. I just got you both in the same room in exchange for a favour. Now's your time to pay up – otherwise, if you like, I can tell *everybody* just how you paid the Piper."

Joey gestured with his hands for Eric to keep his voice down. He didn't want people knowing how he paid his debt. The only ones who knew the secret were Joey, his wife, Aisling, Alan and Eric (although Eric suspected Alan made a video of the encounter, a keepsake he could watch when bored). If word got out that his wife had spent the weekend with Alan Piper in exchange for settling his debts, Joey's street cred would be irreparably damaged. Exposure would make him look weak. In this layer of society, getting the wife to fight your battles put you one notch above child molester.

Joey rubbed his hairy chin and cast his eyes back in the direction of the bar.

"You see them two?"

Eric followed his gaze.

"See the one with the scarred eyebrows?"

He was a stocky six-footer with short, dark blonde hair, uneven eyebrows that consisted mostly of scar tissue, a crooked boxer's nose, and a gaze that despite it all seemed gentle.

"Yeah."

"You can have *him*."

"Why?"

Joey's hands came up to shoulder height, his mouth open with incomprehension. "Whaddaya mean, why?"

"Must be a reason you're pushing him towards me."

"Yeah, it's called repaying that favour you just asked for. Don't be so fuckin' paranoid."

"It comes with the territory."

"I'm not tryna pull a swifty, Eric. I'm just saying that I've got a job coming up that Daz in't part of because the crew's already in place. So if you don't want him, I suggest that you make a beeline for the fuckin' door – because as far as I'm concerned, that's me debt repaid in full."

When he wasn't running the pub, Joey liked to pull jobs on other crews. Normally this kind of behaviour would earn him a one-way trip to the afterlife, but he didn't pull his heists locally. He worked in other areas, paying good money for information from reliable sources, ensuring that his victims thought it was the work of other local crews. Joey always made sure he wasn't anywhere near the action, so needed top-notch teams to do the work. If Joey was using Darren solely as a glorified bouncer, rather than as part of the heist team, it was for a good reason. Eric turned his head back towards Darren, who was still gazing at him with cow-like blankness.

"So what's his speciality?" he asked.

"He's a bare-knuckle fighter and boxer," Joey replied. "And he knows how to use a gun when he puts his mind to it."

"Is he a good fighter?"

Joey smirked. "He can knock fuckers out if that's what you're wondering."

"That's not being a good fighter, and you know it."

The smirk became a snigger. "Well, he's not too good at *throwing* fights."

"Meaning?"

"No fucker'll employ him in the ring at the moment. He was told to throw a bout. Unfortunately, the faggot they put him in the ring with coulda been knocked down by a gentle morning breeze. Darren wasn't to know that, of course, so tried to make the fight look real – in this case, too real. Knocked the guy spark out."

"Then I take it he isn't too bright?"

"Not especially."

"Can he at least follow simple orders?"

"That's summat he *can* do."

"Except in the boxing ring."

Joey nodded. "To be fair to Daz, he wasn't to know he were fighting a spastic with a sugar-glass jaw."

"I'm surprised he still has the use of his knees."

Joey gave him a faint smile. "'Cause when all's said and done, Daz did them a favour. They were grooming his opponent for the big leagues until he got knocked out. It might have cost them in the short-term, but it would've cost a lot more if they'd wasted money on expensive gyms and professional trainers. I watched the fight expecting Joe Frazier, but what shuffled outta the corner were a touch closer to Joey Deacon. Lemme tell you, getting knocked out were the best thing to happen to the dozy cunt."

Eric hitched his thumb in the direction of the bar. "Can I talk to him?"

"Knock yourself out. Not like Daz is going anywhere till he's finished his shift."

Eric started moving, but Joey scooted across the seat and wrapped a fat hand around his wrist. He turned and looked at the bar owner's damp face.

Joey grinned. "When do you need him?"

Eric gave him a brief smile and removed the hand. He didn't trust Joey enough to reveal that information, as it wasn't beyond him to scupper or hijack the plan. "I'll need him when I need him," he replied. "Dunno when that is, yet."

Joey mumbled something, probably offensive, as Eric shouldered and elbowed through the heaving mass of drinkers in the direction of the bar. Those regulars who didn't know him snarled violent threats, and those who did kept their opinions to themselves. The air was thick with body heat and perspiration, and Eric's armpits were clammy with sweat. He wiped the damp off his forehead and nodded at Darren, who returned the gesture. Then he grasped the bar top tightly with both hands, almost as though he would be pulled away by the tide of Friday night drinkers. "Can I get you a bevvie?"

The bouncer's eyes narrowed, and he pulled away slightly. "You're not gay, are you?"

"And what if I was?"

"I'm not into that shite."

"Then you'll be happy to know this isn't a pickup."

"Then why'd you wanna buy us a drink?"

"Because I'm offering a job. And it seems the polite thing to do."

The bouncer turned his gaze in the direction of raised voices and sudden movements in the crowd; his shoulders hunched in readiness, but it was only a group of friends getting boisterous. He relaxed and turned back towards Eric. "You do know that I'm banned from the rings at the mo'?"

"I'm aware of your problems. It isn't that kinda job."

Eric caught a haggard barman's attention, pointed at the nearest lager pump, and raised two fingers. The barman quickly poured a couple and pushed them across the counter. Eric handed over the money and passed Darren one of the drinks. They clinked glasses, swigged, and the bouncer moved closer to Eric.

"Then what kinda job is it?" he said, keeping his voice down.

"The kind that involves you following orders. To the fuckin' letter."

"What kinda orders?"

"The kind I'll give you on the day," Eric replied. "It's a three-man heist and a three-way split, barring five gees to my snitch. That's all you need to know for now."

"What's the big secret?"

Eric's attention turned towards Joey – watching them from his booth seat – before he scanned the crowd for familiar and unwelcome faces. He didn't see any. "Because if I tell you, it also means I'm telling your boss."

"You think he's gonna grill me?"

"Like cheese on fuckin' toast. The less you know, the less you can say."

"And what if I'm busy that day because I don't know enough?"

"I think a potential fifteen grand payday should un-fuck your schedule." Darren came in closer until Eric felt his warm breath on his ear. "Fifteen?"

"That's right."

"That'll tide me and me girlfriend over for a while, like."

"Then I take it your diary's just cleared?"

Darren nodded.

Eric took out his mobile and thumbed through the contacts. "Then gimme your number. I'll phone you on the morning of the job. One thing I *will* let you know: it's coming soon. So don't go planning any holidays or romantic getaways with the girlfriend."

Eric squeezed through a crowd of punters smoking just outside the front door of the Trinity Tavern. The night air was thick with fresh cannabis and tobacco smoke, but it was still better than the clammy warmth of the bar.

He waited near the entrance for a few moments and pretended to check his mobile phone. All the time he kept his eye on the door, watching for anybody pushing through the crowd in a hurry. He didn't put it past Joey to try and tail him.

Nobody emerged through the smokers.

Eric put the phone away and looked around. He noticed his brother's car in one of the parking bays near the tall clock tower of Holy Trinity Church. Its engine throbbed and coughed up clouds of exhaust fumes. The headlights flashed a couple of times.

As Eric crossed the road, he let his gaze drift across the car park. Aside from a group of stationary taxis parked tightly together, the only other vehicle was a blue Vauxhall Corsa. It was situated nearby, almost hidden from view by the cabs. The driver's door was open, and a man stood behind it, smoking within the shadow of a small tree.

Upon noticing Eric, the man dropped his cigarette on the ground and walked to his car. He climbed in and closed the door. The blue glare of a mobile phone illuminated his face for a few moments before the interior returned to darkness. Eric knew instinctively that the man worked for Joey. He was probably texting his boss for further instruction and was likely to be their shadow for the evening.

Eric clambered in the passenger seat of his brother's car and checked the wing mirror. He couldn't see the Corsa, but he did notice headlights sparkling behind the cabs.

Derek shuffled his immense bulk around the seat to get comfortable, and said: "Did the fat fucker give you any trouble?"

"He tried."

"And?"

"I told him you were waiting outside."

"Bet that shit him up?"

"He might've dropped a lump or two in his boxers."

"Did he give us what we wanted?"

"Sort of."

"Sorta? What kinda fuckin' answer's that?"

"Well, he gave us a man."

"What kinda man?"

"That's where the sort of comes in," Eric replied. "I'm not sure yet."

Derek put his foot down. The car screeched into the turn, leaving behind a drifting trail of rubber smoke. After another fast manoeuvre, swerving in and around a couple of slow moving vehicles, he cut right towards Grangetown. When he was on the straight of the A66, he nudged his brother with a hard elbow.

"So Mickey were drunk?"

Eric waved a dismissive hand. "Next stupid fuckin' question."

"All right, then. How drunk?"

"Like he was in the first week of a month-long bender."

"What about Kandinsky?"

"Still can't get hold of him."

"Have you tried his mobile?"

Eric looked at his brother for a moment. "No. I tried sending out fuckin' smoke signals and good vibes."

Derek gritted his teeth. "What have I told you about sarcasm?"

"That it's the lowest form of wit?"

An expression of bewilderment crossed Derek's face for a moment. "No. I told you I'd knock you the fuck out next time you gave us a mouthful of it."

Eric's eyes went to the door mirror. The Corsa overtook a car and settled in behind a Transit van. "Since when did you become Kandinsky's biggest fan? Thought you hated his guts?"

Derek shrugged his massive shoulders. "Just 'cause I don't like the gadgie, don't mean he's not solid. He can fuckin' handle hisself, like. I'll give him that much."

"I'm sure he's thankful for that."

Derek's hands tightened around the steering wheel. "So we are gonna be playing funny fuckers this evening? Is that it?"

"Maybe. I haven't decided yet."

"Then lemme decide for you. Keep the wisecracks to yourself."

"Or what?"

"Or I'll crack wise with me fists. Mebbe crack your fuckin' skull and put your brain to sleep."

Eric leant back in his seat a touch, angling for a decent view of the wing mirror. "Somebody's fuckin' brain is asleep."

"Whassat supposed to mean?"

"Means you're too fuckin' dim to see the nice big bushy tail we've picked up."

Derek's attention drifted to the rear-view. All he noticed were several cars and headlight sparkle. "Which one."

"Two cars back. Behind the Transit. Pre-historic Vauxhall. It was parked behind the taxis. Pulled out just after we did."

"You reckon it's…"

"Of course, it's Joey. Probably sent one of his goons outside to spot and follow you."

"You want me to lose him?"

Eric's hard gaze angled towards his brother. "No, I want you to take him direct to our hiding place."

"And then kick the shit outta him?"

"No. Invite him in for coffee and cuddles."

Derek wrenched at the steering wheel to control his rage. "Just gimme an answer that in't all sarcastic, you ugly fuck."

"Yes. Of course, I want you to shake the bastard, for Chrissakes."

Derek pulled a sharp left at a roundabout and moved in the direction of the river. Then he slowed down slightly and fixed his gaze on the rearview.

Eric slapped his shoulder with the back of his hand. "What the hell are you doing?"

Derek turned towards his brother. "I'm not running from this tit," he remarked, angling his eyes back to the mirror.

The Vauxhall also turned at the roundabout. Derek stomped on the gas, accelerated a hundred yards and cut left into a short road with a dead end. To the right was a small recess covered on both sides by high shrubs and thick bushes. He mounted the pavement as he reversed into the bay until branches were scratching the window and shielding him from view. He flicked off the lights, kept the engine humming gently, and waited.

A long shadow thrown by nearby streetlights stretched in the direction of the dead end and grew gradually darker. A poorly tuned engine sputtered and coughed, and increased in volume the closer it came. The right front wing of the Corsa eased into view. The vehicle rolled forward until it was fully framed in Derek's windscreen.

He stepped on the gas. The car screeched, throwing out exhaust fumes and rubber smoke, and raced towards the Corsa. The driver stared in slack-jawed shock as he realised what was happening, then he threw his arms in front of his face. The front bumper slammed the driver's side door.

Eric was thrown forward until the seat belt snapped tight and halted his momentum. It took him a few moments to regain his focus and realise what had happened.

During those moments, Derek threw open the door and exited the vehicle. He pulled a knife from an inside jacket pocket and moved towards the Corsa. The driver shrieked, tried to start the engine, which sputtered and stalled, then leant across and pressed down the passenger's side lock.

Derek dropped into a crouch and thrust his blade deep into the right front tyre, then did the same again with the left. The driver screamed and tried the engine again. It popped and sputtered, throwing out exhaust fumes, but didn't start. Derek jumped on the bonnet and slammed his right heel into the metal, making deep indents, and then kicked the wind-screen, which spiderwebbed with the impact. He stomped over the car roof, put cracks in the rear windshield, and jumped down. Moving quickly, he slashed both rear tyres and folded the blade into the handle.

Derek ignored the driver of the Corsa, whose terrified face was pressed against the side window, and made his way back to his vehicle. He got in, pulled at the seat belt, and started the engine.

"*That's* how you shake a fuckin' tail," he said, reversing quickly. Then he turned the steering wheel and rounded the obstacle.

As they rolled by, the driver looked at them with a shocked expression, mouthing unheard words, like he was unable to comprehend what had just happened. He tried to force open the damaged door by slamming it with his shoulder. When that didn't work, he scrambled across the seat and opened the front passenger door.

Derek mouthed an obscenity at the man, started chuckling, stepped on the accelerator and drove away.

7.

Harry Sparks heard a familiar knock at the door. Three loud knocks followed by three soft taps. He checked the time on his mobile phone.

Jonno was right on cue.

He switched off the television with the remote, turned to his wife, snuggling next to him on the sofa, and said: "You might wanna make yourself scarce, Babs."

Barbara rolled her big blue eyes and sighed. Sweeping a hand over her long blonde hair, she gathered it in a bunch and made a ponytail. She brushed food crumbs off her jeans and got to her feet.

Her smile was uncomfortable. "I'll be upstairs, reading, while you men talk *business*," she said. "Try and tell Jonno to keep the conversation about my tits as quiet as possible."

Harry shrugged and coughed. "Soz about that, sweets," he replied. "I'll try and steer the chat to summat a bit less offensive." His eyes wandered to his wife's huge breasts, snuggled in a support bra but still prominent even in one of Harry's cast-off polo shirts. The sight of her deep cleavage gave him a semi, which he hid by shuffling in his seat.

"Just having him in the house is something I consider offensive," she said.

Harry held up his hands. "Duly noted."

Her gaze was cold and hard. "You *note* a lot of things these days, Harry. But you don't do anything about them." Full lips turning down at the edges, she allowed some warmth back into her stare. It seemed like there was something she wanted to say but for whatever reason she let it drop. "Just keep the volume down."

Harry knew what was on his wife's mind, though not because he was particularly intuitive. He'd seen the same facial expressions, heard the same sighs and non-verbal communications, and noticed the same coldness in her eyes a lot over the past six months. It came down to repetition.

He'd learned all of these non-verbal ticks during many intense conversations about his criminal life and associates. Somehow these exchanges remained civil, but Harry had noticed an edge recently. Barbara was growing weary of his career and his secrets, and one day very soon all this sublimated anger would tip over into a full-blown argument.

When that day arrived, it would come down to a choice between his family and his associates. In theory, it seemed simple: love always wins. However, in practice, simplicity had nothing to do with it.

Jonno had treated Harry with less respect since the Kevin Nicholson incident. He regularly insulted him in front of the crew, made less than veiled comments about Barbara, and gave him a hard time.

Considering Jonno's current antipathy towards him, leaving the fold was something that he needed to do with care. There was always the possibility that Jonno might get offended if he just walked away without the proper respect. He might even take enough offence to consider Harry as an enemy. And his boss had a violent, low tolerance threshold for enemies.

Harry didn't fancy being on the business end of a splintered broom handle.

Only one person had left without consequence: Bobby Manning. And only because his heroin habit was so bad his lifespan was measurable in months rather than years; drugs were saving Jonno the hard work.

Harry didn't have that option. He knew that if he left, it would need to be with a firm exit plan in place. Preferably something that made a profit.

Barbara turned and moved towards the hallway. Her ample buttocks bounced as she exited the room. Harry couldn't help noticing that she had put on weight. Then he felt guilty. His wife's weight gain was due to comfort eating her way through their marital issues.

He was the last person who could comment on her increased dress size. He only needed to think about buying a takeaway pizza or curry for his belt to move out another notch. Harry groaned as he got off the sofa. Then he went into the hallway and opened the door.

Jonno scowled at him, but he was too good-looking to do it successfully. With big green eyes and sleek cheekbones, his anger always resembled a male-model smouldering for the camera. It was what made him so dangerous: his opponents always noticed the beauty rather than the ugliness that simmered below the surface. The way he dressed compounded the effect. It was hard to believe this well-presented man in a pinstripe jacket, crisp white shirt, blue jeans, and expensive brogues were capable of thieving, torturing, and murdering his way into a very successful career dealing drugs.

Harry knew Jonno well enough to stand aside and allow him to charge into the hallway. He didn't react when his boss looked him up and down a couple of times. "Took your fuckin' time, didn't you?" he said.

Harry closed the door. "Soz, fella," he replied.

Jonno dropped the small Adidas holdall he was carrying on the floor and ran both hands through his fashionably high hair, primping and teasing his waxed locks into position. "Don't tell me you're getting so fuckin' fat that it now takes you several minutes to get from the sofa to the front door?" He laughed at the witticism; it was a nasty, mocking sound that raised the hairs on Harry's neck.

"Was upstairs chatting with Babs."

Jonno sneered. "Chatting or *shagging?*"

Harry maintained composure. "Just chatting."

"If it were me I'd be slamming my length between those big fuckin' jugs."

Harry winced and lowered his hands towards the ground. "Chrissakes, keep it down," he hissed.

Jonno picked up the bag and shook his head in disgust. "Behold, the big man of the house."

"Come on, Jonno, it's not like that," Harry whispered. "Babs can hear this shit upstairs. Think about how you'd feel if you got an earful of summat like that?"

Jonno did an exaggerated pout. "Didn't realise you were one of these feminists, Aitch? When's your next period due?"

Harry sighed and looked at the ceiling for a moment, letting his anger subside, and finally gave his boss a thin smile.

Jonno rubbed Harry's shaved head in patronising fashion, tugged roughly at one of his jowls, and leant in. "Chill, mate, I'm just fuckin' with you. Lead the way, for Chrissakes, before you have a heart attack or stroke." This was another fat joke Harry had to ignore.

He waved his boss into the living room. Jonno sprawled across the sofa and dropped the holdall on the carpet, which left Harry with the armchair that couldn't support his weight. He sank into the cushion and struggled to get comfortable. It didn't work. The more he moved, the worse it got.

Jonno laughed when he noticed his discomfort. "You should see yourself, mate. You look like you're gonna disappear inside that fuckin' thing."

Harry saw that Jonno wasn't in a hurry to offer up space on the sofa. Instead, he shuffled forward, so that his backside rested on the edge of the cushion. It still wasn't comfortable, but it was an improvement on sliding inside the armchair.

Jonno kicked off his brogues and made himself comfortable. Harry didn't want it to be a long evening of abuse and humiliation, so he coughed and waved his hand at the shoes. "You might wanna put those back on, mate."

Jonno raised his perfectly shaped eyebrows. "Oh? Not welcome?"

Harry laughed uncomfortably. "Nah, nowt like that, fella. Babs is feeling a bit under the weather at the moment. So we wanna grab an early night's kip."

Jonno's eyes narrowed momentarily, but then his gaze softened, and he gave Harry a big white grin. "Furry muff," he said. "Just dropping this off, really. Can't hang around."

"Doing owt special?"

The grin tightened into a barely suppressed smirk. "Doing two college girls, as it happens."

Jonno beckoned Harry with a quick wave of the hand, then fumbled in his jacket pocket for an iPhone. He told Harry to pay attention to the screen.

It was a dark, grainy video from the camera operator's point-of-view: Jonno in bed with a couple of girls in their late teens. He switched from one to the other in a constant merry-go-round of filth as each girl moaned and groaned like a porn star as he thrust inside them. At one point in he pulled an enormous length of cock from one of the girls. The condom barely covered three-quarters of the shaft. Both girls were fighting to pull off the rubber when Harry told him to turn off the movie.

It seemed unfair that Jonno was both handsome and had a cock that was double the length of his own. A twinge of penis envy made Harry's balls shrivel. His stomach tightened, even as he attempted a smile to disguise his sense of inadequacy.

Noticing his discomfort, Jonno grinned and put the phone away. "That's what I've got to look forward to – second helpings."

Harry tried to smile, but his heart wasn't really in it.

"Nice," he croaked.

Jonno put on his shoes, then unzipped the little Adidas bag. Inside were tight stacks of money heaped together haphazardly. He zipped it up again and handed it to Harry. "After this trade, we're gonna need to start looking at alternative locations," he said, getting to his feet.

Harry blinked in disbelief. "Alternatives?"

"You do know the Forum's closing, right?"

"You're shitting me?"

"You not read the locals, mate?"

Harry shook his head.

Jonno shrugged. "They're sprucing the place up, apparently. Report said it's gonna take a couple of years. Judging by the fuckin' state of it, I thought that might've been a typo or summat. Two *hundred* years seems more appropriate."

Harry's stomach turned over, and his thoughts moved from drug deals to worries about his son. "How long before it closes?"

"Not long. Three months, I think."

"Shit. Terry'll be gutted."

Jonno's gaze frosted over. "Your son's happiness is the least of my fuckin' worries. In fact, if I gather together and total the fucks I give about Terry's happiness, I think you'll find the number is precisely none."

Harry held up his hands. "Soz, Jon, I'm not thinking straight."

But he was thinking straight. What he enjoyed most about making deals in the Forum was watching the joy on his son's face as he circled the ice rink. The huge grin of delight crinkling his face, small arms performing ungainly windmills as he tried to remain upright in the turns, and the way his mouth formed a perfect circle when avoiding obstacles; these were the reasons he enjoyed making the swap at the Forum. The deal was now so smooth that Terry didn't realise his presence was a cover for something illegal. For him, it was a chance to spend more time with his Dad.

Jonno nodded at Harry's lie. "We need to start thinking about this shit. Needs to be somewhere public, but not *too* public. Somewhere with lotsa distractions."

Harry grinned. "Maybe we could meet them at a funfair?" he said glibly.

Jonno didn't get the joke and shuffled his shoulders aggressively. His beautiful face contorted into something slightly less handsome. He leant close enough for Harry to feel the heat of his breath against his skin. "My heroin deals aren't opportunities for you to have quality time with your son, you tubby fuck."

Harry held up his hands in a gesture of surrender. "It was a joke," he replied, "Just a joke."

Jonno eyeballed him. "*You're* a joke."

This exchange reminded Harry of their school days: Jonno picking on the other kids, taking their money, administering beatings, while he looked on and laughed. Harry always tried to smile, even when it stopped being funny, because he was afraid that Jonno would turn his attention on him if he didn't look like he was enjoying it.

He lifted his hands again, his voice soothing: "Was just trying to lighten the mood, fella. Sorry if it came out wrong."

The tension left Jonno's face, though his shoulders remained tight and hunched. "Just make sure the deal goes through without a hitch, okay?"

Harry nodded.

"Then we can all laugh and joke as much as we want."

8.

Darren Travers pressed against the living room bay window and peered through a gap in the curtain. Streetlights reflected off the windscreen of the dented blue Corsa parked in one of the resident spaces up the street. A cigarette tip glared briefly on the driver's side, and faint plumes of smoke drifted up from the half-open driver's window.

"They're still here," he whispered into the phone.

They had been following him for just over a week. As predicted, Joey pestered Darren for details about the job. Whenever he told his boss that he didn't know anything, Joey responded with uncomfortable silences or threats to his livelihood. Soon enough, cars started appearing in the rear-view mirror whenever Darren left the house, shadowing him from place-to-place. A few people even followed him into the supermarket and lurked in pub crowds as he tried enjoying evenings out with his girlfriend. They weren't trying to be subtle about it, either; they wanted him to know that they were there. Now he sensed them everywhere, lurking just out of eyeshot, which was making him paranoid and twitchy.

Eric sighed. "These men – do they have superpowers?"

"What?"

"Can they hear you from outside?"

Darren's brow wrinkled. "No?"

"Then stop whispering, for fuck's sake. I can barely hear you."

"Fine. How's that?" Darren replied, raising his voice. "Now whatchoo want us to do?"

"Now you go out the back way."

"How do I know it's clear?"

"It isn't."

"Then I'm fucked, aren't I?"

Eric scoffed. "Hardly. I went for a walk a little while ago. Joey's got another car watching the alley on Bedford Street – a green people carrier with two blokes inside. I don't think they noticed me."

"Then I'm definitely fucked."

"This isn't as bad as you think. You need to come outta yours, go left, and stay down until you're past the alley on Bedford. Then cut through onto Samuel Street, jump the gate into the next passageway and cut through unto you get to Craggs, then go over that gate and follow the path until it takes you through to Ezard. Then you just cut around the corner from there, making sure the pricks in the people carrier can't see you, and make your way over to Bishopton Road. We're parked there."

"Christ! I've lived here five years, and you know more about the place than I do."

"Planning, mate. I cased the area soon as you told me where you lived. It's the details that fuck you. So get a move on."

Darren ended the call and pocketed the phone. He turned on the living room lights, to keep his visitors' attention on the window, then he went into the entrance hall and grabbed a dark hooded top off a coat stand. He found a balaclava in an old holdall wedged behind the base of the stand and pushed it in one of the pockets. Putting on the hoodie was harder than Darren had anticipated – it was tight around the waist and working the zip was tricky – making him think that the time was right to resume running and training.

Darren went upstairs, into the main bedroom, where his girlfriend was curled up in the centre of a King-size bed with her legs wrapped around a bunched up duvet. He crouched down and stroked her dark bob. Without opening her eyes, she brushed his fingers away with a quick flick of her small, delicate hand and turned over. Then she muttered something in her sleep and let out a contented sigh. Darren smiled and thought about all the fun they would have with the money he'd earn. He mumbled I love you under his breath, almost embarrassed to say the words, and left the bedroom.

He went downstairs to the kitchen and exited through the back door into the rear courtyard. He stayed still for a few moments and listened for suspicious noises and the sound of footsteps. When he realised that he was alone, Darren opened the courtyard gate, crept outside, tiptoed to one of the tall walls at the end of the alley and peered around it.

Darren recognised the green people carrier behind the gate at the other end of the path. It belonged to one of Joey's bouncers. He pulled the hood as far over his head as it would go and tugged the ends of his jacket over his hands to ensure that he was as dark as possible. Darren dropped to the ground and edged forward on his elbows and knees. Once past the alley, he jumped to his feet and stared at the vehicle.

Mobile phone glare illuminated the interior briefly, revealing two silhouettes in the front seats. Neither figure appeared to be in any hurry. The car doors didn't open.

Darren walked on tiptoes until he emerged on Samuel Street. Then he crossed the road and tried opening the gate to the next alley. It was locked. He clambered up and over it and did a slow jog until he came out on Ezard Street. Keeping small, he cut behind a few cars at the bottom of Bedford, ensuring he remained unseen, and took a left on Bishopton.

As soon as he knew it was safe, Darren pulled down the hood and ruffled his hair. A small four-door hatchback flashed its lights twice. The front passenger door opened, and Eric waved him over.

"Any trouble?"

Darren shook his head.

Eric smiled and got back in the car.

Darren climbed into the rear seat and almost gagged on the stench of stale farts and body odour. He lifted a hand to his face until he'd adjusted to the smell. The interior was small and lacking in legroom. He shifted his weight to get comfortable, but it was impossible. He settled instead for a sideways sprawl that was only mildly uncomfortable.

When he finished shuffling, he looked up and noticed the huge bruiser of a driver staring at him. His face might have been handsome if it wasn't for the broken nose, the cauliflower ears, and the rage in the eyes. It was a gaze Darren recognised from many weigh-ins and before bouts. He extended a hand in greeting.

"You must be Derek?"

Derek's dark eyes lingered on the hand, then he sniffed and turned away. Darren's hand dangled uselessly in mid-air until he finally let it drop on his lap. Eric slapped his brother's shoulder to get his attention and hitched a thumb towards Darren.

"Where are your fuckin' manners?"

The two brothers scowled at each other. Derek started the engine and said, "Same place as me fuckin' patience. Been waiting on this cunt for ages."

Usually, Darren would have reacted, but he knew Derek Stanton's reputation well enough to know it would be wise to keep his mouth shut. The man had reshaped more faces than the average plastic surgeon over the years.

Eric tried to say something in response, but Darren interrupted: "Let it slide. I don't care. Water off a duck's back."

Derek twitched his head in the direction of the passenger. "You heard the man, like. He doesn't give a fuck."

"He's just being polite, which is a skill you could do with learning."

Derek didn't bother responding to his brother's slight. Instead, he pressed gently on the accelerator and guided the car away from the kerb. They followed the winding road towards Lustrum Beck.

When he realised the brothers had no intention of continuing the conversation, Darren coughed to get Eric's attention. "But I would like to know the plan if you don't mind? Where we're going? What I'm supposed to be doing, like?"

Eric turned to him. "Right now we're gonna go for a nice long drive in the country, to make sure we haven't picked up any tails, and to pass several tedious hours. Then we're gonna spend the afternoon in Billingham. Gonna see some friends who're having a little meet and greet at the Forum."

"And then what?"

"Meet and greet them."

"With what? Fingers in jacket pockets?"

Eric reached into the footwell and pulled a green canvas holdall onto his lap. He unzipped it, giving Darren a glimpse of the contents: three guns, several knives, and enough assorted snacks and drinks for him to assume they would be waiting for a while.

"And is there a plan in place?" Darren asked.

"I'll explain all that once we've parked up."

Derek craned his head in the direction of the bag. "You got any pasties or owt in there?"

Eric zipped the carryall, threw it back in the footwell. "No. Just crisps and nuts and stuff like that."

Derek snorted angrily. "So, no proper food?"

Eric sent a hard stare in his brother's direction. "Whaddayou think this is? A fuckin' gourmet restaurant? It's summat to tide us all over while we wait."

"And you didn't think to get pasties?"

"Well, you didn't say, did you?"

"Probably 'cause you didn't fuckin' ask us, like."

Eric folded his arms. "Jesus, have I gotta think of *everything?*"

"Well, you do seem to fancy yourself as some kinda fuckin' brainiac," Derek replied, tapping his temple with a finger.

"Then I guess my intelligence doesn't extend that far."

"Can fuckin' say that again," Derek said. "I'm stopping on the way to pick some up."

"We don't have time for this stupidity."

"I need summat proper, like. And fuckin' Pringles and shit aren't gonna cut it."

Eric unfolded his arms. "Aw, sorry, mate, I forgot to put the shit in there. If you'd told us beforehand, I would've stopped on the way and put some dried turds in the bag for you to snack on later."

Derek leant towards his brother. "You know summat? You're a right cheeky cunt, you. You know full fuckin' well that I like some pasties and steak slices when we're waiting around."

Eric jabbed a finger in the driver's direction. "And you know full fuckin' well that I give the sum total of zero fucks about your dietary requirements."

"Then I'm stopping on the way."

"Swear down, if you go on a shopping expedition, I'm gonna drive off without you."

"And how the fuck're you gonna do that without the keys?"

The brothers jabbed their fingers at each other and argued all the way to Barnard Castle. Darren tried to enjoy the lovely market town with its quaint sandstone buildings and tree-lined pavements, but the brothers wouldn't shut up. During a lull in the anger, as they approached Mickleton, Derek announced that he needed to fill up the car, as it was getting low on fuel. A quick glance at the fuel gauge revealed there was more than half a tank left.

Derek pulled the vehicle onto a quiet petrol station forecourt and filled the tank. Then he entered the shop and took his time perusing the fridge snacks. Eric grumbled foul-mouthed insults under his breath that gradually increased in volume the longer his brother made them wait. Even Darren wondered how it could take somebody so long to buy snacks.

Eventually, Derek sauntered out of the forecourt shop carrying a plastic bag full of Ginsters products and wearing a big grin. As he reached for the door handle, Eric stretched across and pressed down the driver's side lock and kept his finger on it. Derek yanked at the door handle a few times, then jammed his key into the lock and tried to turn it. Eric put all his weight on the button, laughing as his brother snarled insults and demanded that he opened the door before he lost his rag and smashed in the fucking window.

As he watched with open-mouthed incomprehension, Darren wondered what he'd done wrong in his life to end up in the back of a car watching two overgrown children wind each other up.

9.

Terry Sparks turned his attention from the television and looked up at his father with a shy smile. He was small and large at the same time: undersized for a five-year-old, but much chubbier than most of the other children in his year. Harry always felt overwhelming guilt whenever he saw his son struggle to run during sports day and football games. Despite knowing it was wrong, Harry spoiled the boy with too much bad food and found it difficult to refuse when he pleaded for a bit more of this and a little extra of that. Harry loved him too much to say no. His heart always broke a little bit whenever he noticed the boy was upset.

But on days like this, when Terry gave him that beautiful smile, Harry felt like the best father in the world. It wasn't easy to ignore the fact that he was using his son as cover for a drug deal, but Harry did his best to put it to the back of his mind. Instead, his focus was on how happy the boy looked. Through a combination of ignorance and self-deception, he convinced himself that Terry wasn't in any danger.

He patted the boy's shoulder. "Yes, son?"

"Can we stop for McDonald's on the way back, Daddy?"

Harry ummed and ahhed. "Maybe."

Terry's smile faltered, and his eyes widened a tad.

Harry felt a familiar twinge of guilt. He knew his son was working him like a mark, but he hated to disappoint him.

"We'll see. If you go particularly fast on the ice today and get plenty of exercise, I think that'll deserve a burger."

The smile returned. "A Happy Meal?"

"Just a burger."

The boy's bottom lip jutted in an exaggerated pout.

This time, Harry wasn't falling for it. "If you're gonna be greedy, you won't get owt at all."

Terry stopped pouting and nodded. The message was understood.

Harry drained the last of his coffee and pointed at the ceiling. "Now, go on up and get changed."

Terry got off the sofa, pulled at the backside of his Teletubbies pyjamas and rushed from the room. The moment he heard the boy's feet on the stairs, Harry removed the holdall from behind the sofa and looked inside. The carelessly stacked money was tempting; there were better ways to spend it than buying Heroin.

Harry often considered gathering his family together, taking the money, and running somewhere sunny. A lot of British expats made good lives in Thailand and Vietnam. There were lots of hiding places, and the living was cheap and easy.

Fifty grand, plus another twenty he'd saved and stashed over the years, would last several years in Southeast Asia. He'd put the time to good use by learning the local language and acquiring a trade. The family would eat better, exercise more, and sweat away the pounds beneath the hot sun. There was more to life than drug deals and the grey skies of Teesside.

His mind drifted for a while, through visions of golden beaches, swaying palm trees, sunlight glittering on the sea surface, and his wife's body glistening with suntan lotion. His son emerged from the water. He was much slimmer with a healthy glow. He smiled, waved and ran towards them…

Harry snapped back to reality. Letting his imagination wander was dangerous. He knew what would happen if he stole the money. Jonno would catch, torture, and murder him. Though not before he made Harry watch the prolonged and painful deaths of Babs and Terry.

He zipped the holdall and got off the sofa. "Come on, son," he shouted. "We need to get going."

Terry hollered a distracted reply. He was dawdling and probably hadn't even put on his clothes yet. They weren't running late yet, but if the traffic was bad or some other problem occurred it would put them behind schedule.

Exaggerated footsteps resounded through the ceiling, though they all seemed to be coming from the same spot. Harry smiled bitterly. It was a trick he'd used as a boy. He sat on the bed, reading a comic or watching TV, and stamped his feet on the ground to suggest movement and urgency.

His parents never fell for it either.

"*Terence* Sparks, stop playing that bloody Nintendo and get down these stairs *now!* If you're not dressed and down here in one minute, I'm gonna smack your bum and leave without you."

Now *that* sounded like movement. Harry heard the frantic thump of footsteps, the slam of drawers and wardrobe doors, as Terry realised he was in trouble and needed to dress quickly, and then there was the sound of the boy taking the steps two at a time. Terry entered the room. His face was red, and he was breathing hard as he adjusted his jumper. He looked at his father with wide eyes. "I wasn't playing Nintendo, Daddy. Promise."

"If you're lying, there'll be no burger afterwards."

Terry pouted silently and put on his little blue puffa jacket. The padding made him look morbidly obese. Harry thought a burger might not be a good idea after all, but decided to keep the information to himself. A temper tantrum wouldn't get them to the Forum any faster.

10.

Eric hunkered down in the driver's seat and looked around the car park. It was barely half full, and the vehicles were well spread out. He studied everybody entering and leaving the architectural eyesore that was the Billingham Forum.

Windowless and drab, the grey and black slab of the primary structure sat on a sea of faded tarmac. Back in the Sixties, when it was built, the Forum's large, square wall panels had been silver, and when the sun struck them they gleamed. To northerners raised on red brick and concrete, this was probably what the future seemed like – all shiny and new. But time, weather and neglect had transformed it into a symbol of the dull and dismal past.

To the left of the main building was an ugly adjunct that resembled the watching post of a greyhound track. Neither structure looked like they belonged together. Instead, it appeared as if the two buildings had collided at high speed in some cataclysmic event.

Eric averted his gaze for a moment and looked at the dashboard clock. These dealers were obviously pretty relaxed about the schedule.

Derek farted loudly and guffawed pastry shreds into the air like wet confetti. He rolled down the window to allow the rotten egg stench out of the vehicle. Eric wiped damp crumbs off the sleeve of his leather jacket and glowered at his brother.

Derek ignored him and shook his head at the view. "I fuckin' hate Billingham," he said through a mouthful of cold Ginsters pasty. "It's fuckin' grey as fuck," he added, peppering the glove box and dashboard with another spray of food.

Eric glared at the mess. "I didn't know that fuck was grey?"

Derek snorted. "You know what I mean."

"Actually, I don't."

Derek grinned. Half-masticated slivers of beige pastry covered his teeth. "Thought you were supposed to be the brains here?"

"I *am*," he shouted, looking his brother up and down. "You can't even eat a fuckin' pasty without pebble-dashing the inside of this car with half of it. I mean, look at the fuckin' state of the dash."

Derek had been irritating him for the last hour. Constant eating, usually with an open mouth, incessant moaning about the conditions he was being forced to work in, and punctuating his banalities with loud, stinking farts that forced them to open the windows. Brother or not, Eric was giving serious thought to ditching him.

Derek sniffed. "What's your fuckin' malfunction?"

"*You*. You're my fuckin' malfunction," Eric replied.

Both men's posture stiffened in readiness for a fight. They leant close, until their noses almost touched, and scowled at each other in silence, occasionally tilting their heads slightly to accentuate the menace.

"Look, lads, chill out, right?" Darren said from the back seat. He grabbed a shoulder each and used his strength to prise them apart. Then he pushed forward until his face poked through the gap between the seats. "We gotta work together, right? Turn the other cheek to each other's failings, yes? Co-operation?"

Derek looked at the hand on his shoulder until Darren realised his mistake, withdrew both hands, and sat back. Derek sneered at his brother, then flicked his head in the new man's direction. "Listen up, Backseat Jesus, keep your fuckin' teachings to yourself," then he turned back to Eric. "What's this retard's problem?"

"Leave him alone," Eric said. "If Joey says he's okay then that's good enough for me. Adequate means he won't fuck up, which makes him a viable alternative to you."

It was too early to tell what kind of bloke Darren was, but first impressions hadn't counted for much. Almost everything he said ended as a question, and he hadn't come across as even halfway bright.

The fact that Darren ruined a fixed fight was a bad sign, but what worried Eric more was that nobody had kneecapped him for the mistake; as though everybody expected him to screw up. And if Darren really was so competent, why was Joey so quick to get rid of him? Eric pondered these issues in silence. Still, it was too late to send him packing. They needed an extra body, and he was the only person available at such short notice.

Derek shifted his massive frame in the driver's seat and groaned softly. "They're late."

Eric glanced at the dash clock again. They weren't late yet, though they were cutting it extremely fine. "Not what the clock says."

"Fuck the clock. Manning probably lied to get three hundred outta you," Derek said, snorting. "He's fuckin' seen *you* coming. The great Eric Stanton, outsmarted by a pincushion."

"Just because Manning's a pincushion doesn't mean he's lying," Eric replied. "He worked with Jonno for a long time. He knows the routine."

"Routine might've changed since he's been tripping the shite fantastic."

Eric shook his head. "If summat works you don't change it." He neglected to mention that the reason Bobby passed along the information was due to the Forum's imminent closure. Things were going to change regardless of how slick the deal was.

Derek's hands squeezed the steering wheel. "I'm telling youse now, if this is some kind of junky windup, I'm gonna hunt down Manning and kick him into the afterlife."

Eric geared up to reply when he noticed something and pointed in its direction. "You were saying?"

A blue Mondeo pulled into the car park and stopped beneath the Forum sign. A fat man emerged from the driver's side carrying a small black holdall. He wore an unzipped shabby-chic military jacket, baggy black jeans and a pale blue shirt that might have been stylish if it hadn't been stretched in several directions at once by his gut. There was a look of irritation on his scarlet bulldog face. He rubbed his stubbled scalp several times and turned his head towards the vehicle. He called out to somebody they couldn't yet see.

Eric grinned. "According to Bobby that's Harry," he said, adding, "and in that holdall is *our* fifty grand."

Derek shrugged. "Means nowt. Could just be some fat boy carrying his skates."

Harry stretched and groaned. Lifting his hands high over his head, it looked like he was presenting the bag as a sacrifice to God. He stopped stretching and shouted a name angrily.

A small, bowling-pin-shaped child emerged from the other side of the car and waddled over. He looked up at his father and held out his hand. Harry took the boy's hand, and they marched around the corner, the child scuttling four steps for every one his father took to keep up.

"Believe you owe Bobby an apology," Eric said.

"He'll be waiting a long fuckin' time," Derek replied.

A couple of minutes later an old black Nova cruised the car park. Slowing as he passed, the driver craned his head and looked at the Mondeo. Then the car slowed down and came to a stop in a space beneath the adjunct.

The driver's door opened, and a tall, skinny white man in a baggy grey hoodie emerged. He adjusted his low-hanging jeans, pulling them up towards his waist, and looked around the car park on reflex, though he didn't notice Eric and his associates.

The man admired himself in the driver's side window and ran bony hands across his tight blonde cornrows. He had an angular face with jutting cheekbones and deep-set eyes. This idiot had to be ToJo.

He pulled up his hoodie and put on some wraparound shades. Then ToJo reached inside the car, removed an Adidas holdall, and placed it on the roof while he locked the door. The only difference between his carryall and Harry's was its dark blue colour.

ToJo walked away with a cock-eyed gangsta gait, dragging his right leg like it was lame. He tugged at his pants to stop them from sliding down to his ankles.

Derek sniggered. "Didn't know the circus was in town?"

"He might look like a clown, but he carries a couple of blades, and he's got a piece in his glove box."

Derek grinned. "*Ooh*, scary."

"Just keep it in mind."

"I will."

"Glad to hear it," Eric said, looking at his partners. "So let's do this."

11.

The men followed ToJo at a distance. They didn't hurry because they knew where he was going. Eric cut through a group of teenagers milling around near the entrance and made his way to the counter. He bought three tickets from a dour middle-aged woman and they moved in and around the crowds towards the ice rink.

They entered the arena. The chill in the air was immediate. Eric shivered and buttoned his jacket. Bass heavy pop music and loud shrieks echoed off the walls and ceilings and made the room seem busier than it was. About thirty people did laps of the large rink. Most of them moved clumsily, though a few experts weaved with skilful grace through the dawdlers in the middle of the arena.

A raised, tiered seating area gave spectators prime views of the rink. There were about thirty people dotted across the platform, but the majority of the seats were empty. Most of the spectators watched their phones rather than the ice. Of those not staring at their screens, Harry was the only one who didn't look bored.

Eric moved to the back row and used the high vantage point to study Harry and ToJo. Derek took the middle-row and fiddled with his mobile phone. Darren sat a couple of rows ahead of Derek and pretended to read a leaflet he'd found in the lobby.

Harry sprawled his bulk across two seats and watched his son stagger and skid uncontrollably around the rink. The boy waved his arms every time he approached a corner in an effort to stay upright, then lowered his limbs in the straights. Occasionally he grinned and waved at his father, who shouted words of encouragement and waved back.

ToJo sat ten seats to the left of Harry but paid him no attention. Once or twice he removed his shades and watched slender teenage girls twirl and laugh, but most of the time he kept his eyes on his phone.

Over the next twenty minutes Eric and his associates swapped places, left the room, wandered around and tried to look as inconspicuous as possible, but they always ensured somebody was near the rink watching the targets.

Eric removed his jacket and sat a few of rows behind ToJo. Checking the time every couple of minutes, he began to wonder if the deal was going to happen. His patience wore thin, and he started cursing under his breath. Deciding that the best thing to do was go outside and calm down, Eric texted his brother and Darren and left the room.

Cutting through the crowds in the lobby, Eric went outside. He leant against a wall and took several slow breaths until he regained his composure. A ponytailed teenager smiled in his direction and edged towards him.

She fixed him with her beady blue eyes and asked for a light. When Eric shrugged and told her that he didn't smoke, she came closer and whispered: "I'll suck you off for a tenner, Mister."

Her short skirt and halter-top combo displayed pale rolls of midriff and flabby white legs. Neglect and poor life choices had bloated her face and rotted her teeth. Needle marks darkened the crook of her right arm.

"No thanks," he replied.

"You can cum in me mouth for twenty." Opening her mouth, she waggled her long, furry tongue lasciviously and edged forward until their bodies were inches apart.

Eric ignored the girl's fake smile. The bags under her eyes and her lack of colour suggested she'd worked the last twenty-four hours without a break. A yellow bruise on her collarbone was most likely a gift from her pimp. Unseen anxiety flexed and tightened her jaw muscles. She was running on the fumes of her last fix.

Eric knew the look from his childhood. It was on his mother's face every time she finished working the streets. A moment of pity made him rummage in his pocket. He pushed a tenner at the girl. "Here's some money. Buy summat to eat. Now leave me the fuck alone."

She nibbled her bottom lip nervously and reached for the note. Her hand wavered as if expecting the offer to be withdrawn.

Eric's phone beeped. The girl snatched the money and stared at it in disbelief. He waited for her to move so that he could check the message, but she was slow on the uptake.

"Go now, before I take the fuckin' money back."

The girl stormed away without a second glance.

Eric read Darren's text: *D Dn. T cm y wy.* He was still trying to decipher the jumbled consonants when ToJo walked past with the black holdall. Eric looked around for his brother, but couldn't see him.

Deciding not to wait for backup, Eric went after ToJo, powerwalking two steps for every one the dealer made. Eric put his hand in his jacket pocket and fingered a pistol grip. He took a deep breath and picked up speed.

Just a few feet behind.

It was now or never.

12.

Harry's son wobbled through a crowd of skaters, who somehow managed to avoid colliding with him, and grabbed the barrier. He clung on tight and edged clumsily towards the exit gate.

ToJo stood and fiddled with his low-hanging jeans. He walked in Harry's direction, tripped over the fat man's feet, and dropped the blue holdall. Both men made a big deal of apologising. ToJo brushed himself down and picked up the black holdall. Then he sauntered to the end of the row, turned right, moved up the stairs, past Darren, to the top of the viewing platform and cut left towards the upstairs exit.

Darren typed a shorthand text on his phone and pressed send. He congratulated himself on sending it so quickly, and on making sure that it was easily readable despite the lack of vowels.

If only Joey Judd could see him now. For months his boss had been calling him an idiot in front of the other men. He'd accused him of being unable to follow orders correctly. At one low-point he'd even called him a fucking liability. Well, liabilities didn't get text messages out so quickly, and they didn't think on their feet.

Darren had one job: to ensure Harry and his son didn't step out of the building while the Stantons were dealing with ToJo. If that meant bumping into him and causing a scene then so be it. As long as the Stantons were able to drive ToJo and his car away without hassle then his job was done. Afterwards, he would take their car to the meeting point, and they would go their separate ways.

That was all he had to do.

And yet…

There was an opportunity to prove once and for all that he wasn't a liability, and that he could think on his feet. In the blue holdall was fifty grand of raw heroin, and the chance to double their money. Darren had been thinking about it ever since the Eric told him the plan. For some reason the brothers didn't seem interested in the drugs, which puzzled Darren because all they talked about (besides arguing) was money: having it, spending it, travelling to far-flung places with it. He thought ignoring the heroin was an oversight on their part, due to their focus on the cash. He knew they would thank him later for his quick thinking.

Harry's son sat down and tore at the skates. He was as clumsy with laces as he was on the ice and struggled with the double-knot on the right boot. Every now and again he chewed his tongue to increase concentration.

Harry watched with a blank expression that soon changed to one of eye-rolling frustration. He murmured something that Darren couldn't hear, gently brushed the child's hands out of the way, and worked on the knot with a sure touch. Harry removed the boots and patted the child on the head. Then he picked up the holdall and they made their way towards a counter beside the exit.

Darren hung back as Harry exchanged footwear with a sour-faced counter assistant and told him to cheer up, it might never happen. The man sneered and replied that it already had.

Harry and his son pushed through the double doors and into the lobby. Gradually, as they weaved through and around several groups of people, towards the exit, the boy began to baby-step, and his hands went between his legs. Finally, he came to a complete stop and danced on the spot.

Harry looked down at the boy. "Why didn't you say so you wanted the toilet?"

The boy looked up at his father and whimpered. The fluttery expression on his face warned of an impending bathroom disaster. Harry grabbed the boy's hand and dragged him quickly to the rear of the lobby and through a set of double doors.

Darren followed them into a small corridor, which had doors for male and female toilets. He closed the double doors, bolted them, and pushed them a few times to ensure that they were locked. Then he turned the leaflet he was holding into a wedge and went into the men's toilet.

13.

Eric caught up with ToJo as his key hit the driver's side lock. He picked up speed and knocked the wind out of him with a shoulder charge. Eric used his strength to wedge the dealer against the door and ensure that he couldn't move. To stop him from struggling, Eric pressed his forearm into ToJo's neck and pushed his head forward until his face was touching the car roof. Then he jammed the gun barrel into his back hard enough for him to feel it.

"You keep struggling, and I'll unload this thing in your fuckin' spine."

A few people noticed the two men pressed together and gave them curious glances, but they kept walking. Eric knew he didn't have long before people stopped walking and started asking questions. Even though ToJo let his body go loose, Eric could tell that he remained on edge, like he was ready to go for a blade at any moment.

"Whatchoo after, blood?" ToJo asked. Even though he was from York, his accent blended inner-city London gangsta, ghetto American, and Yorkshire grit to create something wholly unique: Emmerdale Eminem.

Eric kept the gun out of sight of passers-by and leant in. "Unlock the door *now.*"

"Chill, blood."

"I'm not your fuckin' blood, but I *will* spill it if you don't do as you're told."

"Ain' doin' nuffink for you, bruv."

Eric pulled back the hammer. "Then you're gonna need a good fuckin' wheelchair, *blood.*"

"Ai, ai, chill, man," he said and unlocked the driver's door. His hand drifted towards the pocket of his jeans. Eric pressed the gun barrel in hard.

ToJo looked over his shoulder with a curious expression. Eric shook his head and tutted. "You wouldn't be going for a knife, would you?"

"Dunno what..."

"I'm talking about?" Eric said. "Then why don't you empty your pockets and prove it?"

"Nah, bruv. No need for that."

Eric pushed in closer. "I'm gonna empty 'em, anyway."

ToJo's body tensed up, but he allowed Eric to explore his pockets. Eric pulled a wallet from one pocket and a switchblade and mobile from another. "What was that about the knife?"

"Forgot I had it."

"I'll bet," Eric said and pulled back slightly. "Now get in and slide across."

ToJo opened the door and got inside. He shuffled clumsily across to the passenger's seat. Eric got in the driver's seat and pointed the business end of the gun at his captive. ToJo's gaze drifted towards the glove box. He licked his lips. Sweat beads formed on his brow.

"Go for that gun and see what it gets you," Eric said.

ToJo gave him the evil eye. "Ain' got no fuckin' gun."

"Then you won't minding opening it, will you?"

"Fill your boots."

"I said *you* open it."

ToJo's brows lowered and formed two deep ridges over the bridge of his nose. His hands shook as he struggled with the glove box locking mechanism. After a few seconds the compartment door opened. He licked his lips again.

The left side of the compartment was a mess of dog-eared map books and random scraps of paper, but an oily cloth and a piece of chamois leather covered the right side completely. ToJo's hand trembled. His fingertips brushed the oily rag. He shot a sneaky glance at Eric, who smiled back.

"Don't do owt foolish. I know what's behind those rags."

"You're pretty well informed, bruv."

Eric leant forward and pressed the gun barrel against his captive's side. "Pull them out," he said. "But do it slowly."

ToJo nodded once and huffed with resignation. He took the rags out one by one and placed them on his knee.

Eric saw part of a brown, textured handle poking out from the edge of the glove box. He removed out the revolver and put it in his jacket pocket.

There was a sharp tap the glass behind Eric's head. ToJo looked up at the torso of a large figure casting a shadow inside the car. He shook his head and groaned in the knowledge that his day was about to go from bad to worse.

Eric opened the door. "You took your time."

Derek grinned at Tojo. "Was taking a slash when I got the message. Then I spent five minutes tryna read the fuckin' thing. Entire fuckin' message was all constonants."

Eric backed out of the vehicle slowly but kept the gun trained on ToJo. "Unlock the passenger door."

ToJo reached behind and pulled at the door lock.

Derek moved around to the other side of the vehicle and opened the door.

Eric stared at ToJo. "Right, dickhead, you're gonna slide across and take the wheel. And if you try anything funny, the last laugh's gonna be on you."

14.

Darren entered the room on tiptoes and closed the door carefully. He put on the balaclava and immediately fought the urge to scratch. Dropping into a crouch, Darren pushed the makeshift paper wedge under the door and jammed it in tightly. He pulled his gun and took a moment to familiarise himself with its weight. Then he rounded the corner and waited for his moment.

Harry pissed into a urinal and stared blankly at the tiled wall. Tilting back his head, he let out a long sigh of satisfaction. Finishing his business, he did a quick shake and zipped himself up. Harry glanced over at the boy, standing in front of a child's urinal, copying his father's actions. Harry's right foot tapped the blue holdall repeatedly, which was beside him on the only patch of flooring not drenched with piss. He smiled and turned to say something to his son.

Then he noticed Darren.

For a moment Harry stood completely still, his smile fading. When he saw the gun, a momentary flicker of fear widened his blue gaze. Then this expression of fear became a frown. He turned slowly on his heels and faced Darren.

"Son?"

"Yes, Daddy?"

"You finished yet?"

The boy zipped up, turned towards his father and nodded.

"Good lad."

The boy realised that his father wasn't looking at him and turned in the direction of his gaze. He stared wide-eyed at Darren for a few seconds and then instinctively drew back a few steps and bumped up against the tiles. His bottom lip quivered, and he cast another glance at his father. Tears gathered at the corners of his eyes.

Darren's chest tightened when he noticed the boy's confusion and fear, but he didn't let it get in the way of business. As he saw things, it was Harry's fault for bringing the boy along for the ride.

A suppressed sob escaped the boy and tears started to roll down his cheeks, but he didn't quite break into hysterics. "Daddy?"

"It'll be all right," Harry said. "Now, go in one of the cubicles and lock the door."

"Da—ddy?"

"Do it *now*," he said. "And don't come out until I say."

Keeping his eyes firmly on Darren, the boy stepped towards the nearest cubicle and went inside. Metal slammed against metal repeatedly as the boy struggled with the lock before it finally slid into place. The boy's feet shuffled in the gap between the bottom of the cubicle wall and the floor tiles. Stifled sobs and sniffles emanated from within.

Harry smiled, but his gaze was cold. "Think very carefully about what you're doing."

Darren's eyes went to the holdall. "Kick it across."

Harry prodded the bag with his left foot. "It isn't worth the hassle, fella," he said. "Just turn around and leave and I'll forget this happened. Doesn't need to go any further. Let's look at it as a mistake."

Darren tightened his finger on the trigger. "I *said* kick the holdall across."

"If I do that, I don't see any scenario that's gonna go well for you."

"Lemme worry about that."

Harry kicked the holdall. It slid across the piss-soaked tiles until it struck Darren's feet. "You know summat fella, if I didn't have my son with me, you wouldn't have had it *this* easy."

"Turn around."

Something in Harry's expression changed. His face went slightly loose for a moment before a small smile twisted the right corner of his mouth. "How much is Manning getting for this?"

Darren hesitated. "Who?"

The smirk became a wonky grin. "The junky who sold us out."

Darren realised his initial hesitation was a mistake. He tried to correct it. "Dunno whatchoo talking about," he replied with a shrug.

Harry chuckled. "Playing dumb isn't gonna save him."

And with that, Darren realised his mistake. It was now obvious why the brothers wanted to stay away from the drugs. Just grabbing the money looked like a lucky strike, but grabbing both bags screamed set-up. A cold chill raised goosebumps on his skin and the hairs on the back of his neck began to rise. He swallowed his fear and decided to tough it out. "Why would I give a shit about a junky I don't even know?"

Harry raised a hand to his mouth like he was sharing a secret and whispered: "Your eyes gave you away."

Darren ignored him. "Turn around and put your hands behind your back."

"Fuck you," Harry said. "You've got the bag, now piss off."

Darren shuffled his shoulders, ready for trouble. "Don't make us tell you again."

Harry brought his fists up to chest height. He lowered his head and brought his right foot forward until he was in a fighter's stance. "You got what you wanted, but you won't be tying me up, fella."

Darren shook his head sadly. "It didn't hafta be like this."

He transferred the gun to his left hand and made a fist with his right. He knew that this wasn't going to take very long. Although Harry was a bigger man, his bulk mostly consisted of fat. Harry wasn't in the kind of shape to cause him much trouble. He was already breathing hard and hadn't thrown a punch yet.

Darren danced forward a couple of steps, made them look clumsy, and waited for Harry to react. The fat man didn't disappoint and shot his bolt early, swinging a wide, wild hook that was easy to duck. Darren countered with a fast right that hit Harry's chin and spun him around. The fat man's eyes fluttered. He staggered blindly into the wall and slid down the tiles until he was face first in a puddle of piss.

Darren came forward a few steps and kicked Harry in the jaw to ensure he stayed down. Then he rummaged in the unconscious man's coat, found his mobile phone, his keys, and wallet, and pocketed everything. He picked up the holdall, approached the cubicle door and knocked on it once. The boy whimpered.

"Kid, your Dad's down, but he'll be up again soon. I'm gonna leave now. Stay in there and count to two hundred. When you're done, you can come out and help him. Can you do that for me?"

The kid moaned yes and counted in a trembling, uncertain voice. Something about the way the boy was counting triggered a few childhood memories. He remembered when debt collectors arrived at his father's home and made themselves comfortable. Darren's dad told him to go to his room, place hands over his ears, and count to a thousand. Darren always heard his father's screams and breaking bones over the sound of the numbers, even when he was shouting them.

Darren wondered if the fear he felt then was similar to what the boy was experiencing. He hoped the kid was stern enough to remain undamaged by the experience. At the very least, he hoped it toughened him up a bit. The kid hit twenty, stammered, choked back a sob, and continued the count.

Darren made for the exit and pulled the wedge out from under the door. Taking off his balaclava, he ruffled his hair for a few seconds, shuffled his shoulders and got composed. Then he walked into the toilet entrance hall, which was empty. Darren moved to the double-doors, drew back the bolts, opened the doors and stepped into the lobby.

He didn't notice anybody hanging around waiting for the toilet, and thanked his lucky stars for that. But it wouldn't take long before somebody saw Harry on the floor, so a quick exit was required. Darren weaved through groups of people milling around in the lobby. Even though he could feel his heart hammering against his ribs, he tried not to look like he was panicking.

Once outside, Darren took in a deep breath and held it until the moment of panic passed. As he walked in the direction of the car, he dialled Eric's number and willed him to pick up the phone. It went straight to voicemail. He thought about leaving a message but felt this was one piece of bad news that was better delivered in person.

15.

Eric told ToJo to turn into a quiet industrial side road. Then he ordered him to get in the back of the car and lay face-down in the footwell. As soon as ToJo managed to contort his body into position, bending his legs at the knees, Derek placed his feet on his back to ensure he couldn't get up again. The car engine started with a cough, and Eric put his foot down.

Not for the first time that afternoon, ToJo felt fear, but this was different. His adrenaline had drained completely, leaving behind an increasing sense of dread. Was this trip going to end in his death? ToJo suppressed the urge to plead for his life and instead prayed for the first time in years. He mumbled the Lord's Prayer incoherently until Derek told him to shut the fuck up. Then he made a silent vow to clean up his act if he got out of this situation alive.

ToJo breathed carpet dust and counted the seconds and minutes in his head because there was nothing better to do. They had been driving for about forty-five minutes, much of it at very high speed. He didn't know where they were exactly, but the stench of horse shit in the air, and the gravel pinging against the underside of the car suggested they were somewhere in the country.

After a few more minutes they came to a stop, though the engine hummed gently. Derek lifted his feet, and ToJo got to his knees and gasped down air that wasn't thick with grime. He looked around and saw a lot of green and grey. Without his glasses, he could barely make out the inhabitants of the car never mind the outside world.

Eric grabbed ToJo by his jacket and dragged him roughly through the gap into the front passenger seat. He brushed at his torn clothing and, in the faint hope of recognising something, studied the scenery again.

Green inclines dotted through with clumps of purple heather surrounded them on all sides. A narrow road cut the hilly landscape in half. Low clouds drifted close to the peaks. ToJo stopped squinting because it hurt his eyes, but he suspected they were somewhere on the moors.

ToJo assumed his bravest expression, which didn't look a million miles away from lip-trembling terror, and stared at his captors. Hoping that his poor eyesight would make things easier, he tried to meet their gaze but didn't manage it for long and gradually lowered his eyes towards the footwell.

"Now what?" he mumbled into his chest.

Eric reached towards him. ToJo shrieked girlishly and drew back, placing his hands over his face and squealing that he didn't want to die. Eric ignored the histrionics and opened the door. Then he sat back and pointed the gun barrel in the direction of the undulating horizon.

"Now you get out and walk."

ToJo lowered his hands and listened to Derek's laughter with an increasing sense of shame. A flush of embarrassment burned across his face. His show of cowardice had amused his captors. He shuffled his shoulders and tried to reclaim some pride.

"You shitting me, right, blood?"

Eric shook his head and pointed again. "Out."

"We in the middle of nowhere, bruv."

"That's kinda the point."

"You got my owny fuckin' means of communicatin'," ToJo said, patting his empty hoodie to emphasise the fact.

"Again, kinda the point."

ToJo found another dash of some courage and tried to appear like the gangster he wasn't. "You know who I am? You know who you fuckin' messin' wit'?"

Eric grinned. "Yeah. You're that bloke who just got punched in the face for asking pointless fuckin' questions."

ToJo looked at him blank-eyed until he finally realised what was about to happen. By then it was too late, and Eric had already broken his nose with a well-aimed right and kicked him out of the car. He landed on his stomach on a wet patch of long grass that bordered the layby and blinked away tears of pain and shock.

Eric reached for the passenger door and began to pull it closed. "Nearest village is ten miles away," he said. "You get a move on, and don't get too lost, and I reckon you'll make it there in about four hours."

The car let out a weak wet cough and pulled away from the layby. Its underpowered engine whined as it struggled up a small rise. As soon as it reached the top, the car picked up speed and disappeared over the other side. The sputtering engine gradually faded into the distance, leaving only the sound of wind-rustled vegetation.

ToJo got to his feet gingerly and rested against a fence post. He pressed a fingertip against the bridge of his nose. The pain made him cry out and blink uncontrollably. Fresh tears flowed down his face.

He wiped the blood off his chin with his sleeve and kept rubbing until the area felt clean. Then he pulled the jacket hood over his head and adjusted his top until it felt right. ToJo fiddled with his loose jeans, held the waistband tightly as he trudged slowly down the road and used the time to think.

His boss wasn't going to be happy about the money. Ramon Carrasco didn't lose his temper often, but when he did the results were explosive. ToJo had witnessed this rage only once, but it was bad enough that he never wanted to see it again. The sight of his boss – face red, eyes wild, voice thick with anger – breaking a man's kneecaps and shins over five grand was one that wouldn't soon be forgotten. ToJo's troubles were ten times the size, so the sooner he reached civilisation and warned his boss about the problem the less severe his punishment would be.

ToJo's balls beat a hasty retreat into his body whenever he thought about what awaited him. Instead, he tried to think through the robbery and work out what had happened in the hope that he might have something positive to tell Ramon. Replaying the incident again and again, he began to see things clearly.

It was a set-up pure and simple. His kidnappers knew what they were doing and were well informed about the weapons he was packing. Had Jonno pulled a fast one? Maybe Harry had decided to strike out on his own? Or was it possible that other factors were at play?

ToJo thought back to the early days of the deal when Harry Sparks was nothing more than another foot soldier, and Bobby Manning was making the exchanges. Now he was exactly the sort of clown who'd spoil a sweet deal like this. He was stupid enough to sample the stock and weak enough to become a junky. Addicts were dangerous and unpredictable. They were certainly volatile enough to consider betrayal and robbery if they were hungry for a fix, and their cash flow was weak.

ToJo remembered telling Ramon that they should switch locations when Harry took over the drop, but his boss didn't see Manning as a threat. So the blame fell squarely on Ramon and Jonno for not changing the routine when they had the chance. ToJo wasn't brave enough to point it out, though. Instead, he decided that getting to a phone as soon as possible and informing his boss about his suspicions would be much better for his kneecaps.

He picked up the pace and hoped his kidnappers hadn't lied about the village.

16.

It took Harry a couple of minutes to come round. When he finally opened his eyes, he realised that somebody was shaking him and saying his name repeatedly. Harry turned his head slightly to focus on the blurred figure but knew he'd have to turn over if he wanted a proper look. Harry eased over onto his back and stared up at the face of an elderly black man with tight-cropped grey curls. It wasn't somebody he recognised.

The man bent towards him. "You okay, Harry?"

Harry let out a sharp breath and pushed with both hands until he sat upright. Spots popped and danced before his eyes and dizziness made him wobble. The Good Samaritan grabbed his shoulders to prevent him from falling back.

"Yeah, I'm... how d'you know my name?"

The man gestured with his chin towards Terry, crying beside one of the sinks. "Your boy told me."

"Yeah, I'm okay, fella."

The man squinted at the bruises on Harry's chin and cheek. "What happened? Did somebody sock you?"

The child whimpered. Harry gave him a sharp glance. The snivels stopped dead, though the tears continued to flow. Harry turned back to the man and gave him his friendliest grin.

"No. Just passed out. That's all."

The old man smirked briefly and patted Harry's shoulder. It was evident he didn't believe him. Approaching the sink, the man washed his hands and stared at Harry in the mirror. "You might want to sort out a change of clothes, friend. Your clothes are drenched with pee. And it bloody well stinks, if you don't mind me saying."

Harry looked down at the damp patches darkening his jacket and shirt. He grimaced and peeled the wet shirt away from his skin. The stench was vile.

"Thanks for telling me, fella."

Rubbing his hands together beneath an air-dryer that roared like a jet engine, the man smiled and shouted: "No problem."

Then he stopped briefly by the boy and ruffled his hair.

"You sure you're okay? You want me to get anybody?"

Harry pressed a hand against the cubicle wall and used it to help him stand upright. He gave the man another smile and assured him he was fine. The man nodded doubtfully, said his goodbyes, and left.

The moment the door closed, Harry tore through his jacket pockets and rummaged in his jeans. All he found were handfuls of lint, wet receipts, and a few twenty pence pieces. His attacker had taken everything else. He cursed at the top of his voice and kicked the cubicle wall until the wood split and splintered.

Harry now had more trouble than he could handle: such as telling Jonno Fielding that his half a kilo of heroin was missing. Past experiences suggested that this would go one of three ways. The first involved taking a half hour of spittle-flecked, demeaning abuse, and probably a beating, before being ordered to go and find the merchandise. The second way was a savage beating and broom handle rape. The third ended with him in small, bloody pieces, awaiting disposal. Now that the run-in over Kev Nicholson had made their relationship so awkward, Harry had a feeling that if he didn't sort the problem, promptly it was a certainty that Jonno would choose the third option.

He only stopped kicking the cubicle to pieces when he was aware of a thin, high-pitched sound in his ears. He turned towards the noise. Eyes wide with terror, Terry pressed up against the wall and shrieked. Harry knew that he was the source of the boy's fear, and a sudden feeling of guilt turned his stomach.

Harry dropped his hands and softened his aggressive posture. Trying not to alarm Terry, he approached with a smile on his face. The boy flinched and edged away, his eyes angling to the exit, he was ready to run for it.

Harry crouched on his haunches and smiled. He kept his distance because he didn't want to spook the boy. "I'm sorry, son. I'm not angry with you," he murmured. "I'm mad at the man who stole from me."

Terry nodded but didn't seem convinced. Harry needed to allay his son's fears before he could deal with telling Jonno about the lost drugs; as soon as a tantrum began it was almost impossible to calm him quickly. Loud screams and limb flailing hysterics weren't the ideal atmosphere for quick thinking or explaining the situation to his angry boss.

"Daddy's not mad at you. I promise. *Okay?*"

Fresh tears gathered around his son's lashes. He jerked his head up and down and sent them rolling down his face.

Harry held his arms open wide. "Daddy needs a hug."

The boy pulled away again, but it wasn't fear that made him withdraw; he looked down at his father's clothes and wrinkled his nose. Harry felt a plunging moment of heartbreak at the rejection. Then he realised the boy was more concerned about touching his piss-soaked jacket and smiled with relief.

"Oh, yeah, I'm a bit damp."

Holding out his hand, palm up, Harry said: "Then instead of a hug. How about a pound coin, instead?"

Terry wore an uncertain expression and gnawed at his bottom lip.

"The man took my wallet and phone, and I need to make a call. When I get my wallet, I'll give you a fiver back. *And* you can have a Happy Meal with extra large fries."

The boy frowned and rummaged in his pockets. He pulled out a pound coin dusted with lint. Harry took the coin and put it in his pocket with the other change. He placed a hand on Terry's shoulder. "Now why don't we go and sort this all out, son? How does that sound?"

17.

Despite speeding most of the way, slowing only to the avoid police speed traps, it took Eric forty-five minutes to reach Feldman's Scrapyard. He drove through the high-walled gate, past towering corridors of rusted ruins, and into the main scrapyard enclosure. He parked near the dirty prefabricated structure used as the central office.

Darren was already there. He stared into space as a short fat man in army fatigues subjected him to an arm-waving monologue. When he realised the boxer wasn't paying any attention, the man screwed up his rumpled, toad-like face in an expression of disgust and turned towards Eric.

Darren appeared worried and nervous. He devoured the nails of his right hand, working his way from left-to-right and back again, as if in some trance. When Eric noticed what his partner was holding in his left, he knew why. Darren was carrying the one thing he'd been told specifically not to grab: the drugs holdall.

Eric sat silently for a minute and let his rage come to the boil. A few deep breaths dropped it to a low simmer. All Darren had to do was prevent Harry Sparks from leaving the Forum while they were dealing with ToJo. That was it, one simple task. How was it possible to fuck it up?

Eric opened the door and stormed towards Darren, who was approaching with an apologetic expression on his face.

Eric pointed at the holdall. "What the fuck have you done?"

"I made a mistake," Travers replied.

"You're right about that."

Sensing impending violence, the fat man stepped between the pair and smiled. "Girls behave, this is a place of worship."

Derek stood behind his brother and sneered. "Worship? What worship?"

The man shrugged. "What've you got?"

"That supposed to be a joke, Gaz?"

Gary Feldman shook his head and lost the smile. "No joke. When you're here, you'll show me the same fuckin' respect you'd show a man of the cloth. Now, I know you doyles have no interest in churches, except in maybe stealing lead off their roofs, so I'll rephrase it in terms you *will* understand: if you wanna fight, take it outside and don't come back."

Eric looked at him. "But…"

"But nothing."

"This idiot…"

Gary placed his hands on Eric's chest. "I don't give a fuck," he said, glaring at everybody. "Listen up, so I don't have to repeat. I'm not in the fuck giving business, and if I *were* in the fuck giving business, I'd be bankrupt by now. I'm in the disposal business, and that's the only fuckin' reason why you're here wasting my valuable time. You came here for one thing and one thing only, and it *wasn't* to argue. Now, why doesn't one of you pay what you owe so that we can dispose of this hot car problem?"

Eric pulled a wad of notes from his jacket. "Five hundred per car, right?"

Gary nodded. "That's right."

Darren looked at both men and said: "Hows about I pay? Hows about I make it up to you for the fuck up?"

Eric pressed the money into the scrap merchant's hand. "How about you tell me *why* you screwed up in the first place?"

Gary placed his hand over his ears and made a *la-la-la* sound. "I *don't* wanna hear this. I *can't* hear this. Take it over there."

Eric and Darren walked along a passage of creaking, groaning car shells until they were well away from the scrap merchant. Then they turned right, out of Gary's line of sight, and stopped. Eric slapped the back of his hand against the holdall that Darren cradled like a dying infant.

"How'd you manage to fuck this up?"

"I didn't think, did I?"

Eric shook his head. "I wouldn't know, 'cause I wasn't fuckin' there."

"I saw the opportunity, and I took it. I thought we could double our take."

"And who's gonna shift it?"

Darren looked down at the bag and sighed.

"Who do *you* know who'll pay for this kinda weight?" Eric asked. "Who do you know who'll stamp all over it and ship it on?"

Darren's face drained of colour and his eyes angled up towards the grey sky. He looked like he was about to be sick.

"Fuckin' drug dealers, that's who. The kinda people we just stole from."

"I didn't think. I'm sorry."

Eric crowded Darren's personal space. "Sorry doesn't fuckin' cut it.

Sorry doesn't fix it. All you needed to do was follow orders."

"I know…"

"So why didn't you?"

Darren glanced at the holdall again. "Because I got greedy."

"We need to get rid of that fuckin' bag."

"I know," he said, giving Eric a hopeful look. "You know anybody who might…"

"I know *one* fuckin' person who might buy this shit. But we're not on good terms at the moment, and I don't wanna deal with him unless I really need to." Eric said. "Actually, what we should do is weigh the bag down, throw it in the fuckin' Tees, and be done with it once and for all."

Eric put his face in his hands, took a few deep breaths, looked up and said: "You've really fucked this. It won't take both sides long to communicate. And when they do, they're gonna know this was a setup. It won't take much time to work out it was Bobby who fucked them over. And they're not gonna hafta look too hard to find him. You've just killed that poor bastard."

Darren shuffled on the spot, looking uncomfortable like he was itching to say something but didn't quite know how. Eric knew an awkward silence when he encountered one. "Jesus! Did Harry recognise you?"

Darren shook his head. "Balaclava."

"Then why're you looking so uncomfortable?"

Darren paused for a few moments. His face twisted between expressions before it finally settled on worry. "I think he's already worked out who set him up."

"And you didn't think to phone?"

Darren didn't know what to say. He just shrugged his shoulders.

It was getting on for two hours since the robbery, which gave Harry and Jonno a head start in finding Bobby. Instinct told Eric to abandon the junky to his fate, that he was a hopeless cause, but his conscience said this was a mistake.

He'd made Bobby a promise. One he knew he had to keep.

Eric pulled a mobile phone and dialled. It rang through to voicemail. "Bob, it's Eric. Listen very fuckin' carefully. My idiot of a partner fucked up his side of the job, which means you're in trouble. You need to get the fuck outta wherever you are and run.

"Lay low until I can get the money to you. Then you maybe you should disappear for a while. Gimme a call when you're settled. Soz about this, I should pick my partners better."

He walked towards Gary, announcing: "We still need one of the cars."

The scrap merchant pressed his bloated lips together in a faint display of amusement. "You can take back the car, but not the money. I don't do refunds."

"Fair enough. Deal's the same; I just need it for another hour or so."

Gary waved a dismissive hand. "The deal's not the same. You pay again if you drive off the lot. No refunds, no credit."

A heavy scowl lowered Derek's brow. "How the fuck is *that* fair?"

Gary smiled. "It isn't. My lot equals my fuckin' rules. If you don't like it, you can consider yourself blacklisted and fuck off."

Derek attempted to say something else, but Eric interrupted: "We like it just fine."

Gary nodded and walked in the direction of the office. He closed the door behind him and locked it. Loud music emanated from inside. He was no longer interested in their business.

Eric unlocked ToJo's car and waved the others over. Darren prodded him. "What's going on?"

"We're going on a trip."

"Where?"

"I'm not waiting for Bobby to call. He said he'd hide out at his ex-wife's place if shit gets dangerous. If he's not there already, that's where he'll go when he gets my message."

Derek lurked a few feet away and kicked up dirt with his steel capped boots. He wore a thoughtful look. "You know summat, cruel as it sounds, mebbe we should just leave Bobby and split his share. Not like the cunt's got much life expectancy, is it? What with the smack an' all?"

Darren nodded. "Gotta say, I think he's right. Bobby just got unlucky."

Eric gritted his teeth. "We're not fuckin' leaving him."

"But…"

"But nothing. I made him a promise. I told him if things got rough we'd be there as partners."

Derek shrugged. "That were your stupid fuckin' mistake, weren't it?"

Eric pushed a finger under his brother's nose. "Listen up, you. The only fuckin' thing we've got is our word, and if we don't have that we've got *nothing*. If we throw our partners under the bus every time things get hairy nobody's ever gonna work with us. We fight for our partners or we call it a fuckin' day, right here and now. You and me are through."

Worry lines formed above Derek's nose and his eyes clouded over. Then he pushed his brother's hand away. "Fine, we'll go find your boyfriend, if you're gonna be that much of a fuckin' pansy about it."

Despite the attempt at sounding magnanimous, Eric knew his brother was worried about going it alone. Derek had ended up doing two years inside the last time he ran a crew. He didn't have the brains or the patience to plan jobs and needed a partner whether he liked it or not.

"Then we better get going," Eric replied. "The sooner we start the sooner we sort this fuckin' mess out."

18.

Jonno sat back in his armchair recliner and blew the steam off a strong black coffee. He adjusted his dressing gown and stared at the television without actually watching it. Instead, he wondered why last night's session with Sophia and Terri had been so disappointing.

The first time had happened by accident. He met the girls in a club and invited them back to his place for weed. His eye was on the blonde, Sophia, who returned his gaze with interest, but he asked Terri along because he thought it would make Sophia more comfortable. His intention was that when the time came, Terri would take the spare bedroom and Sophia would end up in bed with him.

But the weed changed all that.

It was good stuff; in fact, it was the best he'd ever smoked. The feeling was smooth and mellow and quickly lowered everybody's inhibitions. After some heavy flirting, the girls put on a show for him. They stripped to their underwear and danced by candlelight. Then they unhooked their bras and removed each other's panties. And when he could barely take it anymore, they invited him to join the party.

Jonno didn't need asking twice.

They fucked for hours, changing positions and permutations until, finally, Jonno came so long and hard he thought he might have done some permanent damage. When the girls left the next morning, they all arranged to meet up again as soon as possible.

But last night the magic was missing. The weed wasn't as potent, and the girls didn't look quite so lovely. Nobody seemed particularly aroused, and they all went through the motions. He was sure that both girls faked their orgasms. Even he faked an orgasm after an hour of lifeless thrusting, just to get it over with, and tossed the empty condom before the girls got wise to the deception.

The girls had whispered and hissed as they gathered their clothes at seven in the morning. They crept out of the bedroom to put them on in the hallway. Jonno pretended to be asleep to avoid any awkward and stilted conversations. He breathed a sigh of relief when the front door clicked shut. He was glad they were gone.

When he finally closed his eyes again, he slept until one in the afternoon.

Now he was watching the TV with disinterest. An attractive TV presenter guided a middle-aged couple through the rooms of a Spanish villa. Despite his boredom, he couldn't be bothered to change the channel. Instead, he drank more coffee and thought about wanking off to the TV presenter to pass the time.

The house phone rang loudly. Jonno wondered if the girls were calling to apologise for last night's poor performance and considered not picking up. He ignored it until he realised that it wasn't going to stop ringing until he answered. He jumped off the chair and grabbed the handset off the windowsill.

"*What?*"

"It's Harry."

Just the name alone made Jonno's adrenaline spike. His fingers squeezed the handset. Harry never rang after trades; he just delivered the product to the agreed upon meeting point. Something unpleasant had happened; a problem that Harry needed to discuss.

"Do I wanna hear this?" he said.

Harry paused. "Not really."

"This better be a minor problem, Aitch. You're broke down somewhere and need jump leads, right?"

"Think I'd prefer to know how to hotwire a car, right this second."

"Meaning?"

Harry sighed. "Somebody stole the product."

Jonno squeezed the phone until his knuckles turned white and the plastic began to crack. Then he dropped the handset on the sill and stepped away, drawing in deep breaths. He wanted to hit something, somebody, anybody. Harry repeated his name, each time a little louder and more frantic the longer he waited for an answer. Jonno reached for a cushion and screamed angry expletives into it until he was red in the face.

Finally, he took a deep breath and scooped up the handset again. "Anybody we know?"

"Dunno the prick who robbed me, as he was wearing a balaclava," Harry said. "But it wasn't random job, 'cause Balaclava Boy knew the routine."

"A set-up?"

"Yeah. And I think I might know who arranged it."

Jonno's heart skipped. "Who?"

"Bobby."

"*Manning?*"

"That's right. The guy who robbed me clammed up when I asked him about Bobby. Pretended he didn't know the name, but I saw it in his eyes. I heard it in his fuckin' voice."

Jonno's heart fluttered again. It never occurred to him that in addition to a taste for the needle and the crack pipe his former partner might also have developed a taste for betrayal. It never occurred because Bobby was weak and spineless. He was more businessman than gangster; great at shaking hands, making deals, and building infrastructure, but not so hot when it came to violence and brutality. In fact, the rough stuff affected him so much that he started sampling the stock to numb his response to the blood and screams that Jonno revelled in.

And this was why he'd never changed the routine: he believed there was nothing to fear. Jonno had been so busy thinking about all his other problems that he'd overlooked the possibility of betrayal by a man he once considered a friend.

"I wanna see you. *Now.*"

Harry let out a long sigh. "That's gonna be difficult."

"Why?"

"Guy who robbed me caught me by surprise and knocked me out. Took my money, my car keys, and my phone. I'm stuck here."

Jonno groaned. "Stay right fuckin' there. Don't move a muscle. I'm gonna phone Charlie and get him to pick you up and take you to mine."

"What are you gonna do in the meantime?"

"I'm gonna find out where that fuckin' smackhead's staying, then drop a tonne of shit on him."

19.

Jonno downed a couple of double espressos and snorted two fat lines of madman coke before he called Charlie Wallace. The combination of stimulants heightened his aggression and sharpened his thinking.

He told Charlie to grab Harry and leave the boy behind. Charlie suggested that he was uncomfortable with leaving a kid to fend for himself. Jonno screamed abuse at him until he changed his mind. Then he told him to take Harry to his Dad's derelict garage in Seaton Carew, tie him up, and await his arrival.

Jonno wanted somebody, *anybody,* to pay for this debacle. Although Bobby was to blame for the robbery, Harry was to blame for not changing the routine, for not fighting harder to protect the drugs, for bringing his retard of a son with him, and for being useless and fat. For these things, he had to suffer the consequences.

Jonno made the decision to kill Bobby before he had inhaled his first line of coke. However, he was only now beginning to enjoy the prospect of making the piece of shit suffer. He would take him apart piece by piece. Jonno would force the bastard chew on his own entrails before finally allowing him to die.

He wasn't sure what to do with Harry yet, but he had a few ideas.

Maybe a beating would suffice, or possibly a few broken bones would keep him in line. He wondered if maybe it was time to grease up the broom handle again and turn Harry into an example for others (this one particularly appealed, especially as he was still smarting about Kevin Nicholson). Or maybe he would drag a knife from his pubis to his ribcage and watch his bloated innards slither out like snakes escaping from a wet paper bag. He'd only know for certain when Harry was in front of him.

Jonno phoned Jim Hanway and told him to bring an inconspicuous car, a couple of useful men, some weaponry, and come pick him up. Then he showered, shaved, and plucked a few stray hairs from his eyebrows. He sprayed his underarms and dabbed scent on his neck and upper chest. He put on freshly ironed jeans, a white and blue striped shirt, and bespoke pinstripe smart-casual jacket that draped perfectly across his shoulders. The entire outfit cost more than most people made in a week, and his brown leather brogues cost double that.

Jonno didn't dress like other dealers he knew. He dressed with style, or at least his version of it. There were no baggy tracksuits or low-hanging gangsta jeans, and no stupid bits of jewellery hanging like nuggets of gold plated shit from his neck and ears. He didn't wear fat bling rings or anything that called attention to his occupation. The only gold he wore was on his watch, which was expensive but understated.

Jonno primped and teased his hair with wax. He pushed his face towards the bathroom mirror, admiring its sleek, chiselled lines and flawless complexion. It didn't matter to him that he was about to go somewhere dirty to do dirty work. The only thing that mattered was he looked good while doing it.

A car horn blasted for several seconds, and he received a text message telling him his ride was outside. He admired his reflection one final time and left the house.

A shiny black 4x4 with heavily tinted windows, a large rear spoiler, and polished metal rims purred like a contented kitten opposite his front gate. Jonno felt a moment of blind rage; this was the wrong vehicle. It was anything but inconspicuous.

He wrenched open the car door and jumped into the front passenger seat, slamming the door shut behind him. The three men inside jumped, but none jumped higher than the driver. Jim Hanway's rodent face twitched because he sensed danger, and his jaw muscles flexed and jerked beneath the skin. He wrinkled his small upturned nose when he realised that Jonno was glaring at his baggy yellow tracksuit and matching trainers.

"Summat up, boss?" he asked innocently.

"Didn't I ask for summat *inconspicuous?*" Jonno replied.

"Soz boss, best I could do at short notice," Jim added.

"You've got three fuckin' cars, Jim: so why didn't you grab the hatch?"

Jim's cheeks turned pink. "The engine's fucked," he said. "It's up on blocks at the moment, and the Mazda's only got two seats. Didn't have no choice."

Jonno huffed and stared out of the window momentarily, so he didn't have to gaze at the driver's ugly mug. "This thing looks like a fuckin' pimp wagon. Nowt screams criminal louder than tinted fuckin' windows and massive fuck-off spoilers."

"Soz, boss."

"You can keep your fuckin' apology. You're lucky we're in a hurry. Otherwise, I'd make you go back and fix the hatch."

Jim hung his head slightly, trying his best to appear chastened. When he thought it was safe to look up again, he asked: "Where d'you wanna go?"

"Needle Exchange."

Jim revved the engine. "You sure he's gonna be there?"

"No, but if you know a better place to start then feel free to enlighten me."

A burly, bald bruiser, with a face like a Picasso portrait painted on tanned leather, bent forward and tapped Jonno on the shoulder. "He's got hisself a new bird."

"Has he now?" Jonno replied. "Who is she, Dave?"

Dave Callan rubbed his prominent chin. "Marilyn summat?"

"Monroe? Manson?"

"Clarke, I think."

Jonno turned towards him. "You think? So you don't *know*?"

"Not for certain."

"Then I take it you don't know where she lives either?"

Dave shuffled nervously in his seat. "Not off the top of me head, boss."

Jonno gave him a cold stare. "Not off the top of your baldy, leathery fuckin' head. So what exactly is it you *do* know?"

"Jonno…"

Jonno pushed his face between the headrests.

"D'you even know what she looks like?"

Dave's face creased as he struggled with the question. Sweat formed on his brow. Wiping a hand across his forehead, he turned towards the other backseat passenger, possibly in the hope that he might come to his aid, but Ben Otley kept his gaunt, pinched face in the direction of the houses on the opposite side of the road.

"Come on, Dave. What exactly do you know about Marilyn might be Clarke, Manson, or fuckin' Monroe?"

"Nowt," Dave said under his breath.

"So you've just wasted my fuckin' time with this nonsense, haven't you?"

Dave shrugged and pulled a face. He resembled a chastised toddler. "S'pose."

Jonno turned away and noticed they were still outside his front gate. He waved his hands at the windscreen. "Why the fuck aren't we moving?"

"Thought you was laying down the law?" Jim replied, struggling with the handbrake. "Didn't wanna disturb you, like."

Jonno rolled his eyes. "Oh, and that fuckin' stops you from driving, does it? You not heard of multitasking out in Berwick Hills?"

Jim put his foot down but pulled away too fast. The car screeched, lurched forward and stalled. Jonno gave a sarcastic laugh. "Any time you feel like moving is fine by me."

Hands shaking visibly, Jim struggled to turn the key. Finally, the engine roared into life, and the vehicle raced to the end of the street and screeched into a right turn. Jonno eyeballed Jim and then turned his cold gaze on Dave in the rear-view mirror, almost willing them to display any signs of hostility, but they kept their faces down.

"So have youse got any issues with going to the fuckin' Needle Exchange?" Jonno declared. "Any problems you'd like to share with the group?"

Both men shook their heads.

"Fuckin' thought not."

Jonno's attention went to the speedometer – too slow for his liking.

"Pick up the pace, Jim. I've seen cripples crawl faster than you're driving."

20.

Jim turned off Borough Road onto a grimy terraced street blighted with boarded-up properties. Somebody had covered the street sign with white paint and daubed The Needle Exchange over it in shaky lettering. The council hadn't bothered to remove the sign or the graffiti. Like most of the street's residents, they had ceased caring a long time ago.

Behind the boards and the metal covers were addicts, homeless people, and others who had left the human race for one reason or another. The few houses not covered over were regularly broken into to feed drug, alcohol, and gambling addictions – so their inhabitants treated all newcomers with suspicion. It didn't surprise Jonno to see twitching curtains and worried faces peeking out of windows as the 4x4 moved past.

The vehicle pulled up opposite a house that had suffered years of neglect. Its pebbledash had come away in places, leaving large bald spots. Dry and wet rot had eroded the window frames so badly that the only thing holding the panes in place was putty.

Jonno exited the 4x4, crossed the road and knocked on the warped front door. The wood was so soft with wet rot that Jonno wondered if it might be possible to punch and kick his way inside. It took a while for the occupant to come to the door, and then it took just as long for the misshapen thing to be wrenched open.

A wrinkled man with a shock of white hair and a neck like a used condom panted for breath and stared at Jonno, his blue eyes sparkling with irritation. He rested his weight against the doorframe and wheezed enough air into his lungs to form a few words: "What… brings you… to my abode?" There was anger in his voice. He didn't seem pleased at the disturbance.

Jonno waved three twenties in front of the man's face. "Is that a way to treat a friend, George?"

George Harris eyed the money coldly. "Who said… we're friends?"

Once upon a time he'd been Robert Owden's right-hand man, and the brain to Bob's brawn. Together they controlled Teesside. George oversaw gambling, robbery, bribes, protection, smuggling, prostitution, dealing, and any other racket that turned a profit. However, over the years, their relationship soured and their paths diverged.

Bob moved onwards and upwards, legitimising his empire, and consolidating his power. George slid down into the bottle, developing a thirst he couldn't shake, and his former partner cast him aside.

Nowadays he was content to sell his considerable knowledge of Teesside villainy to the highest bidder, usually paid in alcoholic form. What George didn't know wasn't worth knowing.

Jonno waved the cash until it generated a small breeze. "These do."

Now that he'd caught his breath, George stepped away from the door-frame. "Nice as that feels against my skin; it's not gonna make us friends."

"So what *will* make us friends?"

"When that gentle breeze becomes a hurricane."

"That's not gonna happen."

"Then we're not gonna be friends, which means I'm not coming out to play."

"This is real money, George."

The old man scoffed. "As opposed to what? Monopoly money? Get the fuck off my doorstep with *that* bullshit."

"Beggars can't be choosers."

"This beggar *is* a chooser. And I'm choosing to close the door."

"You do that, and you'll regret it."

A small, thin smile squeezed George's lips. "Are you threatening me?"

"If it comes to that."

"Just remember who I am, *boy.*"

"I know exactly who you are; you're the elderly fuckin' shadow of a gadgie who used to be somebody. And now you're just someone in my way. I want some information outta you, alkie, and I'm not fuckin' leaving till I get it."

George grinned and attempted to close the door. Jonno wedged his right foot between the door and the frame. "I'm not leaving without a conversation," he said. "Open up *now*, before I smack the shit outta you."

They struggled for a few seconds. The old man wedged his entire weight against the wood. When it was evident that Jonno was going to force his way in, George stepped away from the door and let the momentum carry his tormentor into the darkened hallway.

Jonno staggered forward a few steps, righted himself, and then felt something cold and hard beneath his chin. George pressed forward until

Jonno felt the iron sight against his windpipe. He raised his hands.

"Easy there."

The old man ground his rotting teeth together. "What were that about smacking the shit outta me?"

"I was upset," Jonno replied. "I still am."

George forced Jonno back outside. "So go be upset someplace else," he said, pulling the revolver away before any of his neighbours could see it. The gun remained behind his back, in case Jonno tried to get handy again. He retreated into the hallway and put the snub-nose back in his pocket. "If you knock on my fuckin' door again, next time I'll answer it with bullets."

The door slammed shut with a bang. Jonno screamed insults and threats, but he didn't lay a finger on the door. He was angry with himself. He should have handled things better. It made more sense to double the reward than use threats, but his desire to get the drugs back outweighed common sense. Cursing under his breath, he inhaled slowly and gradually let it out.

21.

Jonno turned away from the door, put his head down, and stormed towards the 4x4, brushing aside a small dark haired man without looking at him. He got in the passenger seat, wrenched the seat belt across and clicked it in place.

He was now in the mood to kill somebody, so didn't take it very well when Dave said: "Billy Chin's looking for you. He's…"

Jonno cut him off. "Oh Christ, what does that little fuckin' ching-chong man want?"

"Ow! Who d'you think you're calling a little fuckin' ching-chong man, you? You fuckin' racist round-eyed cunt."

Billy Chin's gaunt, angry face poked through the open driver's side window, his dark eyes burning with hate and drug psychosis. Wide nostrils flaring as he snorted with rage, Billy pushed his head further into the vehicle. Jonno realised that this was the small man he'd brushed aside. The recognition of the error made him sink into his seat. He prepared for trouble.

But, then again, most people prepared for trouble when Billy appeared, because you couldn't rationalise with the kind of crazy that he had in spades. Despite a drug habit of legendary proportions, and self-professed HIV and Hepatitis infections, he was one of life's survivors. He'd been surviving for years by running loosely banded communes of junkies and dropouts.

Billy stole from anybody that could afford it. He borrowed from loan sharks without bothering to repay, stole from other junky communes and low-level drug dealers. He even removed copper pipes and wires from construction sites and sold them to out-of-town contractors. Nobody complained when they discovered who had taken their belongings, and they certainly never considered trying to get their stuff back. Instead, they swallowed their pride and accepted the loss.

The few people who'd been stupid enough to try and take back their property or get revenge had either lived to regret their mistakes or hadn't lived long enough for regrets. Billy Chin wasn't the kind of man you wanted to upset; this was what was troubling Jonno when he turned towards the junky with a forced smile on his face. "Was just winding you up, weren't I? I could see you there, mate."

Billy's face remained screwed up with anger. "Is that another fuckin' joke?"

Jonno stared at him in open-mouthed incomprehension. "I dunno…"

"You making some kinda dig about me fuckin' eyes? You saying your peripheral vision is better cozza your fuckin' *round* eyes? Is that it?"

Billy began to shake. His fingers white-knuckled the window frame.

Jonno realised that Billy might be looking for a fight. He wondered if he was still smarting about what happened to Kevin Nicholson all those months ago.

"Come on, Billy mate. That wasn't what I meant at all."

Jim shook his head and added: "Wasn't what he meant, mate."

Billy got in the driver's face. "And how would *you* know what he meant, you fuckin' ferret-headed freak? Have youse two got some fuckin' human-rodent telepathy thing going?"

Normally, it would have amused Jonno to see his driver taken down a peg or two, but the thought of being this close to somebody as filthy and diseased as Billy made his skin crawl.

"Come on, man, it was a joke," Jonno insisted. "Surely you can see that?"

The moment he used the word *see*, Jonno knew it was the wrong choice of expression. It took everything in his power not to let out a groan when Billy's face tightened in another grimace of rage.

"You saying I can't see through me slitty eyes? Is that it, you fuckin' faggot? Hows about I spray some blood around the inside of your nice, clean vehicle? Hows about I give you all a fuckin' AIDS shower?"

Billy pushed his wrist through the window and put a small, sharp blade against one of the veins. Jim let out a shrill shriek. Dave moaned and slid across the backseat until he was in Ben's lap. Jonno turned his body towards the door and reached for the handle.

"Whaddaya want, Bill?" he said.

"Want? Well, let's see, shall we?" Billy replied, pulling away the blade slightly. "Hows about some racial respect, for starters? Or mebbe just an apology."

Jonno lifted his hands in a gesture of surrender. "I'm sorry for calling you a ching-chong man."

Billy's face lost its tightness. He pulled back further, removed the blade from his wrist and put it back in the pocket of his leather jacket. "I've got some gossip I think you might appreciate. But now, in light of you being a cunt, I'm thinking I should take me information elsewhere."

"I said I was sorry."

Billy sneered. "And I can just hear the contrition in your voice."

Jim's eyes fixed on the junky. "Cont… contrish…"

"It's called a vocabulary, you fuckin' dunce," Billy snapped. "Try reading a book sometime. Mebbe then you'd understand it means *remorse*."

Jonno was tiring of Billy's antics. He decided to placate the junky properly if only to calm him down and get him away from the car as quickly as possible.

"Look, I'm genuinely sorry, okay?" Jonno insisted. "I'm in a bad fuckin' mood, Bill. I tend to say stupid shit when I'm upset."

Billy's lips parted in a rotten brown smile. "Yeah, and I know *why* you're upset."

Jonno's heart kicked up a gear. "You do?"

Billy nodded.

"How?"

Billy came close to Jim and tapped his temple. "*Real* telepathy, that's how. Not any of your fuckin' human-ferret shit."

Jim's jaw muscles jumped.

Jonno clapped his hands to get Billy's attention. The junky averted his eyes away from the driver and fixed them on Jonno. "Real telepathy costs money."

"How much?"

Billy shook his head. "That's not how this works, pretty boy."

"I've got sixty quid."

Billy wrapped his arms around his torso and performed a theatrical quiver of delight. "Ooh, you really know how to spoil a girl."

"Is this the part where I get told to go fuck myself?"

"Precisely."

Jonno paused and took a deep breath. "So what is you do want?"

"What I want is world peace," Billy said. "What I *want* is to feel me dick sliding down Cheryl Cole's gullet. What I *want* is to see Boro win the fuckin' premier league. What I *want* more than owt else in the world is to get me hands on aitch so fuckin' pure I can bathe meself in the shit and still shoot it up afterwards. But what I'll settle for is the contents of your wallets. All of 'em – including the sixty you offered the old man. For that, I'll point you where you need to be?"

Everybody in the car complained simultaneously, getting louder and more aggressive until Jonno told them to shut the fuck up. He gathered the contents of their wallets and pockets and held the notes and coins in his hand.

Billy's eyes lingered on the money. He licked his lips.

Jonno waved the paper around. "So where *do* I need to be?"

"Oh, you don't trust us, right? Well, I know who you're looking for. You're looking for Bobby, right?"

"Maybe."

"Don't get all cryptic. We both know who you're after."

"Fine, I'm looking for Bobby."

Billy grinned. "Well, I just happen to know where that fuckin' delinquent is."

Dave poked his head between the two front seats. "Fuck this, boss. We don't need the hassle. Let's just visit this fuckin' Marilyn bird. That's where he'll be."

Billy's demeanour turned angry once again. "*Marilyn?* Listen up, Ross Kemp; he's not with anybody called fuckin' Marilyn. He's never been anywhere near a bitch called Marilyn. Mebbe there's some confusion inside that shiny fuckin' hundred-watt dome of yours, coz Bobby's bitch is *Marianne.* Now sit back in your seat and let the adults talk, you Kojak fuck, before I jam a blood-filled syringe into your fuckin' eyeball."

Dave lowered his head and sat back slowly.

Billy lifted up his hand and rubbed his thumb and fingers together. "You wanna know where he is, then lemme feel your folding paper."

Jonno pushed the money into Billy's hand. He closed his fist around a fat wad of twenties, tens and fives and stuffed it into his pockets. "So, Bobby comes round earlier, asking to buy some serious weight of aitch from us, right? Silly prick offers to pay with an IOU, sez he's good for it. I let him know where he could stick his IOU and told him to get the fuck out.

"Then he starts claiming he's got nearly five grand due in later today. Now, I sez, where the hell are you gonna get that kinda cash from? He sez he's got some hard lads working for him, and they're gonna clear you out. I told him he could take his imaginary raid and his imaginary stash and make *himself* imaginary before I lost me fuckin' rag. So he pulls a hundred and asks what he can get for that.

"Now, while I weigh up his shit, he turns his phone on and takes a message. I dunno what he was listening to, like, but he goes as white as an albino's cock. He gets on the phone with his *ex-wife*, not his fuckin' girlfriend – so you can fuck right off, Ross *Cunt* – and begs to stay with her for a while. Christ, he didn't even collect his aitch on the way out. That's how spooked he was. Which is how I knew who you were when I saw this piece of shit pull up on The Exchange."

"So Janet agreed?"

"For five hundred? Sure, she agreed."

"How long ago was this?"

Billy shrugged. "Twenny minutes ago, mebbe? Mebbe a bit less. He was driving a beat-up Datsun."

"You mean a Nissan?" Jim said.

"I *know* what I fuckin' mean, rat boy! This thing was ancient. But somehow Bobby fuckin' screamed up the street in it. Round to hers, I presume."

"Where's she living now?" Jonno asked.

"Since they split up she's been out in Hemlington. Now, if you grab a pen I'll give you that address."

22.

Harry and his son waited near the entrance of the Forum car park. He stared at his vehicle occasionally, wishing he had the skills to hotwire an engine. It wouldn't get the drugs back any quicker, but at least he'd feel a little more in control of a situation that seemed to be spiralling away from him.

Terry stamped in wide circles and huffed impatiently. He scraped his soles along the tarmac to make the activity more fun. Wondering when Charlie was going to arrive, Harry checked his watch and told his son to stop fidgeting.

A Ford Focus Coupe turned into the car park and moved towards them. It came to a stop, and the driver's window wound down. Harry stepped forward. A smirking man with a skinny, angular face and tall hair poked out his head. "Jonno's pissed with you."

"Tell me summat I don't know, Charlie."

The front passenger door opened and a man Harry didn't recognise clambered out. He was six-three, with huge tattooed arms and a thickly muscled torso that bulged the fabric of his T-shirt. He had the broken, asymmetrical features of a bare-knuckle fighter, and his narrow eyes glimmered with violence. He rounded the vehicle and approached with a friendly smile that didn't fit his demeanour. His hands curled into fists. It was evident he'd been brought along to ensure that Harry didn't misbehave.

Charlie pointed at the boy. "Here's one for starters," he said. "He's not coming with us."

Cold fear squeezed Harry's innards. The fear and worry must have been apparent on his face because Terry picked up the vibe. He drew close, wrapped his little fingers around Harry's belt and held on tightly.

Harry shook his head. "I'm not leaving my son," he said with an edge, suggesting the decision was final.

The big man smiled again. His biceps flexed as he tightened his fists. "Jonno's orders. Sez it's too important to be bringing a boy along. Let's not make a fuss."

Harry stared at Charlie. "Lend me some money and I'll grab a cab," he said. "I'll see if I can get a babysitter or summat. I know where Jonno wants me to be. Christ, the big fella, can ride in the taxi with us if needs be."

Charlie's smirk faltered. He looked up at the big man. "Whatchoo reckon, Bonnie?"

Bonnie beckoned Harry towards the car with a finger. "Jonno sez no, which *means* no," he replied. "Your kid's gonna hafta find his own way home."

Harry stared into the man's dark, expressionless eyes. "He's five years old. I'm not leaving him here." Then he turned towards Charlie, seemingly his best chance of ensuring that his son wasn't left alone. "You know me, man. I'm happy to come along quietly, as long as we can drop Terry on the way."

The driver shrugged at Bonnie. "Come on, fella. He's got a point; Terry's just a bairn."

Bonnie glared at Charlie, who wilted beneath his gaze. "You not hear me the first time around? I *said* we're not taking him. And that's that."

Harry clasped his hands together. "I'm fuckin' begging here, fella. It's dangerous out here for a child on its own. Fast traffic, paedos, older kids, there's lotsa ways for the lad to get hurt."

Bonnie sneered. "Tell somebody who gives a shit."

At that moment, Harry knew that Jonno planned to torture or kill him. His boss had maimed people for a lot less than the mistake he'd made. Abandoning Terry was just a little extra mental cruelty intended to increase his suffering.

The boy wasn't brave enough to ask for help; he would sit and cry until somebody either helped him or preyed on his vulnerability. Harry had no intention of putting him through that kind of ordeal.

He decided to fight. Nobody was going to expect that.

Harry hitched a thumb at his son. "At least let me say goodbye. At least let me tell him to find someone in charge when I don't come back."

Bonnie thought about it for a moment and nodded once.

Harry crouched down before Terry and studied the boy's pale, chubby face. If this was to be the last time he saw his son, he wanted a mental picture of his pink cheeks, bright blue eyes and brown mop of hair. Harry brushed a finger down the boy's face and smiled.

"Listen carefully, son," he said. "I'm going to be gone for a few minutes with these men."

Terry frowned and worried his bottom lip. "Can I come with you?"

Harry shook his head. "Have to talk to them alone. Men stuff."

Terry's eyes angled up and watched as Bonnie approached. The big man crowded their personal space. Harry allowed him to come closer as it made him an easier target. Harry tightened his muscles in readiness – he would have only one chance, so he had to make sure it was right.

Terry's bottom lip trembled. Tears spilt down his cheeks. He shook his head. "No, no, no, no…"

Harry wrapped his arms around the boy and pulled him close. He felt tears on his neck. Lifting his son off the ground, Harry bumped into the big man, who stumbled back a couple of steps. Now he was within striking distance.

Bonnie attempted to grab Harry's right elbow with the intention of pulling him towards the car. As he stepped forward, Harry straightened his hand and flung back his arm in a fast arc.

His hand slammed against Bonnie's windpipe with a loud *thwack*. The big man immediately clutched at his throat and gasped. Wheezing like an asthmatic, he took several tiny staggering steps forward, lowered his hands and drew in a big breath.

Harry struck him in the windpipe again with an even harder blow. Bonnie let out a breathless squeal and dropped to his knees. Eyes bulging wildly, he scratched at his throat again.

Harry let go of the boy, turned on his heels, and crunched a right hook into Bonnie's jaw. The big man toppled onto his side and stayed down.

Charlie was already out of the vehicle with an open straight razor in his right fist. He swung the blade wildly. Harry ducked underneath and threw his full weight into the driver's legs. Charlie pitched forward and landed on his face.

Harry got to his feet first, turned and kicked out just as Charlie was up on his knees. His right foot slammed into Charlie's balls. The man shrieked and dropped the blade. Cupping his groin with both hands, he pitched sideways, curled into a foetal ball, and hissed like a frightened cat.

Harry grabbed Terry by the hand and bundled him through the open door of the Focus. Then he gathered up the blade and jumped into the driver's seat. The keys were still in the ignition. He stepped on the accelerator and raced out of the car park.

Harry looked in the rear-view and saw both men rolling around in pain on the tarmac. He slammed the pedal down and cut through a light just as it went from amber to red, then turned to his son and asked him how he was doing.

Crying with fear and anger, Terry screamed that he wanted to go home.

Harry knew that if he didn't do something about the drugs or Jonno, then neither of them would be going home anytime soon.

23.

The 4x4 turned into a small cul-de-sac off Earls Court Road and moved slowly towards the parking spaces at the end of the street. They passed small red brick and white panel terraces with tall white fences. Several of the properties were derelict and festooned with crude graffiti. Scruffy kids lounged on an old sofa outside one of the boarded-up homes. They glowered at the vehicle as it eased past. Jim pulled in beside a rust-mottled blue Datsun.

Jonno clambered out of the 4x4 and peered through the Datsun windows. The interior was as dishevelled as the bodywork. Discarded takeaway boxes and drink cartons filled the back seat and the rear footwell. Parking fines and other legal paperwork littered the area above the dashboard. It was disgusting how Bobby had come to this; he'd once been such a fastidious and proud man.

Jonno clicked his fingers at Dave in the manner of one signalling an obedient dog and told the others to stay. He figured Bobby would come along without too much fight; he wasn't psychotic like Billy Chin, and wasn't much of a fighter. Two men would be enough to overpower him.

They walked down the road. The surly youths shouted foul-mouthed abuse at them, though they ran away when Dave rushed towards the sofa. Jonno opened an unlocked gate and entered a garden thick with overgrown grass and discarded objects. Striding up the weed-strewn path to the door, he observed that Janet Manning hadn't changed her ways: she was still stupid and idle.

Jonno knocked on the door. One of the back curtains twitched, a muffled female voice hollered from within. There was a long wait before the door finally opened on its chain. Half of a puffy face appeared in the gap.

"Whatchoo want?" she snapped in a voice made husky by years of alcohol and cigarettes.

"Open the door, Janet."

"Who's it?"

"Take the chain off the door and find out."

"Whyn'tchoo tell us who you are?"

Jonno came close, whispering: "Why don't I just smash my way in and beat the shit outta you?"

As soon as the door started closing, Jonno threw his weight against it. The force snapped the chain, and the door jerked back. It struck Janet in the face, and she fell backwards with a terrified squeal.

Jonno charged into the hallway and picked her up by the throat. She had been pretty once, but years of bad living had made her pudgy, saggy and pale. She was well on her way to a gruesome middle age. He squeezed her windpipe, until she let out a pained croak, and shook her, sending her unkempt, brassy hair spilling in numerous directions. Her bloodshot eyes bulged.

"I know Bobby's here, so don't lie to me," he said. "Tell me where exactly and I won't fuck your arse till it's bleeding."

"Upstairs," she squawked. "Dunno where. Wardrobe, mebbe?"

He let go of her throat. She rubbed at the red fingerprints that began to form. Jonno jabbed her face with his finger, ensuring that it hurt. "Stay right there, bitch. If you move, you suffer the consequences, savvy?"

She nodded and then let her head hang.

Jonno and Dave took the stairs two at a time and then separated at the top.

Dave barged his way into the visitor bedroom.

Jonno entered the master bedroom. Breathy whispers like white noise emanated from inside the fitted wardrobe. As he approached the unit, the sounds grew louder until they were indecipherable shrieks. Jonno pulled opened the door and found Bobby cowering beneath a pile of clothes still on their hangers. He held a phone a phone in his right hand and blinked tearfully at the display. His demeanour suggested that he still had more to say even though the call had ended.

Jonno crouched before him. "I think it's time you came out of the closet, don't you?"

Bobby rubbed away the tears and turned his glassy eyes on Jonno. He attempted a smile, but his teeth were chattering too much for it to hold. When this didn't work, he tried a hammy expression of shock and surprise. "What brings you here?"

Jonno couldn't help but laugh at his bravado. "Your fuckin' stupidity."

Dave rushed into the room and grinned down at them.

Bobby alternated his gaze between the pair. "Look, I can explain."

"I know you can," Jonno replied, "but not here, though."

"Jonno…"

"Save it."

"Jonno…"

He grabbed Bobby's right arm and pulled him from the wardrobe. The junky tried to swat Jonno away with his left hand. Although he caught his face with a few weak slaps, his courage soon disappeared, and he allowed Jonno to drag him out onto the carpet.

Bobby lay on his back, panting with fatigue and fear, and looked around for an escape route. The only option was to crawl beneath the bed. With the last of his fight, he turned on his stomach and scuttled for the narrow gap between bed and floor.

Bobby was halfway under when Jonno jumped in the air and came down with both feet on his right ankle. The crack of snapping bone was unmistakeable. Bobby squealed in pain, then yowled when Jonno twisted his heel against the injury. After several seconds of excruciating pain, his body went limp.

Jonno and Dave grabbed the junky by the belt and dragged him from beneath the bed. His breathing was laboured, and his eyes flickered but remained closed. Jonno slapped Bobby's face a couple of times, but he didn't stir.

Jonno and Dave hauled him up by his arms and dragged him downstairs, past Janet, who mumbled an apology, through the garden, and up the road to where they were parked. They pushed Bobby onto the back seat, beside Ben Otley, and Dave clambered into the vehicle and sandwiched him in.

Bobby came to and whimpered.

Jonno turned to face him. "Buckle up, mate. We're going for a ride."

Sweat trickled from Bobby's hairline into his glistening eyebrows. Further beads formed on his cheeks, which were gradually turning pink. Tight lines of worry were etched deep in his face.

"Where we going?" he asked.

Jim turned the key. The engine coughed once and hummed.

Jonno smiled. "You already know the answer to that."

Bobby screamed for help, filling the interior with ear-piercing noise. Ben silenced him with a right to the jaw. The junky slumped forward, and his head hit the back of the driver's seat. He lolled left and right as the vehicle did a fast three-point turn and raced to the end of the street.

Jonno smiled again. He was going to enjoy torturing Bobby and Harry.

24.

Eric caught Bobby's brief hiss about somebody kicking down his ex-wife's door, but the rest of the call came quieter and faster than he could understand. Eric asked him how many men were in the building. Bobby's answer was a barely audible murmur. Then he screamed that they'd found him, and he needed help now. Finally, the line went dead.

Eric held the phone to his chest and thought about a plan of action. He had nothing.

Derek stared at him for a moment. "Boyfriend troubles?"

"How far are we from the Ex-Missus?"

The car approached Blue Bell roundabout, passing the old hotel on the left-hand side. Derek turned his attention to the speedo. "I'd say about five minutes."

"Well I'd say about three," Eric responded. "So maybe try putting your foot a bit closer to the floor."

"You're having a laugh, aren't you?"

"Wasn't aware I was a fuckin' stand-up comedian?"

"This stretch of road's got more bacon on it than a pig farm."

"We'll hafta risk it."

"With what *we've* got in this fuckin' car? Money, guns and heroin? Christ, we'll be pensioners by the time we get outta holiday camp. Think again, dickhead. I'm not going back inside on account of that fuckin' idiot."

Derek hit the roundabout at fifty and just about kept control on the bend. He picked up speed on the dual carriageway but remained under seventy. Turning right, he slowed down as they passed through the Hemlington estate and kept a watchful eye out for police patrols and speed cameras.

A black four-wheeler raced towards them in the opposite lane. It weaved through the slow traffic, easing through gaps that seemed almost too small. Heavily tinted windows turned its occupants into faceless silhouettes. The vehicle's ludicrous rear spoiler and shiny rims screamed drug dealer.

Judging by the sudden end to the call, Eric was confident that Jonno already had Bobby. He believed that they would panic drive for five or ten minutes until they were as far away from the scene of the crime as possible. Then, they would slow to a less frantic pace.

Eric's eyes went to the wing mirror as soon as the vehicle passed. It screeched and burned rubber going into a left turn. Car horns honked displeasure.

Eric lifted his gaze from the wing mirror. "The four-wheeler."

His brother nodded. "Definitely."

Derek waited for a break in the traffic and jammed on the handbrake. The car shrieked through a one-eighty turn that threw out black plumes of rubber smoke. He put his foot down, rounded several slow-moving vehicles that blared their horns as he passed.

He took the left onto the dual carriageway, narrowly missing the front bumper of an eighteen-wheeler, and raced over the roundabout. When he saw the rear spoiler of the 4x4 in the distance, he slowed his pace.

He dropped in six cars behind and waited for their next move.

25.

Terry unfastened his seatbelt and yelled for attention. Harry pulled off the road and warned him that his behaviour was dangerous. He might get hurt badly without his belt or get Daddy in trouble with the police. Next time around he'd get a smacked bottom. Then Harry buckled him in again and stepped on the accelerator.

Terry opened his seatbelt a second time and screamed at his father to stop the car. Harry ignored his son's tantrum and continued driving, in the faint hope that the intensity of his hysterics would tire him out. But the boy had reached that weird place where his anger became a source of energy. The louder Terry screamed for attention, the longer he could sustain the outburst, and the longer he went, the louder he got.

Finding it difficult to contain his annoyance, Harry gripped the steering wheel, gritted his teeth, and tried to tune out his son's screeching. When that failed, he turned up the radio to drown out the sound. Terry increased his volume in response, modulating the noise to irritating effect.

Harry's right eyelid twitched. He rubbed at it, but that only made things worse. Trying desperately to avoid the explosion he knew was coming, Harry told himself that the boy was scared and confused. He wasn't doing this intentionally. It was just his way of letting off steam. Harry turned off the music and tried to relieve the pressure with a dose of old-fashioned parental diplomacy.

"Please put your seatbelt back on, son. It's dangerous."

Terry continued wailing.

"Please, Terry?" he pleaded. "Do it for Daddy."

Terry shook his head and folded his arms. He at least lowered the volume from ear-splitting to loud. That was something. It just wasn't enough.

Harry pressed his knuckles to his left temple and kneaded gently. Diplomacy had failed, so he decided on a more direct form of negotiation.

"Please calm down, son," he said. "If you calm down, I'll get you a Happy Meal when we get to Nana's. I'll even get some nuggets and dips too."

Terry looked at his father. Paused a moment, as though silently considering the offer, and then wailed even louder.

Something snapped. Harry yelled with rage and swerved off the road. The car mounted the pavement and screeched to a halt.

Terry shrieked as he hit the glove box and cast a terrified glance at his father. Without thinking, Harry turned and swung his right arm in a fast arc. He caught the boy across the face with his open hand. The sound was like a gunshot. The impact threw Terry back into his seat. A pink handprint glowed on his pale left cheek. Then it began to redden and swell. The boy's eyes widened with shock, and he fell silent. His chest went up and down rapidly. Tears spilt from his lashes, but the hysterics stopped.

Guilt tore at Harry and sent bitter bile into his throat. He swallowed it back down and tried to rationalise his actions for a moment, but there were no excuses for what he had done. He should have directed his anger at Jonno or himself for putting Terry's life in danger. Harry wanted to articulate this to the boy in terms he'd understand, but he couldn't find the words. Flapping his mouth a few times, he hoped that something intelligent and soothing would emerge.

The only sounds Harry made were percussive pops as his lips smacked together. The harder he tried to speak the worse it got.

Something changed in Terry's gaze. The blue in his eyes went icy. The waterworks ceased. He turned his face towards the side window. His breath misted the glass.

"Son… I…"

Terry didn't react.

"Look, I…"

Harry tapped the boy on the shoulder gently, hoping to repair the damage and apologise for his mistake. Terry turned towards him, grimaced, and made himself small against the seat. The fear on his face hit Harry like a gut punch. He felt sick again.

"Please… I wouldn't…"

"Leave me alone, Daddy."

"Terry…"

"I don't want to talk to you no more."

Terry drew the seatbelt across and clicked it into place. He pulled away when his father reached across to stroke his hair. Harry's hand hung in the air for a moment and then he let it fall on the handbrake. The car pulled off the pavement and picked up speed.

Harry turned on the radio, just to fill the unbearable silence.

26.

Ten minutes later Harry turned into a quiet cul-de-sac of small pebble-dashed bungalows. He drove to the end of the street, entered a driveway and pulled bumper-to-bumper with an old brown Vauxhall estate car.

He opened the door and stared at Terry, whose face was still swollen and red.

"Please stay in the car, son," he said, "I'm truly sorry about what happened."

Terry didn't acknowledge the words or apologetic tone. He didn't even seem to acknowledge his father's existence; his eyes remained fixed on a point somewhere outside his passenger side window.

"I'm gonna go talk to Nana. I'll let you know when it's okay to come in," he said, adding quietly, "Maybe we should keep what happened earlier between ourselves."

Harry exited the vehicle and approached the bungalow. Knocking on the front door a couple of times, he cast a worried glance back over his shoulder. Under normal circumstances, Eileen Clarke would be the last person he'd approach for help, but at that moment she was the only person he could trust. Although she hated Harry with a passion, she would fight for her grandson with every ounce of strength and until there was no more air in her lungs.

The door opened. For a brief moment, there was a smile on Eileen's face. Then she recognised Harry and her expression soured liked uncorked wine. Not bothering to hide her exasperation, she ran both hands through her silver-blonde bob, held the back of her neck, tilted her head upwards, and let out a long, pained sigh.

Eileen had been good-looking once, and it still showed in her face occasionally, but a hard life of manual labour had leathered her skin and dulled the blue in her eyes. A brief spark of malice made them twinkle again as she gave his bruises a close inspection.

"Somebody gave you a good going over, and no error," she said, fighting the urge to grin.

"And hello to you, too."

Wrinkling her nose and sniffing the air, she moved towards Harry then pulled back with a disgusted expression. "Oh God, is that?"

"Yes, it *is* what you think."

Wafting her hands in front of her face, she turned away from the stench. "Jesus. Did you swan dive into a urinal?"

"That's not too far from the truth."

"If you're gonna be facetious I'll close this door on you, Harold."

"I'm *not* being facetious."

She fixed him with a hard gaze. "I take it this has something to do with your bruises?"

"Summat like that."

"So what do you want?"

"I need a favour."

She scoffed. "From me?"

"You're the one I'm asking."

"I'm not in the mood for jokes."

"I'm not joking."

"Are you sure about that?"

"I'm not here because I enjoy your company, Eileen," Harry said, hitching a thumb towards the car. "I'm here because of Terry."

She stared through the windscreen at her grandson. "What's going on?"

"I need you to look after him for a while," he replied. "At least until Babs gets off from work. I also need you to phone and tell her not to go home tonight. She needs to grab a cab. That's important. And she needs to stay here for a while."

Eileen's eyes narrowed. "Why?"

"Trouble."

"Police trouble? Or *friend* trouble?"

"Possibly both."

Her gaze drifted back to the car. "Is this dangerous?"

Harry nodded.

"Christ! Barbara really knows how to pick them," she said, walking a few steps towards the vehicle for a closer look. "Is that even your car?"

Harry smiled uncomfortably.

"I *really* don't want to know," she said. "Just take care of whatever it is you need to take care of."

"Make sure you tell Babs *not* to go home. That's crucial."

"I know how to look after my daughter."

Eileen smiled as she approached the car and opened the front passenger door. She opened her arms wide. Harry's heart pounded against his ribs. He hoped that she wouldn't see the mark on the boy's face. He knew it was a vain hope. The handprint was enormous, red, and impossible to miss. Harry held his breath as Terry lowered his head and exited the vehicle. The boy avoided eye contact with his grandmother.

"Oh, do I not get a kiss now?" she asked, placing a finger gently beneath his chin. Leaning in, she lifted Terry's face to hers. She stopped moving and lingered just in front of the boy with her lips pursed. Turning his face to the side, she craned forward, eyes narrowing, to inspect the livid mark on his cheek.

She pulled back and smiled. "Go inside, sweetie. Put on the Telly."

The boy stomped into the house. Craning her head, Eileen watched him until he was out of sight. Then she turned her attention to Harry.

"Quite a whack you gave him there?"

"Eileen…"

"Shut up."

"Listen…"

"What did he do to deserve it?"

Harry stayed silent. He gave her his stoniest glare.

Normally this would have been enough to silence his Mother-in-Law, but not on this occasion. Eileen had no intention of letting the issue slide. "Come on, big man, what was the reason?"

"It looks worse than it is."

"That mark on his face is going to bruise," she remarked. "It wouldn't look much worse if you punched him."

"I lost my temper."

"And that's your excuse for *that?*"

Unable to offer any justification, Harry shrugged and let his arms fall limply to his sides. He deserved whatever tirade was about to come his way.

Instead, Eileen shook her head sadly. "I always thought, if nothing else, you were a good father and would never hurt…"

"I've never…"

"That is a full-blown slap," she interrupted, pointing at the house. "I saw the way Terry's eyes angled to you when I looked at his face. You know what I saw in them eyes? Fear, that's what. He was afraid of you."

Harry thought about putting up a more robust defence, but what he'd done was inexcusable. His son's misbehaviour had stemmed from a combination of fear and confusion. The situation had required a calm explanation, not violence. Instead, he lifted his hands and gestured for Eileen to lower the volume.

"You know something, I wasn't gonna ask why Terry was out of school," she said. "I thought better of it. But now, in the light of this new development, I think I will."

"That's none of your business."

"Why?"

Harry tried to think of an answer. Nothing came to mind.

Eileen's mouth tightened until it was as thin as a razor slash. She shook her head in disgust and looked away. "Oh, God… You took him to a drug deal, didn't you?"

"Listen…"

"What the hell is *wrong* with you?"

"Look…"

Stepping into the house, she beckoned him inside with a wave of her fingers. "Let's not have this conversation out here."

"Eileen, I've gotta go…"

"I'll be straight on the phone to the police if you drive away without an explanation. The slap and the stolen car will be enough to put you in jail."

A pink bloom spread across Eileen's cheeks and slowly darkened. Her lips puckered like she was sucking on a boiled sweet and her hands shook with rage. It was obvious she was telling the truth.

Sensing no alternative but to obey, Harry stepped inside.

27.

Jonno looked over his shoulder at Bobby. He was still unconscious, or at least faking it well. A thin sliver of drool dripped off his chin and dampened the neck of his T-shirt. He turned his attention to Dave and then jutted his chin back in Bobby's direction. "Give him a shake."

Dave grabbed Bobby's left shoulder. Bobby flopped right and left like a rag doll and slumped against Ben, who snarled, "Gerroff me, you junky fuck," and pushed him upright.

Bobby mumbled something barely audible and leaked fresh drool.

Dave chuckled and grinned at Jonno. "You want me to slap him awake?"

Jonno shook his head. Even if Bobby was faking it, he wasn't trying to escape or bring attention to the vehicle. It made sense to leave him alone. Besides, there would be plenty of time for slapping later. And then, afterwards, the real hurting could begin.

Jonno's feelings towards Harry were less easy to articulate. Even before the incident with Kevin Nicholson, his right-hand man had been veering to the left. When bones had to be broken, he was always somewhere else. When deals were going down, Harry's attention was back at home with his wife and son. In his paranoid and angry state, Jonno considered this lack of attention to be the real reason for the Forum fuck-up.

In his own way, Harry was an even more disastrous second-in-command than Bobby, who at least had business sense and managed to organise the deal with Ramon almost singlehandedly. With no business brain to speak of, and without his appetite for violence, Harry had nothing else to offer the crew. Beating him severely and casting him back down the ranks made sense. Even killing him made sense. The shock value alone would keep his men in line. After all, if Jonno was prepared to punish his oldest friend and longest serving footsoldier, it meant nobody was safe. Fear was an excellent motivation tool.

But he still couldn't quite decide what to do with Harry.

Somewhere deep down, Jonno knew he had to shoulder some of the blame for this mess. He had considered changing the routine briefly, in the weeks following Bobby's departure, but allowed himself to be convinced by Harry that it wasn't necessary. Why change something when it is working? It only needed a few tweaks to keep it fresh.

At first, the idea of Harry and the boy seemed like inspired thinking. Nobody would think anything strange in a father visiting the ice rink with his son. It was far less suspicious than Bobby and Ramon's people making the swap in the Forum toilets, pushing holdalls beneath cubicle partitions, and the police were less likely to stop and search a parent and child.

Then Jonno realised that Harry was more interested in watching his son having fun on the ice than the actual deal. It irritated Jonno that he could have avoided this whole if he'd followed his instincts instead of the advice of an underling.

Maybe killing Harry was for the best?

Jonno took out his phone and dialled a number several times. Each time it went to voicemail. Just as he was about to give up, the line connected.

"Boss?"

"What took you so long to answer?"

"Er..."

Jonno's heart rate spiked. "*Er* doesn't sound promising, Charlie."

"Er..."

"And there it is again."

"Er..."

"If you say *er* one more fuckin' time I'm gonna pull out your tongue."

"Summat's happened, boss."

"Lemme guess," Jonno replied. "You're saying Harry's not where he's supposed to be, right?"

"Summat like that."

"Summat *like* that? Or *exactly* that?"

Charlie paused, then began to speak but stopped before he could let out another *er* sound. "Exactly that."

"How the fuck did that fat bastard get away, Charles? He's not exactly light on his feet. And that kid of his isn't particularly limber, either."

"Caught Bonnie in the windpipe a coupla times. Fucked him right up. Still can't breathe proper, like. Gave me a fair pummelling too, boss."

Jonno squeezed the phone. "Get that fat fucker back and do it *today*, or you'd better start making preparations to emigrate somewhere I can't fuckin' find you."

"Where we supposed to start, boss?" Charlie whined.

"I don't care. Just start summat soon, before I fuckin' end you."

Jonno ended the call and stared out of the window. The car crossed a small stretch of road bordered by a silver mass of wind-rippled water. Distant industrial towers spewed smoke into the air. Gusts sent the fat clouds moving quickly across the grey sky out towards the North Sea.

"This is gonna be a long fuckin' day," Jonno said under his breath.

28.

The 4x4 was still just about visible in the distance, moving at a steady pace, separated by several cars and trucks. Although they were matching the vehicle for speed, Eric was worried that they were too far behind.

"Don't lose 'em," he said.

Derek lifted one hand off the steering wheel and waved it at the windscreen. "There's no way we can lose 'em. There aren't many turn-offs ahead. And if they *do* turn, we'll see 'em do it. Besides, I don't wanna get too close, in case they make us."

Darren pressed his face between the two seats. "Where are they heading?"

Eric glared at him. "How the hell would I know?"

Darren sat back with a huff. "Just asking, like."

"And I'm just answering."

"No need to be a prick about it."

Eric gritted his teeth. "A prick? Listen up, dickhead; we wouldn't even be here if it wasn't for your stupidity."

"Said I was sorry, didn't I?"

"Sorry changes the sum total of fuck all. If you'd done what we asked in the first place, we'd be dividing the spoils by now. Instead, we're chasing these turds across the north-east."

Eric twisted in his seat and looked Darren up and down with an expression of disgust. "The reason you're working for us is that you fucked up one of Joey's jobs, right?"

Darren looked like he wanted to argue, but stopped at the last second. He slid across the back seat and studied the colourless flat marshland and industrial structures jutting from the horizon like narrow bone fragments. He kept his mouth closed, and his eyes averted. Eric assumed that this was Darren's way of admitting it. His anger simmered as he pondered revenge against Joey Judd.

Joey was a poor target for a cash grab because of his tendency to rack up debt. Whatever he pulled in raiding other crews was usually frittered away in a few weeks. Takings from the bar weren't worth the effort of an armed robbery. Plus, hitting a legitimate business would bring unwanted police attention. Eric wondered if another more subtle form of retaliation was required? He made a mental note of it and marked Joey for retribution when the time was right.

The car moved past the Seal Sands chemical works, across a roundabout, and over a small bridge that spanned winding waterways, keeping pace with the 4x4. They passed another chemical plant on the right, with its drab skeletons billowing smoke into the darkening sky, and noticed that the 4x4 had disappeared. Derek accelerated until he came across a sign for Greyhopes Business Park and a left road into the estate. He kept driving for another couple of minutes, waited for a break in the traffic, pulled a U-turn, and drove back towards the business park. He pulled up a few hundred yards from the turn-off and stared at his brother.

"This is your stop."

Eric nodded and exited the vehicle. He jogged towards the estate, turned the corner and disappeared from view.

Derek delved in his jacket pocket and found a mobile phone. He tossed it at Darren, who caught the thing and studied it blankly.

"When the message comes in," Derek said. "Tell me where I need to go."

29.

Holding a bag of frozen peas wrapped in a towel against his cheek, Terry watched the Chuckle Brothers on TV in stony-faced silence. When Eileen was satisfied that the boy's attention was elsewhere, she closed the living room door and dragged Harry to the brightly decorated kitchen. Then she closed the kitchen door and pushed him away.

Harry rested his bulk against one of the marble-effect counter-tops and waited for the outburst. It didn't come. Instead, Eileen wore a saddened, almost dazed expression and shook her head.

"You took your son to a drug deal?" she said in disbelief. "Of all the low things…"

"I never exposed him…"

"Well that's patently untrue, innit?" she remarked. "The slap in the face, the fact that he's terrified. You exposed him to something – am I right?"

"Right."

"You better hope that mark on his face goes down. 'Cause if Barbara sees it you can consider yourself divorced."

Harry held his breath for a moment; this seemed like a small sliver of hope. "You're not gonna tell her?"

Eileen slapped her hands against the tops of her thighs repeatedly. It was a nervous reaction. She seemed unaware that she was doing it. "I'm not gonna lie for you. There's a distinction. If Terry doesn't bruise – and that's a *big* if – and if he chooses not to tell her himself, then I won't say a word. However, if she asks, I'm not gonna lie. Are we clear?"

Harry nodded. "Why keep quiet? If you hate me so much."

Eileen smiled briefly. "I don't hate you, Harry. I just don't think you're good enough for my daughter. And nothing I've seen over the years has changed that.

"When she met you she was studying for a business degree. She had a future. Then she threw away that future for you."

"I didn't make her quit Uni."

"Bet you didn't fight the decision, either?"

Harry stayed silent. Eileen had him there. Male pride had played its part: he hadn't wanted a wife who earned more than he did. His desire to be the sole provider had outweighed his partner's happiness and well-being. That Eileen had brought the subject up meant Barbara had expressed her frustration and regret about this at some point. More guilt weighed down on him.

"The reason I'm keeping quiet is that my daughter sees something in you that no-one else can. She sees some decency, some sweetness, no matter how faint that may be. Something you hide from the rest of us."

Eileen stopped slapping her thighs and removed a mug from the shelf of one of the wall units. She spooned instant coffee into it and looked over her shoulder at him.

"There's times when I look at you and think you might wanna change," she said, turning on the kettle. "I see something in your eyes that gives me hope. And if that's truly the case, I'm offering you a chance – a one-time only offer – to get your act together and change for her and the boy."

"Which is?"

"Be honest for once in your life. Make me believe you actually wanna change. Show me that you can sort this problem out."

Harry held his breath for a moment and let it out. It was time to tell somebody the truth. "Okay. Ask me."

"How long have you been using the boy?"

"I'm not *using* him. Not in that sense."

"I'm not interested in whatever you consider sense. The only thing that interests me is honesty."

"I am being honest."

"Then what have you been doing?"

The kettle came to the boil. Eileen poured the contents into the mug and lifted it to her mouth. She blew steam off the top and took a sip. Then she smacked her lips together a couple of times and nodded at Harry to continue.

"Once a month, on the same date, I've been taking Terry to Billingham Forum," he said. "We go ice-skating, or more accurately he goes skating, and I go sit in the stand. I take a small holdall filled with fifty grand cash and place it at my feet as I watch. Another man with an almost identical holdall of just a slightly different colour, bumps into me, or ties his shoelaces nearby, picks up the money, and leaves his holdall behind."

"And what's in it?"

"Do you really wanna know?"

"The truth? Yes, Harry, I *do* wanna know what you're exposing my grandson to."

"Heroin."

Eileen was silent for a moment. She threw down a massive gulp of coffee and let out a bitter laugh. "*Wow*. And you think that's an appropriate situation for a child?"

"As far as Terry's concerned we were just going skating and having summat to eat afterwards. He never knew what was going on. I've always minimised the risk."

"Until today?"

"Yes."

"And what happened today?"

"I took Terry to the bathroom. A man followed us inside and robbed me at gunpoint."

"Christ, don't tell me he pointed it at…"

"I made Terry go in a cubicle. He didn't see what happened."

"So much for minimised risk."

"This is the first time owt like this has happened."

Eileen gave him a lopsided grin. "It only takes the once."

Harry didn't see any point defending his position. Eileen was taking the time to understand the situation; the least he could do was explain it without adding extraneous layers of bullshit that she wouldn't believe.

"Does Barbara know?"

"About the deal?"

Eileen nodded.

"She knows I get Terry to play hooky once in a while," he replied. "And she knows I take him skating when we do. But if she knew the rest of it, I probably wouldn't need to worry about divorce because she'd kill me in my sleep."

"You're not lying on her behalf?"

Harry's gaze hardened. "You asked for the truth. And that's what I'm giving you."

"Fine. I believe you."

Harry went loose.

"Now I've got one last thing to ask," Eileen said.

"Go on."

"What're you gonna do to make this right?"

"Whatever I can."

"And will you keep Barbara and Terry outta danger from now on? Promise me, otherwise leave now and don't ever come back."

"I promise."

Eileen scrutinised him, inspecting his face and eyes for signs of dishonesty, then she relaxed and opened the kitchen door. She hitched a thumb over her shoulder, towards the bathroom. "Now go take a shower."

"I haven't got time."

"Then make it. 'Cause you stink."

He pulled at his jacket. "The clothes stink."

"Which is why you can grab some of Len's things when you're outta the bathroom."

Harry curled his lip. "Old man clothes?"

"You're hardly stylish yourself, Harry."

"This jacket's vintage."

"And it smells vintage, too," she replied. "Besides, I don't know many blokes who can pull off that trendy fat man look. But I *do* know you're not one of them."

Having a shower would give Harry time to think, to ponder his options, and decide what to do next.

"Okay," he said. "You win."

30.

Harry was down to his boxer shorts by the time he reached the bathroom door. He took off his pants in the bathroom, jumped beneath the hot jet of water and scrubbed away the smell of piss. By the time Harry had finished showering a plan was in place. He towelled down, wrapped the damp towel around his waist and opened the door.

Eileen was waiting outside. She thrust a bundle of clothes into his hand and went back to the kitchen. Harry dressed in the master bedroom and looked for money in the bedside drawers and wardrobe units. Rummaging through a carefully stacked and folded pile of underwear, he found a wad of folded notes. A quick count revealed five hundred and fifty quid in total.

Even though he needed quick cash for his plan, stealing Eileen's money was a scumbag move, particularly after their moment of honesty in the kitchen. He threw the notes back in the underwear drawer and closed it. He decided to be a man and ask for the money outright.

Harry approached the wardrobe door mirror and stared in dismay at his reflection. The waistband of his blue candy-striped trousers sat halfway between his navel and the sag of his moobs, accentuated by the tight fit of the yellow polo shirt. A large, gaudy green golf club logo sat over the left nipple. The outfit made him look like he belonged in a special needs unit. Pulling the shirt out of his trousers softened the effect, but not by much.

The washing machine sputtered into noisy life. He followed the sound into the kitchen. Eileen rested her back against one of the counters and watched clothes spin around the drum, her expression blank and slack. She sucked on a cigarette like it had life-giving properties and exhaled a cloud of smoke at the ceiling.

"Thought you'd given up?" he said.

She looked at the object between her index and middle finger and realised what was happening. Turning in the direction of the counter, she looked for something to stub the cigarette on. She found a saucer, moved towards it, stopped for a few moments, smiled briefly, and then brought the cigarette back to her lips.

"I had till about five minutes ago," she replied.

Eileen turned her head, looked Harry up and down, and smiled at the stupidity of his new outfit. Then she started chuckling. Soft and quiet at first, the laughter gradually rose in cadence until it sounded like the wild baying of hyenas. She folded her arms across her belly to hold in the hysterics. Tears poured down her cheeks.

A hot flush of embarrassment spread across Harry's face. Typically he would have told Eileen to go fuck herself, but he needed her help. He remained quiet and accepted the mockery, even though it hurt. *Use this anger*, he told himself, again and again, *save it for Jonno*.

Eileen finally composed herself, but couldn't quite shake the smirk. "You look ridiculous," she said.

"Thanks," Harry replied. "Might I remind you they're your husband's clothes?"

"You can, but he doesn't wear them often."

"I can see why."

"Be thankful you've got some clean clothes."

Harry scratched at his polyester pants. They were hot and itchy. "Len must have summat better than these?"

Eileen nodded. "You're right. He does."

"Can I have them, please?"

Eileen stubbed out the cigarette. "I'm not giving you Len's best."

"Fair enough," Harry said, "But I do need a favour."

"*Another* favour?"

"I need to borrow some cash."

Her eyes narrowed. "You really are taking the piss."

"The prick who robbed me grabbed my wallet, my cards, my phone, so I hafta get some cash together. Besides, you know I'm good for it."

"Do I?"

"Look, we both wanna sort this problem. The only way I can do it is with cash. Otherwise, Terry and Babs aren't gonna be safe."

Eileen lit another cigarette. "How much is it gonna cost me?"

"It's a loan."

"Not if you get yourself killed, it isn't."

Harry thought about shotguns. Their prices varied depending on the supplier. A visit to Anthony MacDonald would cost him over a grand, plus extra for cartridges. Visiting John Arnold would set him back seven-fifty.

He could try to negotiate him down to five hundred, or pay five up front and promise the rest, but Arnold was notoriously spiky and might tell him to fuck off. Anything less than five hundred quid took him into junky territory – most likely dealing with a psychopath like Billy Chin.

"I need seven-hundred and fifty."

Eileen choked on cigarette smoke. "That's not gonna happen," she coughed. "I don't have that much."

"You'll get it back. I promise."

"Harry, you're not hearing me, I don't have that much."

"Then make it five hundred."

Her face went blank. She took a long drag of the cigarette. "Don't think I've got that much, either."

He was tempted to tell her about the cash in the underwear drawer but kept the knowledge to himself. "Then as much as you've got."

Eileen ground out the cigarette on the saucer with violent, jerky movements, rushed out of the kitchen and into the main bedroom. Drawers were slammed loudly, mostly for effect, and then she came back into the room and thrust a handful of notes at him.

"Two hundred and fifty," she snapped. "And before you ask for more, it's my Christmas hamper money, all of it, so that's your lot."

Harry knew it was a lie, but took the money without complaint.

"You'll get it back."

"I better."

"With interest."

So it seemed like he was visiting Billy Chin after all. Harry was about to walk into a junky hovel with two hundred and fifty quid in his arse pocket; his odds of making it alive to the end of the day had just shortened considerably.

31.

Derek drove through the industrial estate, past windowless grey units, high spiked fences, and tree-lined verges until he noticed a towering landfill on one of the neighbouring roads. He turned right, parked against the kerb and looked around. The area was quiet, some of the businesses had closed for the day, and others were in the process of finishing up. A few cars drifted by, but there weren't many people on the pavements.

A couple of homeless men with straggly beards and ragged clothing clambered up the detritus mountain, picking through it for items of value. Every now and again they lifted objects that started small landslides of litter. Neither man paid any attention to anything outside of their rubbish-strewn world.

Derek waited until the coast was clear and exited the vehicle. He clicked his fingers at Darren, telling him to get a shift on, then locked the doors and started walking. Darren lagged behind, dragging his feet like a stroppy toddler.

Eric hissed at them from behind a small thicket of leafless skeletal trees and green bushes. He beckoned them forward with a wave of his right hand. They moved up the verge and through the shrubbery. All three men crouched in the shadows as a couple of cars sped past.

"So where are they?" Derek said.

Eric hitched a thumb over his shoulder. Staying close to the walls and fences, they walked until they came to another dense group of trees and shrubs, where they watched and waited. Eric pointed at a windowless building with a sloping aluminium roof, which was separated from the rest of the estate by its own large patch of land and tall, glass-topped concrete walls. It had a dirty sign with faded lettering fixed to the roof that read *J.L.F Car Repairs and Bodywork*.

The place apparently hadn't been used as a garage for years. Torrential rains and large tires had chewed up the tarmac path from the front gate to the main entrance and long grass and weeds grew freely across the rest of the grounds.

A muscular bald man emerged from behind the black 4x4, parked in front of the tall, corrugated entrance door, and patrolled the area. He strode from one side of the grounds to the other and back again. Occasionally he stopped and craned his head in the direction of a random sound, and then he resumed walking.

Loud music blasted out of the building. Eric felt the bass thump. *That's noisy enough to cover the sound of screams,* he thought grimly.

Eric patted his brother's shoulder. "You recognise him?"

Derek shook his head.

"Think you can take him out quietly?"

Derek shuffled his shoulders and bristled. He scowled like he'd been asked the most idiotic question ever. "Do I look like a cunt?"

"Is that rhetorical or a genuine question?"

Derek's face twitched. "What does ret... ret... rhetorical mean?"

"It means you've already answered your own question."

Derek grabbed Eric by the collar of his leather jacket and pulled him close until their faces were almost touching. "Hows about you quit being a fuckin' smart-arse, for once?" he hissed.

The pair scuffled for a few seconds until Eric finally prised his brother's hands off the lapels and pulled away. He brushed at the jacket fussily and noticed a few strands of black cotton twine where the top button used to be. He dropped on his hands and knees and scrabbled through the undergrowth until he realised it was too dark to find anything. He got off the ground and glared at Derek

His brother smirked back at him. "Oh, sorry, *mate.* I guess you're too fuckin' clever for your own good. Certainly too clever for buttons."

"The button would've been okay if you'd left me the fuck alone."

Derek shrugged. "Dunno whatcha getting all pissy about anyway. It's a fuckin' cheap Dundas Arcade knock-off."

Eric rubbed the leather between his fingers. "This is a classic."

"If by *classic,* you mean old and shitty, then you might just be right."

Eric snorted and wafted his hand in the direction of the unit. "Just go and do summat useful, for once, and knock the idiot out."

"Then you better create a distraction."

Derek stepped away from the bushes and edged along the wall until he turned the corner. Eric picked a handful of stones off the floor and held them to the light. He kept the two biggest rocks and dropped the rest. He hefted the largest as far as he could. It clattered against one of the walls on the left of the grounds and skidded across the broken tarmac. The bald man's head snapped in the direction of the sounds. He crouched down and tiptoed left warily. His hand was crammed inside his jacket, just in case he needed to pull a weapon quickly.

Satisfied with his handiwork, Eric stepped back and noticed Darren staring at him with his head cocked in the manner of a puzzled dog, his expression bemused.

"What?"

"Are you two always like this?"

32.

Harry pulled the Ford Focus into the kerb, turned off the engine and exited the vehicle. He felt junky eyes on him, watching through gaps in window boards, assessing his worth, and mentally calculating the second-hand price of the car.

Metal shutters covered the windows and the front door of Billy's squat. However, somebody had tampered with them, so that they opened from the inside, meaning that it was a lot easier for the residents to escape from the building than it was for the police and bailiffs to break in. Being wary of strangers, police raids, and private security firms, they never answered the front door anyway. If you wanted drugs or stolen goods, the only way in was round the back.

Harry walked to the end of the street, turned the corner, and cut through a cobbled alleyway behind the houses. He navigated his way carefully around a carpet of takeaway boxes, shattered glass, dogshit, and used condoms.

A small white man with blonde dreadlocks leant against the rear courtyard wall of the squat. He wore a baggy grey tracksuit that was leopard-patterned with stains and bright blue trainers that were several sizes too big. Lifting a joint to his lips, he drew in a lungful and then exhaled several O-shaped smoke clouds. When he noticed Harry approaching, he dropped the spliff on the ground and stepped in front of the courtyard gate.

"Jog on, bumbaclot," he said in a voice that mingled Middlesbrough whine and Jamaican drawl. Standing on tiptoes, the man puffed out his chest and folded his arms over it. If he was trying to establish his alpha-male credentials, it failed: the poor bastard barely qualified as a Zeta. Harry was unimpressed and unafraid.

Up close, the man was younger than he initially appeared, barely out of his teens, but a life of excess had made his thin face pallid and waxy, and broken blood vessels crisscrossed the whites of his eyes. The herbal stench of Cannabis wafted off him. He tiptoed closer to Harry. "You not understand English, blood?"

"English I understand, but I'm not sure what you're speaking qualifies."

The man bristled. "Wazzat s'posed to mean, mon?"

"It means I wanna speak to Billy."

"Ain' nobody home," he said with a sneer. "An' even if there was, ain' nobody got time for yo' fuckery. We's on quiet time, blood. So best be on yo' way."

"Where'd you get that accent from?"

The man's shoulders tightened. "Is natural, mon."

Harry sniggered. "Seriously, where'd you get your accent, fella?"

"I's jus' done fuckin' told you. This shit's natural, motherfucker."

"It's naturally fuckin' stupid," Harry said. "Go get Billy before I lose my temper."

The man shrugged. "Don' know no fuckin' Billy, batty boy. Now why don' you go and *fuck* in the direction of *off*?"

Harry shuffled forward and slammed his forehead into the junky's face. The man dropped to the floor with a groan and rolled around for a few seconds clutching his nose and muffling high-pitched cries of pain. When he lifted his hands away, he noticed the blood on his fingers, let out a whimper, and then his face hit the cobbles. Harry prodded the man with his right foot a few times. He mumbled but didn't open his eyes. Satisfied that he hadn't done too much damage, Harry stepped into the courtyard and closed the gate.

33.

The courtyard floor was barely visible through a mass of blackened foils, discarded syringes, and crack pipes that crunched beneath his soles. Harry studied the ground for a path to minimise the chances of impaling himself on a needle. When he found his route, he stepped through it carefully and reached the back door.

He entered a bright kitchen illuminated by a LED light on a rusted yellow tripod stand. In the corner of the room, with her back to the wall, a middle-aged blonde woman rested her knees on a cushion of takeaway boxes and sucked the small cock of a fat man in a Boro shirt. Behind him, two thin black men stroked their larger erections and urged him on as he thrust deep into her mouth. They ignored Harry as he passed.

Gradually, his eyes adjusted to the darkness of the living room. A few carefully placed candle lamps and battery powered camp lights cast big black shadows up the wall. Vinegary heroin and stale body odours intermingled in a thick stew that Harry tasted at the back of his throat. He covered his nose and mouth with his right hand and stepped over and around the carpet of sprawling people and made his way towards the door at the front of the room.

Pushing the door open, he entered a dark, narrow hallway lit only by a single oil lamp. There was just enough illumination to make out the staircase. A naked couple had made their bed on the steps. Harry stepped over them as he made his way up the stairs.

The narrow upstairs landing had three doors. Harry opened the first door on his right. A toxic miasma of unflushed shit and piss overwhelmed him. He gagged and slammed the door shut. Eyes watering, Harry staggered left and stumbled into the next room.

Billy Chin sat against the wooden headboard of an old double bed reading a battered Thomas Pynchon paperback by candlelight. A thin joint glowed orange between his lips and then he exhaled smoke through his nose. Realising he wasn't alone, Billy stubbed out the joint, threw the book on the floor, and studied Harry carefully, his top lip curled in a contemptuous sneer.

"What's with the get-up?"

Harry tugged at his trousers. "Fancy dress."

"So what did you come as? A cunt?"

"A golfer."

"What golfer?"

"Nick Faldo."

"I don't remember Faldo weighing about forty stone, fat boy."

"I didn't come here for insults."

Billy swung his legs off the bed. "No? Then why *did* you come here? In fact, I don't remember inviting your fat fuckin' arse into me home. I sent the boy to the gate to turn away visitors. Quiet time, Harold."

"And I sent your boy to the floor with a broken nose."

Billy approached Harry. "What the fuck did he do to deserve that?"

"His stupid accent offended me."

Billy got in close, rising on tiptoes until their faces were only a few inches apart. "Your stupid fuckin' face offends *me*, round eyes. Hows about I slice it off with a fuckin' scalpel?"

"Bill…"

"Don't fuckin' Bill me, fat boy," he said, his voice rising. "You're spoiling me calm."

"I need a favour."

Billy scoffed. "From me? Didn't anybody ever tell you that favours cost money?"

"I have money."

"Oh, do you now? Well, bully for you. What makes you think I wanna take your fuckin' moolah? I've had me fill of your mob today."

This set Harry on edge. Chilly sweat frosted his skin. Had Jonno been snooping around earlier? Had he been looking for Manning, or was he putting the feelers out for him?

"My mob?"

"Yeah, that pretty-boy boss of yours came around for info. The racist prick insulted me, too. The cunt's lucky he drove out in one piece."

"Info? What info?"

Billy paused and eyeballed Harry. "That shit's between Jonno and me."

"Fair enough."

"D'you know what that bastard called me?"

Harry shook his head.

"Called me a ching-chong man. You fuckin' believe that? In this day and age?"

Billy's lips tightened, and pink blooms of anger flowered on his cheeks. Harry sensed an opportunity. When he'd entered the squat, the odds were fifty-fifty on Billy selling him what he needed. But now, if Harry played Billy's anger the right way, he knew he'd walk out with a shotgun and as many shells as he could carry. Although, if he played things wrong, he probably wouldn't leave at all. At least, not alive.

"That's well outta order, that is," Harry sympathised. "But it's not the first time I've known Jonno say shit like that."

Billy sought his gaze. "Meaning what?"

"Jonno's not exactly Mister Sensitive when it comes to race."

Billy's eyes went dead as he came in close. His rotten breath warmed Harry's face. "Like what, *exactly*?"

"You want me to go into specifics?"

"That's what exactly means."

Harry remembered past examples of Jonno's racism. "Billy Chink," he said. "He called you Billy Chink."

Billy's mouth twitched. "So did the kids at school. Little fuckin' faggots. So what?"

Harry searched his memories for something more powerful. "Whenever you bought weight from Jonno, he always called it a Chinese takeaway."

Another twitch. "Chinese takeaway? That's funny as fuck, that one. Did youse all have a laugh at me expense?"

Harry chuckled at the time, even though it was wrong, but didn't think it would help his cause to admit it. "Thought it was well outta order, Bill."

"Did you now? I'm feeling your solidarity right here, white brother," Billy said, putting his hands over his heart. Then he bared his teeth in a humourless smile.

"What else did that prick call me?"

Harry remembered a few months' back. A junky had tipped him off about a rival crew holding a bundle of unlaundered cash. He'd passed the tip to Jonno, who put together a successful raid. Afterwards, he brought Harry his cut of the profits and watched Teletubbies on the sofa with Terry. Later that day they sold Billy some weight and then went out for drinks. After a few too many beers Jonno let slip a Teletubbies related wisecrack about Billy in the pub. The insult stayed with Harry for some reason.

"He called you Chinky-Winky."

Billy's face took on a vicious expression, and he jerked forward suddenly. Wondering if he'd pushed him too far, Harry flinched in fear. At the last moment, Billy pulled away and, howling with rage, kicked an old bedside cabinet to pieces. "Fuckin' *Chinky-Winky*? He called me that?"

"You know, from the Teletubbies?"

"I know what it's referring to; you fat sack of shit."

"Sorry, Bill."

Breathing heavily, face red, Billy stared at the broken furniture. His hands clenched and unclenched in a constant rhythm. He looked ready to kill.

Harry heard rapid footsteps on the landing. The door opened, and two naked, skinny men rushed into the room. Both men were flushed and out of breath. "You okay, boss?"

Billy turned in their direction and looked them up and down. "I'm less okay than I was thirty fucking seconds ago when I wasn't looking at your greased-up, flaccid dicks."

The two men stared at each other in confused silence.

"That means try not to trap your swingers in the door when you close it."

They closed the door as they left the room.

Billy turned back to Harry, who was grimacing at the mental image of naked flesh now imprinted in his brain.

"You look perturbed, Harold?"

"It's like Sodom and Gomorrah in here."

Billy sneered. "Sodom and Gomorrah? *Hardly.*

"I'd like to think the Sodomites had a wild fuckin' time of it. Nobody's *here* for fun, Harry. They're here coz there's nowhere else to go, coz they're fucked up on some kinda addiction, or coz they're just plain screwed up. But at least while they're here they're protected. Somebody comes to one of me squats to fuck with *my* people, like you just done with Desmond, and I'll send the cunt screaming to hell."

Billy came in close and looked him up and down. Harry understood the implied threat and avoided Billy's glare. Things weren't going as he had hoped.

"Believe me, there's worse places than this shithole," Billy said. "And d'you wanna know how I know?"

Harry humoured him. "Go on."

"Because I've been in most of them. In fact, if you really wanna talk about *your* idea of Sodom and Gomorrah – a genuine fuckin' abomination, Harry? Then you wanna be talking the first time I went to the slammer.

"Got sent down for six months on a possession of stolen goods charge. I should've been out in three, but because I had a mouth on me, and pissed off the screws summat rotten, I served every fuckin' day of me sentence and I got put in the Bomb Squad, too."

Harry shook his head. "Bomb Squad?"

"The Bomb Squad are the poor bastards who hafta clean up every time prisoners stage a dirty protest."

Harry looked confused. "Dirty protest?"

"Christ. Have you never been outta Boro, fat boy? Well, you do know what a fuckin' protest is, right? Tell me you at least know that much?"

"Yeah, of course."

"And what do people do when they protest?"

"Get radged, shout, and throw shit about – stuff like that?"

Billy brought his hands together in a round of sarcastic applause. "Give the man a fuckin' prize. Well, in a dirty protest that shit they throw about is literal – as in literally their own shit.

"Whenever the head screw brought in some new fuckin' directive or took summat away, these fuckin' animals would toss their shit around like monkeys in a zoo. They'd lob big chunks of shite out of their windows, and the Bomb Squad would come in and sweep it up with a dustpan and brush. As an old cellmate once said: *'There's only so much shit a man can take in life unless you're working the Bomb Squad. Then there's not enough of the stuff.'*

"The screws had us out in the yards in wellies and rubber gloves but gave us nowt for the stench. You had people gagging on the smell, spewing their guts up, which meant we were picking up vomit and shit. The stench got in your clothes, your hair, even your fuckin' skin. Bomb Squad members had to band together at lunch, 'cause nobody wanted to sit with us. You could smell us coming from thirty feet away. And, believe me, it were enough to put you off your fuckin' food.

"And if that weren't bad enough, every so often somebody would get shanked.

"It'd be in the showers, or in a corridor, or some other secluded space, and all of a sudden there'd be that fast *thump-thump-thump*. I didn't need to turn to know what it was. But everybody always turned to watch – human nature, I guess.

"It'd be a buncha lads surrounding their victim, like pack animals, putting him down with fast, short thrusts. These things were nearly always razor blades, pieces of broken glass or an off-cut from shop, melted into old toothbrush handles. They'd go for soft tissue – gut, neck, cock and balls – because the blades were too small to go deep.

"It'd be over in seconds. The victim went down. The shanks got tossed or palmed off. And then there would be blood everywhere. And then that awful fuckin' screaming, when the victim realised just how bad things were."

"Then you'd hear fellas fuckin' in the night, sometimes really close by, and not always consensual either. Or you'd hear men crying after lights out, for their wives, or mothers, or children, and sometimes you'd hear some sad fucker commit suicide."

"Then one day I got me own little taste of how bad things could get.

"I used to make me own masks for Bomb Squad duty. It would be an old rag, which I'd thread with string, and rub some Vaporub or Olbas Oil into the fabric, and tie it over me face. It was pretty good at covering the general stink of shit.

"Now, a couple of bruisers on the squad stole me mask. We got into a fight over it and spent a couple of nights in solitary to cool off. And if it had ended there it would've been forgotten."

"So what happened?"

"A day or two later the bruiser I got into a scrap with had his peter tossed.

"Peter?"

"His cell."

"Oh. Because of you?"

Billy shook his head. "Totally random. The problem was that the screws found some hidden contraband – a joint if I remembered correctly – and took the fat bastard straight back to the hole for another week of anger wanking.

"Well, once that blubbery piece of shite got back to civilisation he went on the fuckin' warpath. Blamed me for it, but he was too fuckin' stupid and angry to see that it were just bad luck.

"So one day, while I had a shower, fatty and a couple of his mates paid some screws to go for a long walk. They told the other lags to turn their backs, or come back later, and then they held me down on the floor and raped me. No condoms, no lube, unless you count shower water and spit, which I don't, and they really fuckin' went for it. Tore me up so bad I had to spend a week in medical.

"Once they finished, they showered me blood off their dicks, got dressed and left the place, laughing. But before they left, Fatty got on his knees and told me a little secret. He whispered, 'I've got AIDS, Billy,' in me fuckin' ear the way a lover whispers sweet nothings to his favourite girl.

"Contrary to popular belief, I didn't get what I've got from a needle,

I got that shit given to me. Now *that's* what prison does to you. That's Sodom and Gomorrah, Harry. Hell on earth. And that was the last time anybody got the chance to fuck me over. Those who try that shit now, who enter me squat, *my* fuckin' sanctuary, to mess with me and mine, come to very nasty ends. And you've just made that egregious error, me fat fuckin' friend."

Harry backed away towards the door. "I'm not after trouble, Billy."

The anger returned to Billy's face. He pulled a switchblade from his pocket and hit the button. The blade twinkled briefly in the candlelight as it snapped into place. "Then why did you come here? Other than to compare me with some fuckin' Tellytubby."

"That was Jonno."

Billy moved forward, knife at the ready. "You're not answering me fuckin' question, Harold."

"I'm sorry about hurting your man."

Billy came closer. Harry thought about the razor in his pocket as a last resort, didn't believe it would help. The junky grinned; there was a nasty glint in his eyes. "You're not sorry yet. But you're gonna be…"

34.

Derek grabbed the wall and pulled himself high enough to peer over the edge.

A stone arced through the air and landed in the courtyard behind the units with a thump. Baldy turned in the direction of the sound and lowered into a half-crouch. His hand went inside his jacket, and he tiptoed away warily.

The moment he was out of sight, Derek scaled the wall and scuttled behind the 4x4. He crouched by the left rear wheel and picked a brick half off the ground. He bounced it in his hand, feeling the weight.

Lowering his head, Derek peered beneath the vehicle. The man emerged from behind the building and patrolled the grounds again, his feet crunching gravel and broken tarmac. Derek tightened his grip on the brick and tensed his muscles in readiness.

The man walked past, moving towards the gate. Derek rose up into a crouch and matched the man step-for-step. Then he took a couple of fast strides, scuffing across the ground. Alerted, the man half-turned in the direction of the sound. Derek swung the brick like an extension of his fist. The jagged edge caught Baldy on the left side of the face, tearing his flesh and breaking his jaw. The man lifted his hands to his face, stumbled a few steps, and dropped on the ground.

Half expecting somebody to hear the commotion and come rushing out, Derek dropped the brick, pulled his semi-automatic and aimed in the direction of the garage. The thumping music must have covered the sound because nobody emerged to check it out. He relaxed a touch and put the weapon back in the waistband of his jeans.

A piercing shriek cut through the bass slam, which Derek assumed was Bobby. He felt nothing for the man because he considered it to be a wasted emotion – sooner or later Bobby was going to overdose or contract some deadly disease. Derek preferred to save what little compassion he possessed for those who deserved it.

Derek beckoned his brother and Darren with a wave the hand, and then dragged Baldy around the side of the unit and removed the man's jeans. Using a knife, he cut improvised bindings from the denim and fastened them tightly around the man's legs and wrists, and then removed the man's socks and stuffed one of them in his mouth. Derek cut a final strip of denim and wrapped it around the man's face to keep the makeshift gag in place.

Eric and Darren clambered up and over the wall. They scrambled forward, keeping low, and dropped on their haunches beside Derek and his victim. Eric examined the unconscious man and paid particular attention to the deep gash. He placed his fingers against the neck and checked for a pulse. When he found one, he breathed a sigh of relief.

Derek found his brother's compassion amusing; in the same situation, he had no doubts that Baldy would stomp Eric's head into the stony ground. "Mebbe you should worry less about Lex Luthor and worry more about Bobby."

Eric scowled at him. "Meaning?"

"Heard him scream a few minutes back."

"They're torturing him?"

Derek shrugged. "How the fuck would I know? I can't see through walls. Mebbe he's having withdrawal pains? Or fuckin' period pains, for all I know?"

Eric stood up and removed a gun from beneath his waistband, checked the clip and the barrel, and screwed on a silencer. Then he turned in Darren's direction. "You think you can follow simple orders?"

He rolled his eyes. "Yes, I can follow orders."

"Not seen any evidence of that so far."

"You say it and I'll do it, alright?"

"When we go in, you keep your finger off the trigger," Eric said, hitching a thumb at Derek. "Leave the bullet play to us."

35.

Billy was very close, almost within stabbing distance. Harry tried to think his way out of the situation. The only thing he could come up with was a plea.

"I was desperate," Harry said, backing away. "I *am* desperate."

Billy's eyebrows arched up. "Desperate for what exactly?"

"I need a shotgun."

Billy stopped moving forward. "Why?"

"I'm in trouble."

"You've got me attention," Billy said. "Be careful you don't lose it."

Harry rested his back against the door. The handle pressed into his flesh. He reached around with his left and let his fingers brush against the metal. Just in case he needed a quick escape.

Billy smiled and shook his head. "You're not fast enough, fat man. Your best bet's to keep me interested."

"I need a shotgun."

"You already said that. And I warned you about losing me attention."

"Jonno's after me."

Billy chuckled. "That's a shame. Take it you fucked up?"

"Summat like that."

Billy lowered the knife slightly. "What? Like poor Kev Nicholson?"

"Worse than that," Harry replied. "That's the only reason I hit your fella. He was in my way, and I needed to see you."

"About a shotgun?"

Harry nodded.

"You not got any weaponry at home?"

"I can't go home," Harry replied. "Not yet, anyway."

"Well, firearms cost money, Harold," Billy said. "And judging by the clown outfit, I'd say your cash flow's pretty fuckin' weak at the moment."

"I've got enough."

"You planning to kill Jonno?"

Harry thought about the answer and what it meant. Jonno had killed several rivals over the years, but Harry had never done the deed himself. He'd beaten men within an inch of their lives, and even turned a few into cripples, but that was business, and he hadn't enjoyed it. Killing another person, even a piece of shit like Jonno, was different. There was no coming back from it.

Something about the idea of murder disturbed Harry and made him pause for thought. He wondered if he would be able to look at his wife and son afterwards? He wondered if his family would feel the moment on him? Or see it in his eyes?

Harry told himself it was about self-preservation: he knew Jonno would kill Babs and Terry if he wasn't available, and take great pleasure in it.

So Jonno had to go. As simple as that.

"I'll kill him if it comes down to it."

Billy pressed the blade against the wall until it retracted inside the handle. "It *will* come down to it."

"So be it."

"How much you got?" Billy asked, pocketing the handle.

"Two-fifty."

"Not much for a shotgun."

"And the car outside will fetch a bob or two."

Rubbing his jaw as if deep in thought, Billy stared at the wall for a few moments. Then he scrutinised Harry again. "You know where he's going?"

"He's gotta place over in Seaton."

"I've heard a lot about it. Never knew it were in Seaton, though. Jonno kept that pretty close to his chest."

Harry didn't bother telling Billy that visitors were either blindfolded or unconscious when they arrived. And by the time they left, if they left, they weren't usually in much shape to remember anything about it. Only a few people in Jonno's crew knew the location, and they knew better than to talk about it with friends and family. Although he did say:

"I'm surprised Bobby didn't tell you."

Billy grinned. "I'm not. Bobby talked about lots of things, but he never gave up that piece of information. Guess he didn't trust me with it."

"Or maybe he had plans of his own?"

"Knowing Bobby, you're probably right."

"I *am* right."

"So that's where your bruises came from."

"That's a good guess," Harry said.

"It wasn't a guess."

If Billy knew how he'd got his bruises, then it meant that he was also aware of a few things about the job.

"So you talked to Bobby? You knew about this?"

Billy shook his head. "Bobby talked, I listened. The fool wanted to pay for drugs with an IOU, and I informed him that he could fuck right off. He said he had summat going on. I told him I didn't care. Said he had *big* money coming in. He didn't quite say how, just that it had summat to do with Jonno. As far as I was concerned, it was junky talk. Ninety-five percent of the words that come out of a user's mouth are lies. Nobody takes owt they say at face value unless they're a cunt. But when your boss turned up earlier in a stinking mood I knew Bobby weren't bullshitting. And now you're here with a face full of bruises and threads that'd shame a Seventies pimp, I've come to realise that mebbe Bobby hasn't completely fried his circuits. That boy's been keeping his big brain a secret."

The nasty glimmer returned to Billy's gaze. Something about his manner suggested he had a few secrets of his own. Maybe Bobby had discussed things with him, after all? Or maybe it was something else entirely? The fact that Billy had mentioned Kevin Nicholson wasn't lost on Harry.

Billy had been the first person to visit him in hospital after the business with the broom handle. It was possible that Kevin had seen or heard something about the place, a piece of information valuable to Billy. Maybe he hadn't been unconscious? Or maybe he'd come around and seen something when Harry had left the garage to find Jim?

The realisation that he was in the middle of something he couldn't yet grasp put Harry on edge. Billy appeared to be improvising, getting him to lower his guard. Harry wasn't quite sure why, although he guessed it involved either money or drugs.

"So two-fifty then?" Billy said. "That's what you offered, right?"

"Plus whatever you can get for the car."

Billy made a big deal of rubbing his chin again. Then he grinned. "Okay, fella, you've got yourself a deal."

It was at that moment that Harry knew Billy was plotting something. He was renowned for driving a hard bargain, for quibbling over each and every penny. There wasn't a deal he couldn't improve with a few hours of persistent haggling. His willingness to accept the offer without complaint wasn't through sympathy or weakness. Harry remained wary.

Billy clicked his fingers impatiently. "Gimme the cash."

Harry rummaged through his inside jacket pocket and handed him the money.

"Now go downstairs," Billy said, pointing at the door.

"Why?"

"Coz I said so, that's why. I don't want you knowing where I keep me stashes."

Harry left the room and made his way downstairs. He stepped over the sleeping couple again and entered the living room. He rested his back against a graffiti covered wall and waited awhile. Several people stirred from their slumbers and looked in his direction. When they realised he wasn't a threat, they went back to sleep.

36.

A few minutes later, Billy entered the room with two shotguns and a big black holdall. Harry eyeballed the second weapon and instantly knew that he was coming along for the ride. "Are you trying to tell me summat?" he said.

Billy tossed him a shotgun. Harry caught it in mid-flight and studied the battered barrel and stock. The little man came in close, his manner threatening.

"I'm going with you."

Harry didn't blink.

"You're taking me with you. Otherwise, you can have your money back, and we can resume our earlier argument. It's up to you. Take it or leave it."

"I'll take it."

"Good."

Harry stared down the sight. "What's in it for you?" he asked.

"I wanna be the last thing that racist piece of shite sees before the end."

"Why?"

"I don't like bigots."

It wasn't lost on Harry that Billy called him *round eyes* and *white boy* and other insults, but he kept those thoughts to himself. Despite his silence, Harry wondered if something more compelling than racism was influencing Billy's decision.

Billy had lived longer than most drug users because he knew how to play the game and more importantly he knew how to play it well. The man probably was as crazy as everybody made him out to be, but he still needed to be smart enough to make everybody think he was *that* crazy in the first place.

Other addicts swarmed around him the way moths get drawn to a flame because he knew how to manipulate people. Billy could leave Middlesbrough, move into any junky squat in the land, and be running the place within 24-hours, turning the inhabitants into his private army.

Harry wondered if Billy was also manipulating him, by using racism as a smokescreen for a much less noble reason: money. He intended to watch him carefully.

Billy threw his shotgun in the holdall. "You ever killed anybody before?"

Harry shook his head.

The little man took the second shotgun out of Harry's hands and zipped up the bag. "That's why I'm tagging along," he said. "To make sure the job gets done. You don't give a prick like Jonno a second chance."

"Did you make sure they're loaded?" Harry asked.

Billy's gaze was chilly. "You take me for a fuckin' idiot? Course they're loaded. What fuckin' good would they be if they weren't?"

37.

Music cannoned off the walls and filled the room with a distorted envelope of ear-splitting sound. And yet it still wasn't loud enough to cover the screams.

Bobby shrieked for help at the top of his voice. He twisted his body left and right to loosen the ropes that bound him to the chair. When that didn't work, he tried turning his head away.

Grinning, Jonno raised a bloodied straight razor.

"Hold him steady."

Ben moved behind Bobby, grabbed both sides of his face and prevented him from struggling. Jonno pulled the man's left earlobe until fully stretched and drew the blade across it. The flesh came away easily. Bobby squealed. Blood trickled down his neck and soaked the fabric of his t-shirt.

Jonno held the small piece of rubbery flesh between his forefingers and thumb and waggled it in front of his former friend, who was now missing both his lobes.

"You shouldn't have betrayed me," Jonno said, leaning in.

"This is fuckin' crazy, man," Bobby yelled. "I dunno whatcha talking about."

Jonno flicked the lobe away and wiped his fingers on a blood-spattered apron. He chuckled. "I'm glad you're not talking. The longer you hold out, the more you have to lose. You've got fifty grand's worth of body parts on you, and I'm gonna take every penny I'm owed one way or another."

Bobby winced and tried a more soothing tone. "If you tell us what happened, I might be able to help. There's no need for torture."

Jonno turned away with a snort. "You've got some serious fuckin' balls."

Ben patted Bobby on the head and laughed. "Now there's an idea, boss. Let's take his hairy fuckin' nuts."

Jonno grinned. "I like your thinking."

Bobby shrieked again. "No, no… I'll talk. I'll fuckin' talk."

Jonno grasped Bobby's balls and squeezed until he winced. "I know you will. If you tell me what I wanna know, I might just let you keep them. Now gimme the names of the dickheads you're working with."

Bobby kept his eyes down. He shivered and stuttered. Every time he opened his mouth nothing emerged but vowel sounds. Jonno squeezed his balls until tears of pain ran down his face.

"Look at me, Bobby," Jonno insisted. "Or I'm gonna tear off your fuckin' swingers."

Bobby stared at him for a moment, before focusing his eyes towards the front of the garage.

"You better start naming names," Jonno hissed. "Before I fuckin' castrate you."

Bobby began to grin. It was so unexpected that Jonno's grip relaxed momentarily.

"What so fuckin' funny?"

Bobby's smile grew wider and cockier. The glint of fear left his eyes. Jonno backed away slightly, confused by the man's show of defiance.

The junky locked eyes with him. "They're called the Stantons."

"And how are you gonna arrange for me to meet them?"

"You're gonna meet 'em sooner than you think."

Something about Ben's demeanour made Jonno cast a glance in his direction. He had ceased laughing, and a worried expression was stripping away the last traces of his smile. His hands fell away from Bobby's shoulders and dropped to his sides. Fingers scraping nervously against his jeans, he stared past Jonno's shoulder in open-mouthed shock and stepped back slowly.

Bobby laughed. "Jonno, meet the Stantons."

He whipped his head in the direction of the door.

Three men were pointing guns in his direction, all of them smiling.

"Stantons, meet Jonno."

38.

Eric placed his ear against a small door to the left of the main entrance. Beneath the thumping bass line and the whine of the melody came a high-pitched scream.

He peered through the keyhole, but the view was limited to part of the far wall, some shelves and mechanic's tools. He twisted the handle slowly, pressed his shoulder against the door, and applied his weight carefully, but there was no give. It was locked.

Eric cursed under his breath. Although he was capable of picking the lock, it would probably take a while. If the music turned off during that time, or somebody noticed the handle moving, the chances were good that whoever went in first would be walking into gunfire.

He turned and went to where Baldy's jeans had been discarded and groped through the pockets. There were two sets of keys: a bunch of house and car keys on a ring and a single Chubb key.

Eric walked back to the door and put the Chubb in the lock. It slid into place, and the mechanism turned. Putting his shoulder against the wood, he pressed the handle and readied his gun. Darren and Derek breathed down his neck as the door opened. A wall of distorted sound hit him. He shut out the noise and maintained his focus.

Bobby was bound to a chair towards the far end of a large, high-ceilinged room that stank of old engines and rusted metal. Both his ear-lobes had been removed. Blood trickled down his neck and soaked the collar of his T-shirt. He wore gore-spattered jeans torn at the right leg, revealing a grotesquely swollen ankle.

Two men stood over him. The one with his back to the door was tall and slim. He was wearing neat clothes covered by a blood-flecked apron, and in his right hand was a bloodied straight razor. The other man was gaunt and scruffy with dark, greasy hair that clung to his scalp. He held Bobby's head tightly, to prevent it moving, and grinned as the man with the straight razor gripped the junky's balls and said something.

A third man sat on a long wooden workbench near the right wall and ignored the torture. He prodded the buttons on a massive stereo unit and watched the LED display lights jump in time with the music. Something must have caught his eye because he turned in Eric's direction. His jaw dropped for a moment, and then his rat-like face twitched. It looked like he was about to raise the alarm.

Eric angled the gun in his direction and shook his head slowly. The man raised his hands in a half-hearted gesture of surrender. Realising he presented no further threat, Eric edged forward and let the weapon drift back towards the main event.

Bobby looked up from the ground as they approached. A grin of recognition spread across his face. The man holding Bobby followed his gaze and went stiff. His mouth formed a perfect O of surprise. He took two small steps back, and his body loosened, ready to turn and run at a moment's notice.

Bobby's smile grew wider and flashed teeth. His mouth moved briefly, and he cast a nod in Eric's direction. The man holding the razor whipped around and scowled at the intruders. There was something troubling about the shifty expression on his face, and the way his fingers tightened around the handle, as he edged closer to Bobby.

Eric squeezed off a warning shot. The bullet kicked up a chunk of concrete near the man's feet. He stumbled back awkwardly and then righted himself. Shock slackened his handsome features, and his eyes blinked rapidly. He loosened his grip on the blade.

The music stopped. The sudden overwhelming silence magnified every shuffle, sigh, and scrape of sole on concrete. All eyes turned to the rat-faced man. He prodded the stereo buttons with an air of embarrassment. His awkwardness increased when he realised that he was the focus of everyone's attention.

Sensing opportunity, the gaunt man moved back slowly, almost imperceptibly, towards the office structure at the very rear of the building. Just as he was turning to run, his soles scuffed the floor.

Derek jerked in the direction of the sound and aimed his weapon. "Ow, daft cunt, where d'you think *you're* going?" he snarled.

Realising he'd been rumbled, the man winced and raised his hands high. He gazed at the office with an expression of longing.

"Try it," Derek said. "Let's see how far you get with a bullet in the spine."

"Easy, fella."

"I'll calm down when you're back where I can fuckin' see you."

He scurried back to his original position. Then his hands dropped to his sides. He looked ashamed to be caught so quickly.

The man with the straight razor recovered some of his earlier bravery. Spreading out his arms in a Jesus Christ pose, he asked: "What the fuck do you want?"

"Right this second, I want you to drop that blade," Eric said, emphasising his demand by pointing the silencer barrel in the direction of the ground.

"And if I don't?"

"You'll never hold anything in that hand again."

Jonno looked over his shoulder at Bobby and took a firm grip on the knife handle. "If you're smart you'll turn and run," he said, edging back towards the addict. "D'you even know who you're fuckin' with?"

"Credit me with a little intelligence, *Jonno*."

"So why the fuck have you come here?" he asked. "Considering you're the pricks who stole from me."

Eric's eyes fixed on Bobby. "Because of him."

Jonno let out a roar of laughter that echoed off the walls. "You exposed yourselves for a fuckin' junky?"

Eric smiled. "When you put it like that, it does sound kinda stupid."

"Now there's a fuckin' understatement. This piece of shit would lemme slit your throat if the roles were reversed."

A deep red flush spread across Jonno's cheeks. His eyes turned in Bobby's direction. He started twisting on his heels towards the addict. His hand tightened around the knife handle.

Eric lowered into a shooter's stance, his aim steady. "Unless you wanna spend the rest of your days wanking off with an Abu Hamza hook, you better drop that fuckin' blade."

Realising that things were about to go badly, Jonno opened his hand and let the knife fall. It clanked against the hard floor.

"Now what?" he asked.

Eric angled his gaze towards the man with the stereo. "Now, rat boy gets off his arse and joins you."

"The name's Jim," he replied.

"Who gives a fuck?" Eric said. "Get a fuckin' move on before I use your knees as target practice."

Jim hopped off the workbench and double-timed across the room. He shivered beside his boss and stared at Eric. He tried putting some bravery in his glare, but it didn't work. Eventually, his gaze drifted down to the ground.

"Now get face down on the floor and kiss concrete," Eric said. "Hands behind your backs."

Jonno lay flat on his stomach, rested his face against the concrete, and crossed his wrists behind his back. Jim quickly followed suit.

The gaunt man hesitated.

Eric aimed at him. "Would you like me translate that to a language you *do* understand, or would you just prefer a sex-change operation performed with bullets?"

The gaunt man assumed the position.

Jonno lifted his head. Concrete dust peppered his left cheek. "Where's Dave?"

"Outside having a nap," Eric replied, approaching the three prone men carefully. "He'll be joining you shortly."

Jonno tried to say something else. Eric rushed forward and kicked him in the jaw before the words left his lips. His face hit the concrete and blood trickled from his mouth. Then Eric stepped over Jonno and kicked the other two men into unconsciousness.

Eric plucked Jonno's razor off the ground and used it to cut Bobby's ropes. The junky rubbed at the livid red marks on his wrists and swung his arms around to get the blood flowing again.

"You okay?" Eric asked.

The addict gazed at his grotesquely swollen ankle and whimpered. He prodded it with his fingertip and yelped with pain.

"Really need to get a move on," he replied. "Could lose me fuckin' leg without proper treatment."

Eric sniggered and shook his head. Although the injury looked terrible, it wasn't something a cast or a few steel pins couldn't fix. Even his ears would heal with only a few scars.

Eric folded and pocketed the razor, saying: "You heard the man, we're in a hurry. Let's find some more rope and tie these pricks up."

39.

Harry put his foot down, and the car picked up speed along Seaton Carew Road. Daylight now consisted of a thin band of orange that hovered just above the western horizon. Industrial lights twinkled against the rapidly darkening sky. Cold air swept through Harry's open window. The faint odour of the chemical works wasn't quite enough to cover the vinegary stench of Billy's sweat.

His passenger was becoming increasingly agitated. He gnawed his fingernails and spat the pieces in the footwell. It was hard to tell if there was something on his mind or if he needed a hit.

"Why'd you save Kev Nicholson?" he asked without prompting.

Harry squeezed the steering wheel briefly. "Who says I did?"

"Kev sez you did."

Harry smiled. "So he was awake?"

It was now obvious why Billy was here, and why he'd subjected Harry to a constant barrage of questions throughout the journey. Sly little queries about the building and its layout, where things were situated, and if there were likely to be any unwanted visitors. Kevin had seen something when everybody else was out of the room. Something he'd only told Billy.

"He said you fought his corner good style and lied about his importance. Said we were *tight*."

Harry nodded but didn't reply.

"So why'd you save him?"

Harry thought about his son for a moment and compartmentalised the guilt. "I've got my reasons."

"Such as?"

"He didn't deserve it."

"I doubt Jonno sees it that way."

"Fuck Jonno. He didn't deserve *that*. Shit, it wasn't even about punishment. It was about humiliating him. It was like some fuckin' pack animal thing. They were enjoying it."

Billy grinned. "Are you *really* tryna tell me you've never enjoyed kicking the shit outta somebody?"

Harry sighed. "I used to."

"But not no more?"

Harry remembered visiting a rival dealer and beating him in front of his children. The man had made the mistake of doing deals in territory that Jonno considered his own, an error that required swift punishment. Harry and Dave Callan visited the man's home, pushed their way inside, and smashed him with hammers in front of kids not much older than Terry. They cried and screamed at them not to hurt their daddy. The man begged his children to leave the room, but Dave just laughed and told them to stay and watch. At one point, the elder sibling wrapped his arms around his little brother and buried his face in his chest to prevent him seeing his father's humiliation.

A deep sense of shame overwhelmed Harry. He stopped swinging the hammer and stepped back. Every glance at those terrified children only increased his embarrassment. Dave didn't notice he'd lost his partner and continued the assault.

By the time it was finished, the man had two broken arms, a shattered nose, fractured cheekbones, three smashed ribs, and a mouthful of tooth shards. The kids shivered and stared blankly at their Dad. Then the youngest looked at Harry with an expression of fear and disgust that cut him to the bone. It was a look he never wanted to see again.

After that day, everything felt different. His taste for violence diminished to the point where the thought of it made him feel sick. He either used excuses to back away from the rough stuff or did it halfheartedly. He tried to participate in other ways and earn money for Jonno's outfit by using his brain as opposed to brawn. He wasn't very good at it. His relationship with Jonno deteriorated. And now his family was falling apart at the seams, and he had no idea how to put it back together again.

"I haven't enjoyed it for a long time. In fact, I fuckin' hate it."

Billy spat another fingernail shred into the footwell. "Then whyn't you just leave?"

"You think I haven't already thought of that?"

Billy smirked. "Who the fuck knows whatchoo think about, Harry? Aside from your next hit of junk food."

Harry squeezed the steering wheel again. "Bobby had to develop a drug habit for Jonno to wash his hands of him. That's how fuckin' paranoid he is. He certainly doesn't wanna let anybody go. At least not while their heart's still beating."

Billy nodded. "That's why you gotta get in first."

Harry smiled bitterly. "Gotta kill my way to a peaceful life. Isn't that ironic?"

"Yeah, if you're Alanis Morissette. That's a fuckin' paradox you're describing, Harry."

"Paradox, irony, who gives a fuck? I'm still gonna have to put Jonno down."

"Better him than you."

"I suppose."

"That cunt deserves what's coming to him."

Harry shrugged.

Billy sneered. "Don't go all gay on me. Kev told me what happened, you know, in *exhaustive* fuckin' detail. He told me how your mob beat the shit outta him, snapped his fingers, kicked out his teeth…"

"I don't need a recap. I was there."

"Mebbe you *do* need one," Billy replied. "Just to remind yourself why you're putting him down."

"It's not summat I wanna relive."

Images of the ordeal flashed in his skull. Jonno and Dave lifting Kevin off the ground and for some inexplicable reason pulling down his pants. Everybody laughing at the man's fear-shrunken penis until he began to cry with shame. Jonno playing up to the crowd, describing Kevin as more woman than man and asking what it was that women like most? Then he recalled Jim and Ben bundling Kev to the ground and holding him down; a broom handle lubed up with washing up liquid and spit, Kev's face when the handle went in, the screams of pain, the blood… so much fucking blood.

"If I hadn't done summat, they would've killed him," Harry said. "I could see it in their eyes. They weren't gonna stop."

"You want that to happen to your wife? Your son?"

The possibility sent a brief, hot rage through Harry. He didn't say anything. Instead, he shook his head.

"Then it's not murder," Billy added. "It's a public fuckin' service, like putting down a mad dog."

Harry decided to change the subject. "Did Kev ever tell you who grassed him up?"

Billy cracked a broad smile. "You seen Ben Moody around lately?"

They passed an oil refinery dotted with vast white silos on the left, and a chemical plant spanned with skeletal structures and thin chimneys on the right. They weren't far away now.

"Can't say I have," Harry replied. "Figured he took his money and split."

"You figured wrong."

"Dead?"

"Fixed him a dose that was too hot by anyone's standards," Billy replied. "Buried the cunt somewhere out on the moors."

Harry noticed the Greyhopes sign ahead and flicked the indicator. He turned left and drove through the featureless estate until he came across a small stretch of road with a broken streetlight. He parked within its shadow and killed the engine.

Billy picked up the holdall and exited the vehicle. Harry waited a moment, drew in a deep breath and exhaled slowly. This was it. He got out of the car and locked it.

They walked across the road and up a small verge, shuffled through a gap between a couple of leafy shrubs and into a small, dark alcove created by overhanging tree branches. Using this shadow as cover, they peered over the wall at a windowless building with a sloped roof. Jim Hanway's black four-wheeler sat in front of the large, drive-in door.

"You see owt?" Billy asked.

"No," Harry replied. "And that's what worries me."

"Why's that?"

"Jonno usually has somebody patrolling around outside, especially when they're torturing someone, just in case of surprise visitors. Plus, I can't hear any music."

"Music? Is Jonno planning to torture Bobby through the medium of dance?"

Harry grinned. "Nothing drowns out screams quite like dance music."

They stuck close to the wall and went around to the front gate. Billy scaled the wall with the agility of an athlete, which Harry considered impressive for a forty-something heroin addict with HIV and Hepatitis. Harry, on the other hand, huffed his way over with all the dexterity of an obese man with Type-2 Diabetes.

Doubling over, Harry gathered his breath in long, hard gasps. When all this was over, he was finally going to do something about his weight.

Billy sneered and shook his head in disgust.

"Am I gonna hafta resuscitate you?"

Harry couldn't speak yet. He answered with a shake of the head.

"Are you sure? Coz I sure as shite don't wanna be locking lips with you."

Harry managed to gather enough air in his lungs to form a few words. "I'll be fine."

"You better be," Billy replied. "Coz if we've gotta run, I'm leaving your fat arse in the dust. You hear?"

"In Dolby."

40.

Billy crouched beside the four-wheeler and opened the holdall. His eyes narrowed as he studied the shotguns, then he handed one to Harry. He grabbed the other weapon and put the holdall over his shoulder.

Both men heard a rustling sound, like shaking branches. Billy jerked his shotgun to the right, in the direction of the noise. "You hear that?" he hissed.

"I hear it."

Following the sounds, they moved to the right of the building, towards the rear of the plot, where they discovered a small thicket of shrubs beside the boundary wall. The leaves and branches shook violently. Beneath the rustle of foliage was an insistent mumbling.

Billy pushed to the front and approached carefully. He rounded the bushes, sniggered into the palm of his hand, and waved Harry forward with the shotgun.

Dave lay on the ground in his polo shirt and boxer shorts. His limbs had been bound tightly with strips of denim. A sock had been pushed into his mouth as a makeshift gag and tied in place with another piece of denim. He kicked out his legs for attention.

Harry crouched on his haunches and studied Dave's face. A deep gash ran a few inches from his chin towards his left ear, and every time he made a sound, fresh blood flowed from the wound. It was a recent injury; the coagulated blood on the lower half of his face was still damp.

A jolt of fear passed through Harry when he realised that they weren't the first arrivals to the party. He was about to remove Dave's gag and ask who was inside when Billy let out an unpleasant chuckle.

"If it isn't me old mate, Ross Kemp," he said. "Where's the Ultimate Force when you need 'em?"

Harry stared up at him. "What the fuck are you on about?"

Billy grinned back. "Just a little in-joke between Baldy and me."

Harry began working the knot that tied the gag in place. Billy pushed him over before he could finish the job. Harry jumped to his feet and dusted himself down. "Seriously? What the fuck?"

Billy pointed the shotgun barrel at Dave. "We're not here for this piece of shit."

Harry drew back on his tiptoes, so that he had a good six inches height advantage, and glowered down at the man. "Don't ever push me again."

Billy wasn't intimidated in the slightest. "Then stop being a prick. You're wasting me time."

"I wanna ask him what happened."

"Would you like me to summarise what happened?"

Billy spun on his heels and slammed the shotgun butt into Dave's head. The man stopped struggling. Billy hit him again, but this time much harder. The impact resounded with a loud crunch. Smiling at a job well done, Billy stepped away and watched as Harry got on his knees and placed his fingers against Dave's neck. The pulse was faint. A significant dent at the top of his skull was beginning to redden and swell. Harry figured he didn't have long to live without treatment.

"Did that encapsulate what happened sufficiently?" Billy said. "Did that illustrate that somebody hit him pretty fuckin' hard? Now let's stop playing silly buggers and go sort out Jonno."

"You didn't have to hit him," Harry hissed. "He was already tied up."

"For a man who's come here to kill, you're showing an alarmingly yellow streak."

Harry got off the ground and removed one of Eileen's cigarettes from his pocket. Using the time to think, he lit it, took a big drag that made him feel lightheaded and blew smoke at the darkening sky.

Things weren't happening as he'd hoped. Billy had no intention of playing the game by anybody's rules, but his own, and Harry wondered if anybody, including Billy, knew what they were. Without some semblance of control, this was likely to turn into a massacre. Indiscriminate murder wasn't part of the plan.

"What're you *really* here for?" Harry asked. "'Cause it sure as shit isn't racism. And I'm pretty fuckin' positive you're not here to help me."

Billy smiled. "You certain about that?"

Harry spat the cigarette. "Sure as I'm standing here."

Billy shuffled on the spot as if readying himself for trouble. "Mebbe I'm here for revenge – for Kev, for Bobby?"

Harry stomped the still smouldering stick beneath his heel. "I don't think it's that either. I think Kevin told you summat about this place. Summat he saw. Summat only you know."

Billy licked his lips nervously. The smile started fading.

Harry sniffed the air, and whispered: "I think I smell money."

Billy lifted his arms and inhaled from both armpits. "Just a bad case of BO, mate."

Harry pointed his shotgun at Billy's chest.

The junky sneered. "Such a shame. We coulda been friends."

"Drop the weapon," Harry said.

Billy studied Harry for a moment and shook his head.

"I'll pull the trigger."

"Even if I believed that, which I don't, it wouldn't do you much fuckin' good."

Harry knew he shouldn't have taken Billy at his word. He should have checked the weapon for shells.

He pulled the trigger.

Click.

Billy's grin widened, became quiet laughter. He put the barrel of his shotgun beneath Harry's chin. "But this one is loaded. So unless you fancy having your head turned inside out, I'd drop yours on the ground and get in front of me, where I can keep me eye on you."

Harry dropped his weapon. As long as Billy didn't frisk him, he still had a chance. Charlie's straight razor was in his trouser pocket. Harry only needed Billy to avert his attention elsewhere for a moment – to concentrate on corralling Jonno and the others – and he would drop the bastard with a couple of well-aimed swipes.

Harry turned around, raised his hands, and waited, but Billy didn't bother to frisk him. Instead, he jammed the gun barrel against Harry's lower back and pushed him forward.

"Walk, and be careful about it. Start getting all wobbly, or make any sudden movements, and I'll sever your fuckin' spine and leave you where you land. You understand me?"

"Loud and clear."

"So move," he said, prodding him again.

Harry marched forward with Billy matching him step-for-step to the door. Listening out for recognisable voices or screams, Harry gripped the handle and waited. There were a few murmurs, but nothing to help him understand his predicament. All he knew at that moment was Billy intended to use him as a human shield if the bullets started flying.

"What the fuck you waiting for?" Billy hissed.

"The right moment."

"Fuck the right moment. Get on with it."

Harry turned the handle.

41.

Bobby fumbled through his pockets, pulled a crushed cigarette box from the front of his jeans, and managed to stop shaking long enough to put a crooked cigarette in his mouth. He also found a lighter, flicked the wheel until it made a flame, and burned the tip. Bobby puffed out smoke and stared at the severed earlobe on the ground.

Eric placed his hand on Bobby's shoulder for a moment and squeezed tightly, which was as close as he could get to a show of compassion. Sympathy wasn't going to fix what had happened. They couldn't afford to slow down.

"What's done is done," Eric said.

Bobby turned towards him. "Gimme the blade."

"Why?"

Bobby's attention went to Jonno, who was still unconscious on the floor. Eric shook his head. "Forget it."

Bobby studied him with glassy eyes. "Would you forget it?"

"Probably not."

"Then why should I?"

"Because you're nearly five grand richer than you were yesterday. You won."

Bobby took another drag of his cigarette.

"And I – no, *we* – could win again."

"What're you getting at?"

Bobby wiped perspiration from his forehead and brow with his left palm before rubbing it on his jeans. "Jonno's got money here."

"And you're only telling me this now?"

Bobby shrugged. "This place is alarmed to the fuckin' ceilings. Three separate codes on three different panels, in various parts of the building," he said. "And only Jonno knows the codes. Normally this wouldn't even be on the menu."

There was a panel by the main entrance, and another situated on the wall beside the rear office door. Eric couldn't see the third keypad.

"The only way to get in would be to have three separate crackers working the codes at once," Bobby added. "And you have a minute to do it. Otherwise, the alarms go off and trigger a warning at a private security firm near Hartlepool. They can be here in under ten minutes. That's what Ben was heading for earlier."

Eric looked in the direction of the back office. "You can't get out that way?"

"You can, but Ben were heading for the panic button. The firm's alerted immediately. They phone the office and private lines. If nobody answers, they send a patrol and inform the police."

"Wouldn't that put Jonno in the shit?"

Bobby took another drag of the cigarette then let it drop on the ground. "If he has to press that button, then he's *already* in the shite. Besides, all that's here is money. I seriously doubt there's drugs on the premises. As for incriminating evidence, he goes over this place regularly with luminol and a UV light and bleaches the fuck outta it."

"And your ankle?" Eric said.

Combined shock and anger seemed to have made Bobby forget about his injuries momentarily. "Can wait."

"Do you even know where this money is?"

Bobby hesitated. "No, but I know it's here."

"How?"

"Kev Nicholson told Billy Chin."

"But not you."

Bobby shook his head.

"Then it's probably some junky pipe dream," Eric said.

"Mebbe it is, like. But why alarm the shit out of a place if there's nowt here?"

"Good point, but you still don't know where it is," Eric replied, turning on the spot and waving his hands around the hangar-sized space. "And there's a lotta ground to cover."

Bobby nodded "That's where a blade comes in handy."

Part of Eric wanted to know if this money existed, but he knew there was no guarantee that Jonno would spill, even under duress, and he wasn't foolish enough to risk what he'd already earned on the rumour of more. And he certainly wasn't about to let Bobby waste valuable time torturing Jonno for something that might not be real.

"Are you sure this is about money?"

"I deserve payback."

Eric shook his head. "No. You *want* payback. Assuming ToJo's not a complete fuckin' idiot, he's probably found a village by now. He'll be spilling his guts about everything. They might already be on their way. They're not gonna be pleased about losing fifty grand. They'll be out for blood."

"But…"

"But nothing. We have the money. We have you. Our job is done. If you wanna hang around and carve up Jonno, you're on your own. We're not hanging around."

Bobby stared at Jonno's prone figure for a moment. Eric pulled the razor from his pocket and held it in front of his face. "What's it to be? Stay and torture Jonno or are you gonna smarten up and come with us?"

Bobby waved the blade away. "Let's go."

Eric crouched down and let Bobby wrap an arm around his neck.

"Come on, you two, we're moving."

Derek finished binding Jim's ankles and checked it was tight enough. Darren finished tying off Jonno. Derek double-checked his work to ensure it was done right. "We're done," he said. Both men moved over to the door and waited impatiently.

Bobby stumbled a couple of small hops for every step Eric took, and each landing kicked off a series of grimaces and sobs. He was playing up the pain for an unsympathetic audience.

"Whyn't you try acting like a fuckin' man?" Derek said.

"You try having a broken leg," Bobby shrieked. "See how you react."

Derek sniffed. "I've tried several, along with arms, fingers, ribs and nose. Don't recall acting like a fuckin' mincer, though."

Eric was about to tell the pair to shut up when Derek and Darren pointed their weapons at the door and made a hasty backpedalling retreat. They scuttled to the workbench and used it as a shield.

"We've got visitors," Derek whispered to his brother.

Eric hissed a flurry of swear words and rushed Bobby back to the chair. The junky whimpered as his injured ankle struck the ground and smothered a squeal with the palm of his hand.

Eric dropped into shooter's stance and steadied his aim.

The door handle turned.

Eric prepared himself for the worst. His finger brushed the trigger.

The door opened, and Harry Sparks entered the room with hands high. Bruises darkened his face, and his clothes appeared a lot more eccentric than they had been earlier in the day. A small man holding a shotgun lurked in the shadows behind him.

"Throw down your fuckin' weapon," Derek roared, "and step out with your hands high."

The small man cackled. "Hows about I remove this idiot's spine and then throw some fuckin' buckshot your way?"

Narrowing his gaze, Derek tilted his head and studied the figure. He cursed under his breath, looked over at his brother, and mouthed the words, *Billy Chin.*

Eric didn't need his brother's help to recognise the high-pitched, nasal voice. Their paths had crossed several times during his time as a debt collector. The last occasion had involved Billy holding a syringe of blood to Derek's throat while Eric pleaded with him not to press the plunger. Somehow he'd managed to talk him down.

Derek let out a rumble of laughter. "Who gives a fuck about Fatty Beltbuckle? By the time he hits the deck, you'll be nothing more than a fuckin' memory. I'll drop you, Billy."

"You better make that a fuckin' kill shot. 'Cause if you miss, I'm coming straight at youse with a syringe full of fuckin' AIDS."

42.

Cold sweat rolled down Harry's spine and nestled between his butt cheeks. Fighting the urge to fidget, ignoring the raised voices, he focused only on his predicament. Negotiating his way through all this greed and aggression was the only way he was going to get home to his wife and son. That was all he wanted now. No amount of money was worth this trouble.

Eric stepped away from Bobby and fixed his gun sight on Billy. "If you drop the fat boy, then I drop you. You won't even get a chance to go for that syringe."

"How do we settle this?" Harry pleaded. "I don't want any trouble."

"Shut the fuck up," Billy snapped.

"Whatever you're up to has nowt to do with us," Eric said. "We came here for Bobby, and we're leaving with him."

Billy shuffled. "Not with me fuckin' money, you're not."

"D'you see us carrying any fuckin' money?"

"You two greedy fuckers are always up to summat," Billy said. "And it's always about money."

"Billy, there *is* money," Eric replied. "But it's in a car not too far from here – in drug form."

The pressure of the shotgun barrel on Harry's spine eased a little.

"Aitch?" Billy asked.

Eric nodded.

"Pure?"

Harry let his right hand come down slowly. He waited for Billy to notice, but the junky was more interested in heroin at that moment.

"As pure as a virgin's honeypot," Eric replied.

Billy swallowed audibly. "Pure enough to bathe in?" he asked, voice breaking.

Harry's hand rested at his side. Any second he expected Billy to scream at him to raise it again, but the demand never came.

Eric smiled. "If that's what takes your fancy."

Harry's fingers brushed the hem of his pocket.

"Why the fuck should I believe you?"

"Why would I lie?"

"Because you're a cunt?"

Eric shrugged his shoulders. "There is that, but there's also *this*: we've got more guns than you and could drop you and fatty before you even have a chance to react – yet you're still alive, and we're still talking. What does that tell you?"

"That mebbe you're on the up-and-up."

Harry's fingers pushed past the hem and into the lining.

"If you wanna hang around after we've gone, that's on you, but we are leaving through that door. And you're not stopping us."

Harry felt the knife handle, put his fingers around it. He no longer sensed any weight against his spine. Holding his breath, he retracted his hand carefully.

Billy took a half step back. "What kinda weight we talking?"

"Ask your hostage," Eric replied. "He's the one who was carrying it."

"Half a key," Harry answered quickly through clenched teeth. "Fifty gees of it."

"Why're you giving the drugs away, man?"

"Because we're not fuckin' dealers, Billy. We weren't supposed to grab the drugs at all."

"Then why did you?"

Eric tipped his head in Darren's direction. "Because of *this* clown."

Billy chuckled. "Good old Thrombosis."

Darren groaned, and his gun wavered momentarily.

Eric craned forward. "What?"

Billy's lips parted in a yellow and brown grin. "That's his fuckin' nickname, man. One of Joey Judd's boys buys weight from me. He used to talk about a guy called Thrombo, said the cunt was so inept he could ruin a cup of instant coffee. Joey likened him to a fuckin' thrombosis – you know, an annoying clot that goes around fuckin' with the system. There in't a job too small for him to mess up.

"Watched him spanner a fixed fight not so long ago. Cost me a fuckin' packet – 'cause I had me money on the other gadgie."

The knife handle was halfway out of Harry's pocket. He fingered the back of the blade, ready to snap it into place. There was one chance at this – a half chance, at that – and if it failed, he'd have just enough time to see his entrails spray across the room before he died. All he could do now was wait.

Darren edged away from the bench and towards Billy. His face darkened. "You wanna watch that mouth of yours, you junky prick."

A momentary silence fell on the room. Harry heard Billy's sharp intake of breath. "Whatchoo fuckin' say there, *Thrombo*?"

Eric turned his head in Darren's direction. "Let's take it down a notch. We're all still friends here."

Darren inched forward, lining up a shot. "He's not me fuckin' friend."

Billy swivelled slowly to face the boxer. Harry couldn't see where the gun was pointing, but he was positive that the junky's attention wasn't on him. He brought the knife handle fully out of his pocket and began prising the blade into place.

"Back down, *now*," Eric said. "You've already fucked this up once, don't do it again."

Gritting his teeth, Darren moved on another few steps. "I won't be mocked by a junky piece of shit."

"Who're you calling a piece of shit?" Billy said.

"Don't be fuckin' stupid," Eric snapped. "We can all leave this place happy."

Harry's heart thumped. His body stiffened, and he closed his eyes, ready to go down in a hail of bullets.

Eric coughed. "Warning shot."

Derek pulled the trigger. The bullet smacked into the ground by Darren's feet, peppering him with concrete shards. He stopped moving and turned his head slowly in Eric's direction with his mouth open and his eyes widening with surprise.

Eric kept his focus on Billy and Harry. "The next one goes in your fuckin' head. I won't let you fuck this up."

Darren loosened, lowered his gun slightly, and inched back towards the workbench.

Billy guffawed, moving slightly to Harry's right. "Not so fuckin' bold now, are we, *Thrombo*?"

Harry fully retracted the blade and kept it flat against his thigh. He took in a long, slow breath, held it, and angled his eyes right, towards Billy. Leering and laughing, the junky pointed the shotgun barrel away from Harry's body.

This was it. His chance.

Harry turned on his heels, swinging the blade in a fast arc.

Billy saw the movement late, his leer turning to a grimace, and tried to get off a shot. Harry heard the blast, felt something hot tear through his flesh, and completed his swipe.

The blade cut Billy's right ear in half, sliced through the right cheek, and embedded deep in his nose. Dropping the shotgun, Billy shrieked loudly and grabbed at the knife sticking out of his face. He sliced his fingers as he attempted to yank the blade from the bone and fell on the ground.

Harry dived for the shotgun. As his fingers wrapped around the stock, a silenced gunshot spattered his face with concrete. Harry blinked the dust from his eyes. There was a fresh hole in the ground a few feet away. He relaxed his hand and let it move slowly away from the weapon.

Eric squinted at him through a faint plume of gun smoke. "Don't be fuckin' stupid. Nobody needs to die here."

Harry put his hands in the air. Sharp pains sliced across his stomach. He removed his jacket. Blood seeped through the shredded white fabric stretched across his midriff.

Lifting the polo shirt, he realised that the injury wasn't too bad – most of the blast had missed him, but a piece of buckshot had mangled a chunk of flesh just above his belly button. Despite the pain, it was only a flesh wound. He kept his hand on it to stem the blood flow.

Eric maintained his aim. "That's nowt a hooky doctor won't cure. But if you go for that shotgun again you'll have a wound even the good Lord Jesus won't be able to fix."

Harry put on his jacket, got to his feet, and turned towards Billy.

The junky rolled around on the floor with his face in his hands. He kicked his feet against the concrete and screamed like an upset toddler. Blood oozed through his fingers in a steady stream, making spatter patterns on the ground.

"What now?" Harry said.

Eric exchanged glances with his brother.

"That's up to you."

Harry raised his hands. "I don't want any trouble, fella."

"What *do* you want?"

"I came here to take care of Jonno," Harry said, looking down at the unconscious men. "But it seems like you've taken care of him just fine. Are you gonna kill him?"

Eric shook his head. "No, and neither will you."

Harry took a deep breath. "He's gonna kill me if I don't. Hurt my family."

"He's not gonna be in a position to hurt anyone."

"And why's that?"

Billy removed his hands from his face, mumbled incoherently, and unleashed a thin stream of vomit on the ground. His eyelids fluttered for a few seconds, and he pitched forward face first in the puke puddle. Harry moved towards him, then remembered what was in his blood and took a few steps back.

Eric nodded at the prone man. "Because he's likely to do it for you."

"Assuming Billy gets up again. That blade in his face looks pretty fuckin' bad."

Eric lowered his weapon a touch and placed his finger on the trigger guard. "If you know Billy well enough, you'll know his tricks. He's caught out more than a few people with the old passing out trick. He's expecting somebody to fall for it and rush to help him. At which point he'll jab you with one of the several syringes of blood he's carrying in various pockets. Or maybe he'll slice you with the blade that's currently in his face. If he cuts you open it's game over – if the HIV doesn't get you, the Hep definitely will."

Harry stepped even further back. "Good point," he said. "Doesn't help my situation, though. Even if Jonno disappears there's still Ramon to contend with; he's gonna be looking for his fifty grand. When he can't find Jonno, he'll no doubt turn his attention to me."

"Can't give you that money back."

Harry gave him a rueful smirk. "Can't or won't?"

"You decide."

"Then I'm gonna need running money. Otherwise, I'm dead."

"That offer I extended to Billy's still open."

"The drugs?"

"Yeah."

"Not really sure they'll help," Harry replied. "Unless you know somebody who can buy that kind of weight quickly."

"I know a bloke."

"He'll pay market price?"

Eric laughed. "Half if he's feeling generous."

"Then I guess I'll take the aitch."

Harry gave Billy a wide berth before stepping outside. Eric kicked out and sent the shotgun scraping across the ground into the far right corner of the garage, before also walking around the prone junky.

Derek and Darren lifted Bobby and carried him out of the building. When they were all outside, Eric closed the door and locked it with the key.

43.

The key clacked in the lock before being removed. Voices and footsteps faded as they moved away from the building.

Billy figured it was time to open his eyes. That movement alone was enough to make him wince. He didn't need a mirror to realise Harry had done serious damage, so he focused on something other than the pain. He fixated on how angry he was that nobody had fallen for his ruse.

It would have been good to give them something unpleasant to remember him by. Maybe wipe the smug expression off Eric Stanton's smirking face forever? Or give Darren Travers a gift that ensured nobody would ever get in the ring with him again? Or guarantee that Harry would never be able to fuck his wife without a condom?

Still, if Eric had been telling the truth, he would make a tidy profit from the trip. Plus he'd get the added benefit of giving Jonno the worst and last day of his life. It was worth the scars for that alone.

Billy wailed as he sat upright. Bracing himself, he brought up his hands and let his fingers brush against the razor grip. Splinters of pain radiated from the wound. Billy huffed twice, clenched his muscles, wrapped his fist around the handle, and got to work.

As he pulled at the deeply embedded blade, Billy suffered agony like nothing he'd ever experienced before. He screamed until his voice cracked. Just before he passed out, Billy finally wrenched the blade free.

He came round a couple of minutes later with the razor still in his right hand. His wound throbbed unpleasantly, and blood oozed from it in a continuous trickle. With a massive effort, he managed to sit upright, although it took a while for his heart to return to an acceptable speed. Every time he thought about the pain his stomach lurched and he suffered new dizzy spells. He knew that if he was to get anything done, he needed a fix to take the edge off things.

Billy reached into a pocket and found a small nasal spray bottle filled with liquefied heroin. He removed the cap and inhaled a few drops, along with some of his blood. Then he lay back and waited for the effects to take hold.

A brief surge of euphoria passed into a general sense of wellbeing, and a flush of warmth tingled his face and body. Billy swayed as he got to his feet but managed to remain upright. He pressed his fingers against the wound. The pain was still there but disembodied, as if it belonged to somebody else. He wiped the fresh blood off his chin.

Fighting the urge to sleep, Billy plodded around the garage and rummaged through piles of detritus and discarded engine parts, until he found what he wanted behind a pallet of dusty boxes. He pulled out an extendable ladder, walked to the rear of the building, and placed it against the wall beside the office. Then Billy found an old rag and wiped the oily rungs until they felt clean and safe and extended the ladder to its full height.

Something moved behind Billy. He looked over his shoulder and smiled with amusement. Jonno wriggled against his bindings, moving his arms up and down and left and right in a constant rhythm. Billy coughed to get his attention.

Jonno's face slackened with disbelief and fear. He shook his head and blinked several times. "What… *What?*"

"You look surprised to see me?"

Jonno rolled across the dusty ground and kicked out his feet, trying to loosen the ties that were tight around his ankles. "Cut me loose."

Billy moved the ladder until he was happy with its position.

"Well, I could do that," he replied, "but I don't think I will."

Jonno shrugged and wriggled more frantically.

Billy groped through his jacket, removed a syringe of blood from his inside right pocket and approached Jonno. Realising what was about to happen, Jonno's body went as still and stiff as a shop floor mannequin.

Billy got on his knees and came in close, resting the sharp point against the delicate flesh of Jonno's neck. He held Billy's gaze as best he could, but eventually averted his eyes. He made no unnecessary movements. His chest hardly seemed to rise and fall.

"Harry told me summat funny earlier. Wanna hear?"

Jonno whispered a barely audible *no.*

"Too bad, 'cause you're gonna hear it anyways."

"What did the racist fuckin' drug dealer call the Chinese junky who bought weight from him?"

Jonno observed Billy with suspicion and murmured *dunno.*

"A little hint: it's a Teletubbies related play on words."

A sudden moment of recognition dilated Jonno's pupils. He drew in a rapid breath and tried to pull away. Billy pushed Jonno flat on the ground and sat on his chest to restrict his movements. Then he found a vein in the crook of the man's right arm and injected the contents of the syringe. Jonno let out a girlish scream of fear and anger and pissed his pants.

Billy got off Jonno and watched with amusement as he writhed across the floor like a dying worm. After a couple of minutes of Jonno stopped struggling and started fighting for breath, his skin reddened, and he shivered uncontrollably. He was too short of breath to speak, but he turned his head in Billy's direction. There was a question in his tear-glazed eyes. Billy decided to answer it.

"You're having an anaphylactic shock, Jonno. The human body doesn't like infusions of foreign blood."

Jonno's eyes widened.

Billy grinned. "By that, I mean blood that isn't your own, like, rather than your Hitler Youth concept of foreign."

Jonno wheezed a lot and tried to sputter words. His swollen tongue ensured they didn't come out very well.

"You're dying, Jonno. There's only one thing that can help you."

Billy removed an EpiPen from his pocket and came in close. "Being a junky, it always helps to have a few of these around. This'll save you from the anaphylaxis. D'you wannit?"

Jonno nodded

Billy jammed the needle into Jonno's upper thigh and held it there for ten seconds. Then he walked back to the ladder and looked up at the whitewashed breezeblocks.

Jonno gradually ceased wheezing, and he breathed little easier. "Still feel funny," he groaned.

Billy paid him no attention, kept his eyes on the wall. "I'm not surprised, as you've just come outta anaphylaxis. Anyways, I don't really know what 2cc of blood does to the human body, but if it's owt like an acute hemolytic transfusion reaction, the chances are the adrenaline's not gonna do you much good in the long run."

Jonno squealed. He started writhing again, but in his weakened state, his movements were sluggish.

Billy jiggled the ladder and made certain that it was secure. "Quit whining, you pathetic piece of shite. It's not like you're gonna live long enough to develop it anyways."

Jonno cried out for help. Billy stepped away from the ladder again, took a running start and kicked him in the face. Something made a loud cracking sound.

The blow had crushed the bridge of Jonno's nose and the area beneath and around his eyes began to swell. Billy turned him on his stomach, so he didn't choke to death on his blood. Even then his breathing was laboured and sounded wet. He didn't want Jonno to die yet.

Billy delved through his inside left pocket and removed a small keypad mobile phone. He pressed a few buttons and put it to his ear.

"Des, it's me… It's Billy, you simple-minded fuck.

"I need you to do summat for me… No, it's not a friendly request, it's a fuckin' order… Grab a couple of capable men and head over to Seaton Carew *now*… By that, I mean big men, strong, capable of carrying heavy loads. Capable of fuckin' handling themselves if shit happens… In fact, fuck it, lemme take a load off your spliff-addled fuckin' brain. Just give Jeff and Ed a call. Tell 'em it's urgent. Tell 'em there's several grand in it.

"I don't wanna conversation about your busted fuckin' nose, Des… In fact, I don't wanna conversation at all… *I'm* fuckin' talking here… So, listen up before I lose me rag. Grab a pen now and write this shit down… 'Cause if you forget owt, I'm gonna fuck you up good style… Have you got a pen?… Good. And have you got paper?… Even better… Now, here's what I want."

44.

The group hurried away from the garage, past the still unconscious Dave, and stopped at the gate. Derek opened it and peered in both directions. The street was clear of people and vehicles. A few lights twinkled in distant units, but they were far away, and it would be difficult for anybody looking out to recognise faces or specific details. Derek told them it was safe to move and led the way to the car with Eric and Bobby bringing up the rear.

Although there were no people on the streets, they kept their heads down, and their eyes averted. When they reached the car, Derek looked around before he put his key in the lock. This was more criminal reflex than because of a specific threat – the landfill was as deserted as the roads and pavements – but he did it again as soon as the boot opened. He grabbed the heroin holdall, removed it, and held it in the air.

As the Harry reached for the bag, Eric grabbed his forearm.

"What's the problem?" Harry said.

"No problem," Eric replied. "Just want you to do summat for us, that's all."

Harry pulled away slightly. "I'm listening."

Eric smiled, to put him at ease. "Don't worry. It's nowt difficult or unpleasant."

"Okay, then. What?"

Eric held up a mobile phone. "I want you to make a call."

Harry recognised it. "Isn't that ToJo's?"

"It was ToJo's, but now it's mine," Eric replied. "Should have his numbers on it. I want you to phone his people."

"Why?"

"Because I asked nicely, that's why, and because I'm about to hand you a bag worth fifty grand."

"You've already told me I won't get that much for it."

Eric shrugged. "What you get for it is your business. What you do for it is all I care about."

Harry grabbed the phone. Thankfully, ToJo was too stupid to password protect it. Harry scrolled the contacts and looked for the name *Ramie* or *Ramon*. The names were a random jumble of letters and numbers, probably in case the police ever found the phone. Harry scrolled back through a list of previous calls and found the right number. He selected it and asked Eric what he wanted him to say.

"Get them over to the garage. Tell them Jonno set it all up."

Harry grinned. "Ramie will never believe that."

"So convince him."

After a few attempts, the other end of the line picked up. "About fuckin' time," the voice snapped. "Where the fuck're you? Been calling for hours. You better have me fuckin' money, lad?"

"It's not ToJo, Ramon."

"Then whosis?"

"Harry."

"Sparks?"

"That's right."

"Where the fuck's Toby?"

Harry put his hand over the receiver while Eric told him. He pulled his hand away, saying. "How the fuck would I know?"

"You what?"

"I expect he's been dumped somewhere."

"Dead?"

"Your guess is as good as mine. And guess what? Mine isn't very fuckin' good."

"Okay, then," Ramon said, pausing for thought. "Which brings me to me next question: why've you got his phone?"

"I got it from Jonno."

"*Jonno?*"

"Yep."

"What the fuck's going on, lad?"

"You tell me? 'Cause I'm still confused myself."

"You not got the aitch?"

"Some Bravo-Two-Zero cunt in a balaclava ambushed me in the bogs," he said, glaring at Darren. "Took the bag, along with my phone and money. *Then* Jonno's boys grabbed me off the street and took me out to Seaton. It was then I realised Jonno was involved."

"Why?"

"Because he had ToJo's phone."

"How'd you know it were Toby's?"

"He showed me once, boasting like he does. Told me it had all the new features. Seemed stoked about how much it cost."

Ramon groaned. "Told him to get rid of that thing a thousand fuckin' times and get some disposables and new SIMs."

"Guess he didn't listen."

"Did you see me money?"

"I looked but didn't see either the aitch or the money. Jonno's gotta have it, though, because he had the phone. Look, I dunno what the fuck's going on, fella, but I get the feeling we're both being played. If you want your aitch back, you need to get down here *now*."

"Where are you right this second?"

"Leaving Seaton."

"I need you to wait around."

Harry snorted. "Not happening, fella. I got lucky once, but if I wait around, I'm committing suicide. I managed to put Jonno and his men down, but that was only thanks to blind fuckin' luck.

"I was gonna torture the location of the stuff outta him, but when he warned me there was back-up coming, I figured I better disappear. And by disappear, I mean like Lord fuckin' Lucan. I'm gone, fella. Good luck getting your shit back, Rame."

"No, wait…"

"I'll text you the address of the garage if you wanna chase, but I'll be long gone."

Harry hung up, texted the address, and hit send. Then he turned off the phone and handed it back to Eric, who gave his brother the nod.

Derek opened the bag, made sure there was nothing but heroin inside and gave it to Harry.

Eric scowled at Darren. "Now it's your turn to make amends."

"How?"

"Phone Joey," Eric replied, pointing in the direction of the garage. "Tell him about *this* place."

Darren frowned. "But if I do that…"

"That's right. He turns up here and comes in all guns blazing."

"It'll be…"

"A massacre?" Eric replied with a shrug. "Possibly, maybe, who knows? Joey's been fuckin' lotsa people over for a while now. He's due some pay-back. Consider this his payment in full."

"Joey's gonna know I set him up."

"Maybe. If he survives."

"But…"

"But make the call. *Now*."

45.

ToJo trudged through a field thick with heather and tough grass. It seemed like he'd been walking this same patch of land for the last few hours. His legs ached and his muscles burned. Every time he dragged his feet, to save energy, his toes caught in the undergrowth and slowed momentum. He spent more time staggering and stumbling than walking, which sent the ache deeper into his muscles. Every attempt to pick up the pace was hindered by having to hold the waistband of his jeans and stop them from sliding to his ankles.

Sudden torrential rain showers made the ground heavy and water-logged, and poor eyesight made it difficult for ToJo to navigate by land-marks. He gasped for breath as he lumbered to the top of steep inclines, but the horizon was never much more than a green and grey blur.

Initially, ToJo stayed away from the roads, because he figured it would be easier for him to travel in a straight line. He soon realised his mistake, because he seemed to see the same trees, stone bridges and brooks. He wasn't sure if it was his eyes, or if he was somehow going in circles.

Vehicles passed infrequently. Whenever a car came towards him, ToJo waved his hands frantically in an attempt to get some attention. Nobody stopped or even slowed for a closer look. Despite his irritation, ToJo didn't blame them. He looked more like a damp chav than a 'lyrical master from da streets'. He wasn't sure he'd stop in the same situation.

The further he trekked the more ToJo pondered his lifestyle. Try as he might he was never going to look or sound like he'd started life on inner-city streets. He could wear as many cornrows or dreads as he liked, and loaf around in pants so baggy they started at his knees, but he would always be a pasty white boy from a privileged background. His father had been right all along – he did look like an idiot.

He'd only assumed his current identity because he wasn't posh enough for public school. The other kids mocked his Yorkshire accent, his par-simonious way with money, acquired from his tight-fisted father, and his inability to adjust to London life. It seemed like he was a square peg in a world of round holes: he didn't fit anywhere. He was a brewer's son and always would be.

As the existential doubts mounted up, ToJo came to a decision about his life. He decided to clean up his act, shorten his hair, tidy his clothes, and prove that he was worthy of a second chance. He would beg his father for a position at the brewery, even if it meant starting at the bottom. By the time the sky turned as dark as slate, he was unwavering in his belief that he'd made the right decision.

It was then he noticed the distant twinkle of lights.

A village.

ToJo ran towards the glow at top speed. Unfortunately, holding on to his jeans meant that his fastest pace was little more than a cockeyed canter. He stopped moving, looked around nervously, and let his jeans drop to his ankles. He scooped them off the ground and bundled them in his right hand. The cold air nipped his flesh. He warmed his thigh muscles by rubbing them vigorously and then sprinted towards the village.

He stopped running just before he reached the outskirts and hid behind a wall. While putting on his jeans, he took a few moments to think of a suitable sob story that would explain his appearance and allow access to a phone.

When he was happy with the story, ToJo hopped the wall and started walking. He held his waistband and tried to walk without dragging his leg. Despite this, the few people who were on the street glowered at him and muttered insults as he passed.

A deep flush of embarrassment burned his cheeks; even his father's scorn was better than this. All he wanted was a pub or a small corner shop, or anything to get him off the street. He noticed the blur of an illuminated pub sign up ahead. He stopped outside the door, took a slow breath, ran the story through his head one last time, and stepped into the establishment.

The place was small and narrow with a low-beamed ceiling, wood floors, and a tiny wooden bar in the right corner. A few matching tables and chairs took up most of the limited floor space.

Most of the action was near the far wall, beside a roaring fire, where a table of four ageing drinkers laughed and joked. Their amusement subsided when they first noticed the new arrival. Then it started up again and louder than ever. They didn't bother to disguise their caustic remarks about ToJo's appearance.

The ringleader was a fat man with an alcohol flushed complexion. His frame was squeezed uncomfortably into a white shirt and tweed blazer. His gut strained the shirt fabric and threatened to pop several of its buttons. He'd wrapped a blue tie so tightly around his neck that it sent folds of fat bulging over his collar. It looked like the world's slowest case of death by strangulation. He swallowed the last dregs of his pint and grinned in ToJo's direction.

"What's wi' the appearance, boy?" he asked.

The other men guffawed and offered their variants of the question.

At least the alpha-male has been established, thought ToJo. He assumed his broadest Yorkshire accent and stroked his nose in an uncomfortable manner.

"Some buggers mugged me earlier."

The man nudged one of his friends, an emaciated man with a face like a schoolroom skeleton, and laughed loudly. "Weren't talking about the phizog, lad. Were asking about the clown costume? You not heard of belts where you're from?"

ToJo pulled at the waistband of his jeans and held them up. He sat on one of the stools near the counter to avoid the necessity of tugging at his trousers every few seconds. He chuckled as though he was in on the joke rather than the brunt of it and replied: "Were at a fancy dress party out in Teesside."

The man snorted. "Tha' place is a right dump, boy. Why would you want t' venture there?"

ToJo shrugged. "A girl."

The man's mouth turned down at the edges, and he nodded in satisfaction. "Aye, fair enough. I'd venture t' tha' dive for the right lass."

ToJo noticed movement to his right. A thin, middle-aged man with hollow cheeks, dressed in a white shirt and black trousers combo, emerged from a doorway behind the bar and watched him with suspicion.

"Can I help you?" he said, scrutinising ToJo's appearance.

ToJo smiled without teeth and lowered his head to appear submissive.

"Can I please use your phone, sir?"

The man jutted his chin at ToJo's swollen nose and bruised eyes. "Somebody gave you a right going over, son."

"That's why I need to use the phone."

Rubbing his chin, the barman hesitated and directed his gaze towards the four men by the fireplace.

The man in the tweed jacket waved his right hand at ToJo. "For Heaven's sake, Bri, let the lad make his call. Look at him – he's harmless."

Brian gave a brief nod and lifted the bar hatch, and then he gestured ToJo through with a few flicks of the wrist. The barman pointed at an open door. "Through there on the right, on a table near the stairs."

"I might need to make a couple of calls," ToJo said. "Sorry."

"Ah, you're all right. Just don't make 'em too long."

ToJo entered the dimly lit, narrow hall and found a dusty portable handset on a small table near the foot of the stairs. He picked up the unit and dialled a number from memory. It picked up on the third ring.

"Alastair Jones speaking."

"Dad, it's Toby."

"What do *you* want?"

"Don't be like that."

"Why not? You've not been pleasant to me, recently."

Toby felt pride tugging at him. There was an overwhelming urge to scream abuse at his father and slam down the phone. Instead, he held the phone in the air, away from his face, while the moment passed. Then he put the phone back against his cheek, saying, "And I'm truly sorry about that."

"Sorry is a good start. I can work with sorry," his father replied. "So why're you calling? I don't expect it's a social thing."

"I need help."

"Do you now?"

"Please, Dad"

His father huffed. "I remember offering you help a couple of years back. A bloody good position at the brewery, as it happens. And I remember you laughing in me face too, lad. Thought you were too good to work your way up from the office, you did."

"I made a mistake."

"Aye, you did at that."

"Please, Dad. Show some compassion."

"Compassion?" he scoffed. "Last time we saw each other, the only C-word that came off your lips were the one that rhymes with hunt. Even called mother one, too. That hurt her, lad."

ToJo winced as he recalled the moment. The look of shock and pain on his mother's face was hard to forget. He despised his father for reminding him of it. "I know. And I was wrong to say those things. And when I see Mam I'll tell her that in person."

"I suppose your new friends have rejected you?"

"Actually, I rejected them," ToJo said. "I don't wanna live like this anymore. I wanna change me life, Dad. But I need your help to do it."

There must have been something genuine in the tone of his voice because his father let out a long sigh. "If that's really the case, then you'll agree to me terms?"

"Aye."

"That means get rid of that stupid bloody hair. Those ridiculous dreads."

"They're cornrows, Dad. But fine, agreed."

"And those ludicrous baggy pants will hafta go, too. They make you look like summat from the circus, lad."

"Fine."

"You'll start wearing proper clothes from now on," his father said. "Suits, good shoes, shirts, like a real man."

"Yes."

"And you'll come into the office on Monday morning at nine. No tardiness, son, and you'll be ready to work your guts out."

"Agreed."

"Okay, then, what d'you need from me?"

"I need you to send a car over to fetch me from…" ToJo went through the open door and looked at Brian, pulling ale for the man in tweed. "Excuse me, where are we exactly?"

The barman smiled. "You got proper lost out there, didn't you?"

The moment he knew the location, ToJo went back into the hall. "*The Wheatsheaf* over in Lower Quigley."

"My God, boy, that there's the middle of nowhere. What the bloody hell you are doing out there?"

"Getting mugged."

"Actually, forget I asked. I don't want to know. As long as you're prepared to turn over a new leaf, I'll send a driver out to you, along with some money."

ToJo thanked his father and ended the call. Then he rang another number from memory. It picked up on the second ring and a voice asked, "Whosis?"

"Ramie, it's Toby."

"Finally," Ramon replied. "I'd given you up for dead."

"Why?"

"'Cause I had an interesting call about you less than an hour ago."

"Oh yeah, who?"

"Harry."

"Fat Harry?"

"That's right."

"Don't tell me he got robbed too?"

"Give the boy a gold star."

ToJo played nervously with the hardened twists of cornrow. "I knew it were a set-up," he said. "Those bastards knew too much about me."

"What bastards?"

"Two of them. One huge, ugly, burly bastard, the other bloke were smaller, but knew how to handle hisself."

"You seen them before?"

"No, but they *definitely* knew me."

There was a brief pause at the other end.

"Harry thinks Jonno set it up."

ToJo thought about Bobby for a moment and his earlier suspicion that the junky might have masterminded the robbery. He considered saying something then felt a twinge that made him pause for thought. The second he opened his mouth Bobby would die. It might not be immediate, but it would be an inevitability. If Ramon believed Bobby was a threat, however remote, then he would deal with him decisively.

The things ToJo told his father weren't lies, but in that split-second of uncertainty, his words felt false. Surrendering to that uncertainty would make him a liar and by proxy a murderer. Letting go of all the old anger was the only way of shedding his old persona. The power to end Bobby's life was on the tip of his tongue, all he had to do was mouth the words. ToJo wasn't the type to show mercy, but Toby could. He thought again about what he wanted in life and chose a one syllable question:

"Why?"

And with that ToJo was gone...

The relief of not having to play the role ever again made Toby grin and stand up straight. Playing the hard man wasn't his concern anymore.

"'Cause Harry claimed Jonno had your phone. In fact, Harry called me from your phone."

"Sounds plausible enough. D'you believe him?"

"Like with religion, I dunno what I believe. I only know there's more to this than what I've been told."

"You going to check it out?"

"Me money's gone missing, lad. The drugs are missing. Of course, I'm gonna check it out. We're on our way now."

"Well, good luck finding them."

Ramon coughed. "*Good luck?* It sounds like you're giving me the kiss-off?"

As scared as he was of his boss, Toby knew what he wanted. He had a lot of apologies to make with his family, but at least he'd have a steady job with plenty of room for advancement. He had to stay firm.

"I've been out in the middle of nowhere for hours," he said. "I've had a gun pressed into me spine, had me nose broken, I'm soaked to the bone with pissing moors rain, and I've had a lotta time to think. You're right, this is the kiss-off, and I'm going home."

"Maybe *you're* in on it?"

"If you really believe that, then I'll be at me Dad's brewery on Monday morning. I won't be hiding, 'cause I've got nowt to hide. If you want your money back, we'll hafta arrange summat, 'cause I'm flat broke. You can break me knees if you want, but it won't get you paid any faster."

"But…"

He hung up and placed the phone back in the holder. He wasn't sure what Monday morning would bring, but he felt better than he had in a long time. The sense of relief was profound.

Toby Jones allowed himself a brief laugh, wiped the emotion from his eyes and went back into the bar. Then he ordered one of his Dad's beers on credit and waited for the car to arrive.

46.

Joey Judd sat in his booth seat and digested both his Lamb Phaal and the information Darren Travers had just fed him. Neither was going down particularly well. He ignored the people milling around the bar, the raised voices and loud music, and studied the problem in his head.

According to Darren, the Stanton brothers were pulling a number on Jonno Fielding and Ramon Carrasco at Jonno's headquarters in Seaton Carew. The take was fifty grand plus the same again in heroin.

Rubbing his itchy beard constantly, he replayed the conversation; studying the inflexion of Darren's voice and the words he used, the tactical pauses, and the awkward moments of silence, Joey came to the conclusion that although there was some truth to the story, it also contained gaping holes and outright lies.

Joey believed the part about the money, but the rest was harder to accept. Watching his junky prostitute mother slowly kill herself with heroin had made Eric Stanton ambivalent at best about drugs and dealers. Although he'd dabbled with weed and coke as a younger man, Eric had never touched heroin and would be unlikely to deal it. So that part of the story didn't add up.

The idea that either Jonno or Ramon would undertake a deal on non-neutral territory made no sense either. Jonno always seemed street-smart and capable. Smart enough not to deal on home turf. Ramon's reputation pegged him as intelligent and vicious. Again, bright enough not to step into a room where his opposite number has a territorial advantage. If these two were going to make a deal, it would be in neutral territory that was either secluded or allowed them to hide in plain sight.

Then there was Darren himself. Since meeting Eric, he'd been evasive and secretive. Somehow he'd even managed to sneak out of his house unseen this morning. Why would he suddenly decide to pass on information about his new partners? The only reason Joey could think of was he had been told to, as he wasn't bright enough to concoct such a convoluted story.

It reeked of a set-up.

Joey could send men to Seaton quickly enough, but if he was being framed the chances of them returning were slim. Maybe the police were waiting? Or maybe the Stantons were hiding out of sight, ready to jump out with shotguns blazing? Or maybe this was some other kind of trouble? He wanted the money, but could do without the hassle.

He picked up the phone and dialled.

"Yeah?"

"Darren put Eric on the line."

"I dunno… What? *Eric?* But I told…"

"Yeah, I know what you said. And we both know it's bullshit. Put Eric on the line now."

"But…"

"No buts. I wanna speak to him."

There was a loud rustling followed by muffled sounds. Muted voices rumbled beneath the general ambience and steadily rose in pitch. Then the sound was clear again.

"Joey?"

"Nice try, dickhead."

Eric huffed. "What tipped you?"

"The drugs, mostly," Joey said. "You're not a heroin man, Eric, and you never will be."

"That was… Darren's mistake," Eric replied. The long pause felt significant; Joey wondered if Eric had glared at Darren during the silence.

"You sold me damaged goods, Joe."

"You mean Thrombo?" Joey replied with a chuckle. "I take it he fucked up?"

"Several times."

"He has a tendency to do that."

"I asked for a competent man."

"No. If memory serves, you requested a man, which I gave youse. Never said either way whether he was competent or not."

"You said he could follow simple orders."

"And he *can*. They just have to be very fuckin' simple, is all."

"Plus you tried to follow Darren around so that you could hijack the job."

"Old habits die hard. I could say sorry, but I won't waste your time with a lie."

"At least you're honest about that."

"Now put the other dickhead back on."

Eric gave Darren the phone. "Whaddaya want, Joey?"

"You think you can fuck me over and —"

"I didn't…"

"—I'll just happily let you slide it in?"

"I didn't…"

"Yes, you did. I think when all this is said and done I'm gonna come and pay you a visit."

"Good luck, 'cause I won't be there."

"Maybe not now, but you'll show up eventually. The money you've just made will run out because you're a fuckin' idiot. You'll squander it somehow – you always do – and then you'll come crawling back to Teesside for another payday. Our paths *will* cross again."

"Mebbe I'll just sell up and move on."

"Then mebbe I'll take it out on your girlfriend."

"You…"

"Your money belongs to me now," Joey said and laughed. "Or your girlfriend will belong to me. And I *won't* be gentle with her. Me and the boys will teach her a few things about the capacity of the human body for punishment."

"You…"

Joey ended the call, dropped the phone on the table, and started rubbing his beard again. He wondered if Darren would show up of his own volition or if a visit to the girlfriend was required?

47.

Darren held the phone against his chest. Face draining of colour, he turned and pressed his forehead against the window. His breath fogged the glass. It was immediately obvious it was bad news.

Eric prodded his shoulder. "What's going on?"

Darren's eyes remained on the dark landscape. "I knew that fuckin' phone call was a mistake."

"What did Joey say?"

"He wants me money. All of it."

"Should've told him to go fuck himself."

"Yeah, mebbe I shoulda said that."

"So why didn't you?"

"Coz he's gonna go after me girlfriend."

"*What?*"

"Unless I give him what I've made today."

"That's not gonna happen."

Darren turned towards Eric. "Don't tell me what to do with me money. If I hadn't made that fuckin' call this wouldn't be a problem."

"And if you'd done what you were told none of us would be here now."

Darren's gaze went steely. "If Joey hurts me girlfriend, first I'll kill him and then I'll come for you."

Eric held his stare. "Hold your fuckin' horses. Let's not start throwing threats around yet. I'm not telling you what to do with your money; I'm saying I'll sort this shit out so you don't hafta give him a penny."

Darren's expression softened. "How?"

"Dunno yet. Let me have a think. But I promise you Joey won't be hurting anybody."

Eric turned to Bobby, wedged between Darren and Harry. His face glistened with sweat, and he winced every time the car moved abruptly or juddered along uneven patches of road.

"How are you doing?"

"Me ankle's throbbing like a bastard," Bobby whined. "I need the hospital, or I need a fix for the pain."

He looked at Harry and offered a shy smile. The fat man scowled for a moment, then turned away with a derisive snort. "Forget it. That stuff'll kill you."

A coughing fit shook Bobby. He tilted back his head and wailed at the roof of the car. "Then gemme to a hospital."

Eric slapped his brother's arm. "You heard the man."

Derek pressed down on the accelerator. "The sooner this whiny fuck's outta the car, the better."

Bobby groaned. "You never been in pain before?"

"I'm in pain now, listening to your bullshit."

"You've got no heart."

Derek sneered. "I've plenty of heart, just not for a smackhead like you."

Eric ignored their continuing argument in favour of Darren, still resting his face against the window.

"Is your girlfriend straight?"

Darren nodded. "Never even had a parking ticket."

"Does she know what you do?"

"She knows I'm a fighter," he replied. "If she knew the rest she wouldn't be me girlfriend for very long."

"So getting her to run isn't an option?"

Darren looked at Eric and shook his head. "She'd never leave her family or her job. She's a local girl and proud. You know the type?"

"Yeah, I know."

Darren's face tightened as he fought his emotions. He didn't want to show his humanity, so he turned away from everybody. Eric noticed a tear rolling down his right cheek, but the fighter didn't make a sound.

Joey had crossed the line. Threatening Darren was one thing, but intimidating his girlfriend was something else. Joey had a right to be angry about the deception – stumbling into any room that contained Billy Chin, anger, and a loaded shotgun was going to be hazardous for the health – and it was obvious that Joey sussed the trap quickly. However, any real man would punish those responsible and not their families and loved ones. The way Eric saw it: Joey was now fair game for any trouble that came his way.

He concentrated for a few minutes, mulling over ways to solve Darren's problem. Then it came to him: it was possible that the same person could solve both Darren's and Harry's problems. Eric dialled a familiar number and waited.

"Yeah? Whosis?"

"Alan, it's Eric."

Alan snorted. "Eric who? Clapton? Estrada? Bana?"

"You know full fuckin' well who it is."

"Sorry, mate, you've got it all wrong. If it's Eric Stanton you're referring to – he died just over a month ago. Cancer of the ego, apparently. Got too fuckin' big for his pea-sized skull."

Eric had expected resistance. His former boss wasn't exactly happy at the manner in which he had left, and was one to carry a grudge. Eric held the phone in the air, capturing the ambient sounds of the car.

"D'you hear that, Alan? That's the sound of me laughing on the inside."

"What the fuck d'you want?"

"A favour for a favour."

"Why should I do *you* a favour?"

"Because I've got summat you want in your life."

Alan paused, sniffed. "Enigmatical, but I'm finding it hard to give a fuck."

"Okay, then, here's summat you do give a fuck about, which is profit."

"What kinda profit?"

"Twenty grand, minimum."

"Oh, would you look at that?"

"Look at what?"

"I've just managed to find a fuck I can give you."

"That's nice."

"Keep talking, Eric, and mebbe I'll find a few more."

"You can keep your fucks, Alan. All I want is that favour."

"Go on."

"How'd you like forty grand of raw for half price?"

Alan paused briefly. "I thought you didn't…"

"I *don't*. This is for somebody else. But connecting you and him is my favour to you. He needs the sale, and you definitely have the contacts to sell it on at full price or even more than that, depending on how you cut the product."

"Consider me interested," he said. "Now my favour to *you*."

"Do you still video all your conquests, Al?"

"I dunno what…"

"Don't take me for a fuckin' chump, mate. Your little love nest in Saltburn is covered with spy cameras. I know this because I was there when you had them installed – remember?"

"What makes you think…"

"Now most of the cameras were hidden in the bedroom. And all of them were pointed at the bed. Lots of coverage, I do believe they call it in the profession. I reckon all that coverage comes together well when you get it in the editing suite."

Alan spat out a single bitter laugh. "I s'pose it does."

"Who edits it for you?"

"Nobody you'd know. Just some young lad who occasionally gets in on the act from time-to-time."

"A bit of double trouble?"

"Summat like that."

Alan said nothing, so Eric decided to fill the gap:

"I want the video of you with Aisling Judd."

"Why?"

"My business."

"That's not how this works," Alan replied. "You wanna favour from me; then I wanna know why?"

"I want Joey off my back."

"That's a lotta weight to be carrying."

"I'm serious, Al."

"So am I. With summat like this, if he's not on your back then he's gonna be on mine. Now, you know I can handle that fat prick, but he's still gonna make me life awkward."

"Twenty grand can smooth a lotta awkwardness. Besides, by the time I've finished with Joey he'll be as meek as a dead kitten."

"That's pretty meek," Alan replied. "But what about the missus?"

"Not like you to give a shit about your conquests, Al?"

"Ash was summat special."

"I'll bet."

"I'm fuckin' serious, Eric. Once Joey's done with her, she'll have more slices than a bread loaf."

Eric laughed. "Don't worry so much. I've got a plan."

48.

Billy climbed the ladder and studied the painted concrete blocks. Even up close it was impossible to determine what was real and what was fake. Billy rapped his knuckles against every block until he came across one that sounded hollow inside. Using a clean knife blade, he carefully cut the Papier-mâché and paint cast away from the rest of the blocks and let it drop. It shattered into several dusty pieces against the hard ground.

Inside the cavity were ten thick wads of money, wrapped tightly with green elastic bands, each roughly about the same thickness. Beside them were three small jewellery boxes. Billy ran his fingers across their black plush exteriors, picked one up at random, and opened it. Within the moulded cushion interior was an ornate, polished steel watch overloaded with dials, a chronometer, and buttons of various sizes. The metal strap had been burnished to a high shine and sparkled beneath the lights. Paperwork and receipts in the box confirmed it was a Breitling worth over five grand.

Billy opened the second case, containing a Rolex with a white and gold fascia and a steel and gold strap. The paperwork put it at double the price of the Breitling.

The third box contained a Patek Phillipe. It was worth more than the Rolex and Breitling combined. He placed the watch back in its case.

Billy counted one of the bundles and then did it again to be sure: five grand in twenties and fifties. If the denominations were similar, it meant he was looking at fifty-grand, plus another thirty for the watches. He dropped the bundles on the ground, put the jewellery cases in various jacket pockets, and scurried back down the ladder.

Billy threw the cash in a shopping bag and turned towards Jonno, who was awake, though spaced-out and confused. Smeared scarlet gore and vivid purple contusions stood out against the whiteness of his skin. His clothes were drenched with sweat, and he seemed unable to stop shivering. Aside from the occasional click of chattering teeth, he watched in silence.

Billy smiled at him. "Bet you're wondering how I knew about your hiding place?"

Jonno nodded once.

"You shoulda checked Kev's condition more closely."

Jonno allowed himself a bitter smile.

"You told your fellas to leave the garage after you finished handle-fuckin' Kev. Then you put up a ladder and very carefully opened your clever little Papier-mâché construction – well, better than I managed, anyways."

"There's a knack to it."

"I'm sure there is," Billy replied, "but I'm short on patience, or on caring much about the exquisite fuckin' delicacy of your arts and crafts skills."

"So what else did Kev see?"

"Saw you grab a fat stack, count off a couple of gees, put your fancy cast back in place and come down the ladder. Then you put the ladder back where you found it and invited your gadgies back inside. You paid ratboy a few hunnerd to drive Kev to a hospital and a few hunnerd more to dump the car with Gary Feldman.

"Then you gave Harry some cash, which he was supposed to give that nasty little baghead Ben Moody for playing Judas.

"You think you're gonna get away with this?"

"I am getting away with it," he replied. "Don't see any fucker coming to your rescue – do you?"

"You let me go, and I'll forget this happened."

Billy crouched down beside Jonno. "You're not gonna live long enough to forget anything."

Footsteps crunched outside and stopped behind the front door. Billy jumped to his feet and moved stealthily in the direction of the shotgun. He scooped it off the ground and approached the door. He jacked out the empty shell and readied himself for unwanted visitors. Then his phone rang. He answered and told the caller that he'd unlocked the door with Jonno's key. He lowered the weapon and turned away.

Three men pushed into the building. Des led from the front, greasy dreads bouncing, as he heaved a massive wheeled suitcase into the room by its handle. Behind him were two tall, well built black men dressed in military-style cotton clothes, one with a shaved scalp and the other with a large, untamed Afro. The man with the Afro wheeled in two even bigger suitcases. The man with the shaved scalp carried an enormous case over his shoulder as though it was as light as a pillowcase full of feathers.

Once they reached the centre of the room, the men dropped their baggage in a messy pile and looked around. Des turned towards Billy to say something but his mouth went slack. He said whoa under his breath. His two companions weren't quite as demonstrative. The man with the Afro leant forward, narrow-eyed, as he stroked his chin. The other man pursed his lips and flared his nostrils.

Des took two steps forward and studied the wound more carefully. "That's some serious damage, bruv? Your face looks like Frankenstein's dick."

"Frankenstein were the doctor, you mongoloid."

Des looked crestfallen for a moment. "But who…"

"You know who."

Des pointed at his broken nose. "The same bumbaclot what did this to me?"

Billy nodded. "That's him."

Des gritted his teeth and muttered Jamaican and American ghetto curses, while the Jeff and Ed exchanged glances, rolled their eyes at his theatricality, and whispered a few obscenities of their own.

Then Des noticed Jonno on the floor and let out a chuckle. Cackling with glee, he slapped his thighs a few times, then approached the prone man with his wonky gangsta-stride, and kneeled in front of him. "My, my, my, blood, how the mighty be falling."

Jonno snorted his amusement into the concrete dust and told him to go fuck himself. Des slapped him across the face and demanded respect until Billy told the young man to leave Jonno alone.

Des brushed down his knees and observed the shopping bag by Billy's feet. "How much we got, bruv?"

"Fifty grand, plus some expensive watches."

Barely able to hide their delight, Des, Ed and Jeff grinned at each other momentarily. Des went overboard and tried to high-five the man with the Afro, "Gimme five, Jeff, my man," but he turned away with a shake of the head and left Des flailing at thin air.

Billy picked up the shopping bag and threw it on the workbench. "Before youse all start getting ideas. I'm taking half, plus all the watches. The rest youse can split as you see fit."

Des twiddled one of his dreads. "Don't you think it should divide equally, bruv?"

"No, I fuckin' don't. This isn't a fuckin' democracy, *Desmond*," Billy responded, aiming the shotgun at Des. "I'm taking half, and that's the fuckin' end of it."

Des noticed the shotgun, and the rising cadence of Billy's voice because he held up his palms as a gesture for calm. "Chill, blood."

Billy's hands tightened around the gun. "I'll chill your fuckin' blood in a minute."

Des' face drained of what little colour it had, making the bruises beneath his eyes and around the bridge of his disfigured nose stand out. He shuffled on the spot. "Christ, Bill, I's just be opening a dialogue."

"And I'm closing it," he replied. "And start speaking like a fuckin' white man, for Chrissakes. You've never been to Jamaica, and the closest your pallid arse has been to black was when you came home to find some playa giving your girlfriend her first taste of a twelve-inch black pudding."

Des' head dropped until his chin rested against his chest. He contemplated Billy with moist eyes. "Dude," he said in a soft voice. "You promised you'd never tell."

"Well, consider it one of the many fuckin' lies I'll tell you in this life."

"Shit, man…"

Jeff and Ed sniggered until Billy scowled in their direction. "What the fuck're you two smirking at?"

Jeff ran a big hand through his Afro and shrugged. "Nowt, Bill," he said in a deep rumbling voice. "Just waiting on orders."

"Did you bring the shit I asked for?" Billy said.

Jeff swung his arm in the direction of the cases. "It's all there."

"Then quit sniggering and start earning your fuckin' pay."

49.

Derek pulled up alongside a deserted bus stop on Ladgate Lane. Eric turned in his seat and handed ToJo's phone to Bobby. "This is your stop."

Bobby blinked nervously at the distance from the car to the bus stop bench. "Can't you drop us at the hospital entrance?"

"There's CCTV all over the hospital, so that's not happening. You're gonna have to phone it in."

"That's a fair old hop," Bobby replied, pointing at the bench.

Eric sighed. "It's about ten fuckin' feet."

Darren helped Bobby out of the vehicle. He hopped quickly over to the bench, wincing and wailing with each landing. By the time Bobby eased himself onto the seat, his face was shiny with fresh sweat, and he gritted his teeth with the pain. He clung to the mobile phone like it had pain-relieving qualities.

"When are youse gonna give us me money?"

"A couple of days," Eric replied. "Tell me where you'll be."

"Marianne's place."

"And what are you gonna say if anyone asks?"

"Got mugged. Din't see me attackers."

Eric nodded. "Good enough. And drop that fuckin' phone down a sewer grate once you've called for an ambulance."

50.

Jeff and Ed opened the suitcases and removed the contents. They laid four big industrial bin liners on the ground, and placed four sharp blades, four hacksaws, a couple of machetes, lots of rope coils, and several big black towels on top.

Billy turned on the spot, scanning the garage for old buckets or large drip trays. He couldn't see anything, so he tapped Des on the shoulder and pointed towards a large pile of discarded equipment near the workbench.

"Go look in that lot," he said. "Then scour the shelves. See if you can find some buckets or owt."

"Buckets?"

"Yeah, or drip trays. Summat they collect oil or petrol in. We're gonna need to drain these fuckers before we chop 'em up."

With the exception of Dave, who hadn't moved at all, Jonno and his men were now awake. They pleaded for their lives, their voices rising in volume and desperation until Billy told them to shut the fuck up. Then they dropped to distressed whimpers. Jim Hanway sobbed gently, repeating," I don't deserve this," under his breath in a manner that suggested he genuinely believed it.

Des blinked at the jumbled heap and curled his lip. "Why're you giving me all the shit jobs, bruv?"

Billy grinned. "Because that's your speciality, Des: all the random shit nobody else wants to do."

"I could help with *them*," he replied, waving his hands at the soon to be dead men.

Billy's grin became a sneer. "How many days did you cry for, again, after we topped Moody?"

"That were different."

"How?"

"Ben were me friend."

"Ben were nobody's friend."

"I liked him."

"That's different," Billy added. "Coz Ben didn't like you. He thought you were a cunt."

An expression of intense dismay made crossed the young man's face. His bottom lip trembled a little. He sniffed and turned back towards the junk pile. "How many buckets d'you want?"

"As many as you can find," Billy said. "I wanna drain them all at once if we can. Don't wanna be here all fuckin' night."

Head hanging slightly, Des dragged his feet to the junk pile and rummaged through it, throwing things to one side with little regard for the mess he made. He mumbled expletives and occasionally turned to glower at Billy.

Jonno raised his dust-caked face off the floor. His eyes were bloodshot, and the lids were red and puffy. "Take the money, Bill," he insisted. "I don't care about it. I can make more. Just, please, don't do this."

Billy crouched in front of him. "And have you come after me, later?"

"I wouldn't."

"Sure you would. I would if I was you."

"Well, you're not me."

Billy came in closer. "Then explain Kev Nicholson? You came after him, later."

"That was different."

A half smile twisted Billy's mouth. "That fella wouldn't hurt a fly."

"He hurt me fuckin' business, though."

"He panicked."

"He threw two packages in the Tees."

"Two *small* packages."

"It's the principle. Kev still dumped them."

"Coz he got collared by the piglets. He had to do summat, didn't he? Otherwise, he'd be doing time."

"Not my fuckin' problem. He cost me two grand."

Billy stood and shook fatigue out of his legs. "Kev woulda paid eventually."

"But he didn't – did he? He had plenty of chances. I gave him plenty of time. And examples hafta be made."

"Then you shoulda come to me. I woulda sorted summat out."

"He didn't say, did he?"

"Kev still wears a bag, if you're interested? They removed several feet of infected intestine. The poor bastard has to be careful what he eats for the rest of his life. Can't drink booze, can't eat owt spicy, the sad fucker eats nowt but rabbit food. You destroyed his fuckin' prostate, too. He's not been able to get it up since. All cozza two measly fuckin' grand."

"Me heart bleeds."

Billy patted his face. "It will, Jonno. It will."

"Look, Bill…"

"Let's talk proportion here. You ruin a man's ability to shit and shag over a couple of grand, so what should *I* do for fifty?"

Jonno looked at the floor, his features screwed up with intense concentration, searching for an answer that might save him, but seemed unable to say anything. Instead, he let out a noise that could have passed for either a groan or a sob. He rested his face against the cold concrete. He sniffed back tears and blinked his eyes repeatedly until the emotion passed.

Des came over with three large black buckets that smelled of oil. He also had a deep drip tray wedged beneath his right arm. "Got that shit you wanted," he said.

Billy eyed the haul with disinterest and hitched a thumb in the direction of an H-shaped hydraulic car lift near the office. "Put 'em over there."

The young man did as he was told, placing them on the floor. Then Billy fixed his gaze on Jeff and Ed. "Tie their legs with a timber hitch," he said. "I wanna hang 'em from the lift beams."

Jim slithered across the floor like a snake, moving in the direction of the rear office, but without much success, his face darkening with effort and panic. Ed attempted to grab his feet, but he kicked his hands away and squealed in terror. Jeff blocked the driver's path and gave him a quick kick to the temple when he tried to slide around him. Then Ed tied his legs in a tight timber hitch knot.

Ben yelled as they approached, rolled on his back, and kicked out his feet repeatedly, making it difficult for them to grab him. Eventually, Ed managed to secure his feet, and Jeff stamped on his face until he stopped moving. Then Ed tied off another knot and used it to drag him across the floor to the lift.

Billy walked over to a small shelf on a stretch of wall near the office. He grabbed a dusty four-button handset off the shelf and pressed the *on* button. The motor grumbled into life. He jabbed up. Creaking and groaning, the black metal H came off the ground gradually. When it was high enough, Billy pressed stop.

Des placed towels, buckets and the drip tray beneath the four points of the H, as Ed tied up Dave's legs. Then he put his fingers against the man's neck and announced that he was dead. Billy gave a nonchalant shrug and said it was probably for the best. Then he nodded in Jonno's direction.

The pair cast long shadows over Jonno as they approached warily as if expecting him to kick and scream. He didn't.

He offered no resistance as Ed bound his ankles tightly, then let his body go loose as the two men dragged him across the floor. His face was devoid of emotion. Billy found it hard to hide his disappointment. He wanted tantrums and shrieking. He wanted some fight.

"No tears? No screams?" he said.

Jonno's expression remained impassive. "What good will they do me?"

"Mebbe I want you to cry."

Jonno cracked a grin as Ed hooked his legs over the beam closest to Billy. Jeff and Ed quickly hung the others to the remaining points of the H and went to get knives. Billy pressed up again, and the lift creaked back into life. The four men came off the ground and dangled upside down, rocking like pendulums.

Billy picked up a bucket and held it just beneath Jonno's head at a slight angle, to catch the initial spurts of blood. Des handed Billy one of the big blades and stepped back. He gnawed at his nails nervously and turned his body so that he didn't have to watch the violence.

Billy let out a loud tut. "You useless bastard. If you're not gonna help then get outta my peripheral vision, coz you're spoiling the moment."

He waited for the young man to edge away, before placing his blade against the knot of hard muscle at the left side of Jonno's neck. "Any last words?"

The drug dealer shook his head.

Billy pushed the blade deep and dragged it across.

Jonno grunted.

Blood sprayed.

51.

Sitting back with a squeak in his leather executive seat, Alan Piper rubbed his black stubble and stared at the four packages of heroin on his desk. In his expensive bespoke suit, with his carefully coiffed hair, and his sharp cheekbones, he looked more like a male model posing than a criminal contemplating a score. Two tall men with muscles packed into much less impressive suits flanked him and tried to look serious.

Alan prodded one of the packages with a finger. "Do I need to be worried about where this came from?"

Eric shrugged and hitched his thumb at Harry, resting his bulk against the wall. "That's his business."

Alan took in Harry's outfit with distaste and raised his eyebrows. "Well?"

Harry folded his arms. "It came via Jonno Fielding, but Ramon Carrasco is liable to be looking for it, too."

"And nobody knows you're here?"

Harry shook his head.

"And I take you're gonna keep your fuckin' gobs shut, right?"

All four men nodded.

Alan flashed a handsome white smile. "Glad to hear it. On the off chance that he does find out, Jonno's not got the muscle to trade blows with me. And I doubt Ramie knows those I've got in mind to move this little lot."

Harry stepped forward with this hand extended. "So we've got a deal, then?"

Alan reached across the desk and shook his hand. Then he left the room and could be heard opening and closing doors as he moved around outside.

Derek looked at one of the big men, saying: "How's life, Manny?"

Manny grimaced uncomfortably, as though afraid his boss would hear, and craned forward, whispering, "I'm the new you," he said. "We're Alan's go-to gadgies now you and Eric are outta the fold."

Derek laughed. "What's he paying youse?"

The other guy nudged Manny with his elbow and hissed. "Boss'll be paying us fuckin' nowt if he comes back through that door and sees you gabbing on his fuckin' time."

Manny shrugged. "Soz, mate."

Derek wafted his hand dismissively. "No worries, gadge."

Alan came back through the door, holding a couple of thick bricks of cash, a DVD in a clear plastic sleeve with the letters AJ DP scrawled on it in red marker, and a laptop. He put the two stacks in Harry's hands and put the computer on the desk. He turned on the machine and held the disc in the air for Eric's benefit.

"This disc comes *back*," he said. "If it winds up in the hands of the local scunners, or on the internet, you're going in the fuckin' ground – I shit you not."

Eric nodded. "You have my word."

Alan tapped the DVD against the desk to emphasise his point. "Swear down, this is for blackmail use only. The only fuckin' reason you're about to see this is because of the cut-price aitch. This copy comes back to me after you've finished with it. And if you've got any fuckin' decency you'll warn Ash that Joey knows and give her time to make her escape. Joey *will* slice her up if he gets the chance, and she deserves better than that. She deserves better than him, anyway."

"Like I said, you have my word."

"Good enough," Alan replied, placing the disc in the machine. Then he looked at Harry, still counting his money, and said: "You happy with the amount?"

Harry finished flicking through the notes of the second brick. "I'm happy."

Alan pressed play, sat back in the chair, and placed his feet on the desk. The four men edged towards the screen for a better look. Alan allowed himself a brief smile as he removed a fat cigar stub from an inside jacket pocket and sniffed it. Plucking an ornate silver lighter off the desk edge, Alan flicked the ignition wheel until it caught, then held the flame against the cigar until the tip burned orange. He puffed the cigar continuously and released cloud after cloud of rancid smoke.

As the on-screen action got hotter and louder, Eric laughed into his palm and looked at his brother, who was shaking his head in disbelief. Even Darren and Harry cracked big smiles and nudged each other from time-to-time.

Eventually, Eric burst into peals of laughter and turned towards Alan.

"Oh, this is fuckin' perfect."

52.

Ramon Carrasco sat in the front passenger seat of the people carrier and watched the smoke and lights of Teesside's industrial landscape as it passed. The driver prodded the Satnav display and told him they were close to the address Harry had provided. Then he pointed left out of the window, at a distant collection of ramshackle low-rise buildings. Ramon nodded once and returned to his brooding.

There was something off about Harry's story, something that didn't quite add up. Although ToJo confirmed the double robbery narrative, Ramon's bullshit detector warned him that things were not as described.

For over three years Jonno had bought raw product from him without a hitch. So it made no sense for him to jeopardise the arrangement with a sudden and uncharacteristic display of greed.

Jonno had never struck him as clever, but he wasn't an idiot, either; and jeopardising a deal to make a hundred grand was an idiot's play. Of course, Ramon had no way of knowing if Jonno was in some financial trouble, or if his aspirations had changed, or if there was something else at play that he couldn't yet see, but he did know that something in his gut warned him Harry's story was just plain *off*.

Ramon trusted his instincts – because they were rarely wrong – but he trusted his brain even more. He hadn't got where he was in life by making stupid, irrational decisions.

Despite the exotic name Ramon Carrasco was Yorkshire born-and-bred. He took after his tough, practical, and street-smart mother, rather than the idealistic father who had fled persecution after participating in student revolts in Franco's Spain in the late Sixties. In fact, the only things he inherited from his father were his name and his swarthy Mediterranean good looks. He didn't even speak Spanish.

His father, José, had settled in York as a political refugee, but always intended to return home to Madrid when the dictator's reign of terror finally ended. Life got in the way of those plans, early in 1975, in the form of Ramon's mother, Louise, an unplanned pregnancy, and a quick wedding. It wasn't a good marriage, and José wasn't a good husband or father, and when he went back to Spain a few years later, Louise and Ramon were glad to see the back of him.

A succession of his mother's boyfriends had steered Ramon towards a criminal life at a young age. They also gave him a crash course in how not to be a villain. He watched these men ignore their gut instincts, he watched them make unthinking, careless decisions, and then he watched them behind steel bars – faces falling as his mother informed them that it was over, and she wasn't going to wait.

In their way, each one of these idiots taught him when to trust in caution and careful planning and when to trust his gut, which was why he wasn't ignoring the alarm bells that were ringing loudly in his skull, telling him that Harry's story smelled of set-up and deception. Still, Ramon needed to know what had happened. He wasn't prepared to lose his money without a fight.

He turned to the three men sat behind him.

"I dunno what's waiting for us out at Jonno's place," he said, "but take nowt at face value. There's summat fishy about this whole thing. I think Harry's telling us fibs, but I'm not sure why."

A burly mixed-race man with a shaved head, a thick black Taliban beard, and a couple of tattooed tears near his right eye, edged forward and touched Ramon's shoulder. "You think it's a set-up, boss?"

Ramon shrugged. "Mebbe it is. But I'm tryna work out why, and I keep coming up short."

"Greed?"

He shook his head. "Harry never struck me that way. This is summat else."

The men nodded silently. They rummaged through bags and pulled out weapons. They checked their clips and screwed on silencers. Then they double-checked them.

The vehicle turned into the Greyhopes estate and did a slow drive-by. Ramon noticed the big garage on the right and nudged the driver. "Drive around the corner and park up."

The car pulled into a small, dark layby and the driver switched off the engine. Ramon holstered his weapon, adjusted his jacket, and then pointed in the direction of the garage.

"We go in as two teams," he said, indicating the man with the tattoos. "Frank, we're going in at the back. Joe, I want you and Col to hit them from the front. We go in on me signal. When you get me text message, you bust in that fuckin' door and charge. But *don't* fire off any rounds unless they start shooting first."

The driver coughed for attention. "And me?"

"Stay in the car, Sam. We might need to get the fuck outta here in a hurry."

Ramon exited the vehicle first, moved up the grass verge, and waited in the shadows between the trees and the wall. Frank pushed through the shrubs and settled beside him, brushing leaves off his black cotton jacket and trousers. Joe and Col – who both resembled Frank without the beard and Tattoos – edged around the trees and crouched on their haunches, awaiting further orders.

Ramon looked over the wall. Aside from a black four-wheeler near the garage, the grounds were deserted. A faint band of light filtered beneath the main entrance of the unit. Indistinct sounds emanated from within, but there was nothing recognisable.

"We're good to go," he whispered.

They moved quickly around the corner to the gate. Ramon grabbed the top, pulled himself up, and peered into the grounds again. All the action seemed to be happening within the unit. A loud voice shouted something unrecognisable, but it was impossible to discern how many people were inside and what they might be packing.

"We're still good," he added, scuttling over the gate. Loose tarmac and gravel crunched underfoot. He tread lightly and kept to the areas of soft damp dirt and grass.

Frank followed suit, crouching at his side within a pocket of dark shadow near the perimeter wall. They stayed in the shade as they crept towards the rear of the unit.

Joe and Col landed with a thump as they came over the gate. Stooping low, their feet scuffed along the rough ground as they scurried for the shelter of the 4x4. One of them must have caught a loose piece of tarmac or a brick fragment with his toe because something scraped and skipped across the asphalt and pierced the silence.

Ramon jerked around and looked over his shoulder. Heart thumping, his breath caught in his throat as he waited for the garage doors to open and whoever was inside to come out shooting.

Joe and Col stood in plain sight, with their eyes down, as if unable to move. Finally, after a short, uneventful wait, Joe turned his head in Ramon's direction and shrugged apologetically. He replied by pressing a forefinger to his lips and then pointed at the car. The two men tiptoed carefully behind the vehicle and out of view.

Ramon and Frank moved away from the wall and sidled across to the rear corner of the unit. Poking his head around the edge, Ramon noticed that the back door was open, illuminating a long band of concrete paving. Within this patch of light was a small dreadlocked man pouring dark liquid from a large tray into a grating beneath a downpipe. There were another three buckets filled with liquid by his feet.

Ramon asked Frank for his opinion. The large man watched the proceedings and then backed away with his expression set in a thoughtful scowl. He stroked his beard and turned to his boss.

"You recognise Dreadlocks?"

Ramon shook his head. "He's new to me. And if he's one of Jonno's then he's scraping the barrel for help."

"Is he pouring blood?"

"Either blood or oil."

"If that is blood," Frank said. "There's a lot of it. Seriously, boss, what the fuck is going on?"

Ramon removed his weapon from its holster. "Only one way we're gonna find out."

Ramon waited for Dreadlocks to turn and grab a bucket, but he didn't seem to be in any hurry. He continued pouring the liquid slowly to ensure that it all went down the drain without spillage. Gradually the angle of the tray got steeper until it was almost upside-down and there was nothing but a slow drip of liquid. Finally, the dripping stopped. Dreadlocks put the tray aside and turned around to collect a bucket.

Sensing opportunity, Ramon sprinted the thirty-foot distance before Dreadlocks had a chance to react. He jammed the silencer against the back of the man's head. "Do summat stupid," he whispered. "I fuckin' dare you."

Dreadlocks stiffened, took one deep breath, and accepted that dare. He shouted the name *Billy* as loud as he could.

Ramon pressed the trigger once.

Dreadlocks grunted and dropped face down on the floor.

Crouching low, Ramon went through the door with Frank on his heels.

53.

Derek parked the car halfway up Kings Mews and turned off the lights. The whitewashed, uplit rear of the Trinity Tavern was clearly visible at the far end of the street. A couple of silhouetted figures lurked in the shadows of a parking recess on the right. A faint amber light glimmered every few seconds. The sweet herbal scent of weed wafted into the vehicle through Derek's window.

Eric unhooked his seatbelt and eyeballed Harry. "If you walk now, nobody will think any less of you. This isn't your fight."

As soon as the money was in his hands, Harry had expected the Stanton brothers to kill him and take it for themselves. He was puzzled that they gave him the drugs without complaint, and it also mystified him that they then let him keep the cash. Every time an engine backfired or the car went over a bump in the road, Harry jumped in his seat and gripped the holdall tightly to his chest.

Eric's gaze drifted to the bag and then back up to Harry's anxious face. "You can relax. If we were gonna take the money, we would have done it by now."

"But why?"

Eric smiled. "Why are we letting you keep it?"

Harry nodded.

He shrugged his shoulders. "You did us a solid with Billy. There was no guarantee he would've backed down. Things might've got bloody. Putting him on the ground took guts. Plus the phone call to Ramon involved fast thinking. In both cases, you did us a solid, so I'm doing you one."

Harry breathed a sigh of relief and relaxed his grip on the bag.

Eric let out a small snort of amusement. "I reckon you've been holding that breath for a while."

Harry nodded. "Since your friend paid me."

"Seriously, you can relax. And… you don't hafta get involved in this. It's not your problem."

All Harry wanted was to get back to his family. He had just enough fight to grab the money he'd hidden at home, along with his family's passports, pack a few mementoes, and take his wife and son into hiding. Then his criminal career was over.

"You know summat," he said. "This is the end of the road for me. I'm finished."

Eric opened the door. "Fair enough. I understand," he said, getting out of the vehicle.

Harry clambered out of the car into the chilly night. Len's polyester trousers had made his legs hot and clammy, so being in the open was a relief. He pulled at the waistband to get some airflow going. Eric's mouth puckered in a small smile of amusement. Harry blushed slightly.

"They're loaners," he said.

"They'd be better off binned," Eric replied.

Harry scratched at a new itch on his outer thighs. "Actually, I think they'd be better off burnt. That way there's no chance of anybody using them again."

Eric held out his hand towards Harry, who went to shake it. Wearing a bemused expression, Eric pulled the hand away and directed his attention to Harry's bag. "I need that last package of aitch."

Harry went *ah* and delved in the bag. He tossed the packet to Eric, saying, "Make sure to wipe my prints before you plant it."

Placing it carefully inside his jacket, he said: "Don't worry. I'm not stupid. Or at least not *that* stupid."

Harry wanted to say something profound, mark the moment indelibly, and encapsulate all the errors that had brought him to this point, but the words weren't there. Instead, he zipped the bag and said: "Being a criminal isn't all it's cracked up to be."

Eric's mouth tightened momentarily, though his expression remained blank and unreadable. Harry wondered if he was bright enough to understand everything he was trying to express in that one short sentence.

Eric fixed him with his calm gaze, and for a moment looked like he was going to reply with something meaningful. Then, after a brief pause, Eric nodded once, smiled, and turned towards the car. "Look after yourself," he said over his shoulder.

Tightening his grip on the bag, Harry walked briskly to the end of the street. He looked back only once. The three men were standing beside the wall of the Trinity Tavern. Eric jumped up, grabbed the edge and peered over it.

Harry went around the corner and came out on Kings Road, a brightly lit street of amusement arcades, betting shops, pound stores, and fast food establishments. Random pedestrians eyeballed his clothes as they went past. A few of them even dropped snide comments as they were walking away. Harry ignored them and rushed along the pavement towards a stationary taxi in a parking bay outside a kebab shop.

He tapped on the window. A young Asian man wound it down, gave his outfit an amused once over, and said: "Yes, boss?"

"Alright, fella. How much is it to Eston?"

54.

Ramon tiptoed into a narrow prefab office of stud walls, plasterboard, Perspex windows and dusty furniture, and crouched behind a grimy desk unit. He made his way to the office doorway and peered around the frame. He'd seen most things in his time, but this one was new to him.

Two large men dressed in black were placing body parts in huge industrial bin liners. Arms, legs, torsos and heads were stacked carefully in the bags, with black towels thrown on top, and they were all placed in oversized suitcases.

On the floor, in a naked pile, was a thing that had once been Jonno. Ramon recognised the severed head. In its mouth was an enormous severed cock that was still dripping blood.

A man with wild black hair, oriental features, and a long bloody scar on his face pointed a shotgun in the direction of the office. His finger tightened on the trigger when he noticed Ramon. He squinted down the barrel and edged forward.

"Throw your weapons through the door, then step out slowly," Billy said. "I won't fuckin' ask youse again."

Frank jabbed Ramon with his finger and asked what was happening. When Ramon whispered the situation, Frank paled slightly and readied himself by wrapping his hands around his automatic in a combat grip.

Billy took another step forward. "Youse are making me ask again," he snapped. "I don't like asking twice – there won't be a third time. Throw your weapons through the door and then step out."

"D'you think I'm fuckin' stupid?" Ramon shouted. "Fuck you."

Billy cackled. "I don't think you're stupid; I fuckin' know it. The cartridges in this blunderbuss are triple-aught buck. Now, if you know owt about guns, you'll know that flimsy stud walls are no fuckin' protection against this kinda ammo. You think you're safe? This shit will blast through the plasterboard, tear you to shreds, and then rape your fuckin' soul as it's slithering outta your corpse. Get the fuck out here now!"

Ramon typed out a quick message to the men at the front door: *Trouble.*

Cum round back. Be fuckin careful. 3 of them. Their armed. We wont be.

He pressed send, deleted the message, and put the phone back in his jacket. He pitched his automatic through the doorway. It scraped across the concrete. He turned to Frank, whispering, "They're coming in through the back. We need to draw their attention."

Frank nodded and tossed his gun out of the office.

"We're coming out. Don't shoot."

Ramon stood and lifted his hands above his head. Frank followed suit. Both men entered the main garage cautiously, taking slow steps. Ramon maintained eye contact with the wild-haired man. "We're not armed. Are you Billy?"

The man nodded. "And the lad outside?"

Ramon shrugged. "Dead."

Billy sniffed and spat on the ground once. "RIP Desmond."

Jeff and Ed picked up the silenced autos and trained them on the two intruders. Billy pitched forward a few steps. "I heard summat outside. Who else is out there? Don't lie."

"That were me," Ramon said. "Me foot caught a stone as I came over the wall. Fuckin' thing went miles."

"Remember that shit I said about lying?" Billy replied, his trigger finger tightening. "Now, I'll repeat."

"I'm not lying. There's a driver around the corner, but that's it. Don't believe me, let's go outside and look."

"Oh, you'd love that, wouldn't you?"

Ramon's right hand lowered slightly. Billy came up close, placed the cold barrel beneath his chin.

"Chill, *Bill*. If you let me grab me phone, I'll call the driver and tell him to come inside. Come on. You've got the big scary gun. I'm not gonna owt stupid."

Billy's eyes angled towards Ramon's hand, and he gave a brief nod.

"If you start speaking funny, or use owt I think resembles code, your fuckin' head becomes a Rorschach."

Ramon brought his hand down in a smooth, gradual movement, maintaining eye contact with Billy. As he fumbled inside his jacket, a couple of thoughts struck him. His men needed as much time as possible to get into place. Plus, he felt he had a right to know why there had been so much bloodshed. Considering it was his property, they were probably fighting over. He decided to engage Billy in conversation to pass the time.

"I don't care if you've got a beef with Jonno," Ramon said. "It's none of me business. I'm just here because I had a deal with him that went south."

"I heard about it."

"Heard? Or can I take it *you* fucked up me transaction?"

Billy leered. "You could take it that way. But if you did, you'd be taking it the way an altar boy takes a Catholic priest's dick – all fuckin' wrong."

Ramon removed the phone. "You know owt about me drugs?"

Billy gave him a rotten grin that opened his swollen scar and sent fresh blood down his face. "You might wanna look at Harry Sparks. He gave me this fuckin' beauty, earlier. And once you're finished with him, you might wanna turn your attention on Eric and Derek Stanton."

"Who're they?"

"Used to be debt collectors. Now they're entrepreneurs," Billy replied.

"Thieves, in other words?"

"Summat like that," Billy said. "I guess they've got your drugs, along with Jonno's cash."

"Let us go on our way, and we'll sort 'em out."

"I *could* do that, but what's to stop you coming after me, later?"

"Because me business in't with you."

"Mebbe not now, but later you might think otherwise."

Ramon edged forward. The barrel pressed against his windpipe and made it hard to breathe. "Then you don't know me very well," he croaked. "This don't hafta get any bloodier than it already is."

Billy's eyes angled towards the suitcases. "Oh, I dunno, there's plenty of room for more corpses."

55.

Joe Tolliver wasn't a smart man, but he was smart enough to follow orders to the letter. So he waited by the front door watching his mobile phone. Even when somebody shouted the name Billy he didn't move.

Col jabbed him in the back and hissed in his ear. He demanded that they storm through the entrance and take everybody by surprise.

Joe stood firm. "We wait," he said.

Prison had taught him the art of patience. Time had a habit of dragging if you let it. He had filled his prison days with yoga and meditation, and his nights with learning to read. Patience helped him struggle through the alphabet and helped him form words; it gave him the strength he needed to survive the monotony of jail time, and now it was going be the difference between life and death in this situation.

Joe let the seconds drift. He wasn't going anywhere until he received a signal or until he knew for certain that his boss was in danger. Indistinct voices emanated from the garage, but he couldn't make out the words or the tone. Ramon shouted something, but it didn't sound like a signal. Joe ignored Col every time he pulled at his sleeve. He even kept his nerve when his partner threatened to go in alone.

Then he was rewarded for his patience. His phoned vibrated and the screen lit up: *Trouble. Cum round back. Be fuckin careful. 3 of them. Their armed. We wont be.*

Joe displayed the handset to Col so that he could read Ramon's orders for himself. Joe moved quickly and quietly, with his partner close behind, watching the ground for detritus and loose tarmac. He knew that another noisy mistake would be deadly.

Joe reached the rear of the unit and poked his head around the corner. A small figure lay face down on an illuminated patch of ground near the open back door. It didn't move as he approached on tiptoes. Blood matted the thick dreadlocks at the base of its skull. Joe stepped around the corpse, hunkered down low, and went into a narrow, dusty office. He removed his shoes carefully and put them to one side. There would be less noise if he had to move fast. Col also removed his trainers.

Joe shuffled through the tight space, using the furniture to maintain balance. He felt Col's warm breath on the back of his neck as they reached the doorway. Joe poked his head around briefly and took a mental snapshot of the situation.

Ramon and Frank had their backs to the door and their hands raised, although Ramon had a mobile phone in his right. A small man with wild black hair and a sliced-up face held a shotgun beneath Ramon's chin. Two tall men provided cover with silenced automatics.

Ramon said things that he thought his captors might want to hear in a soothing tone, but the man with the shotgun was having none of it:

"Oh, I dunno, there's plenty of room for more corpses."

Col hissed in his ear that they needed to act now, but Joe wasn't prepared to make his move until somebody made a mistake. He wafted away his partner, whispering: "We wait. I'll take shotgun you take the other two. On me signal."

He knew that it wasn't in his partner's nature to wait, or to act in anything other than a highly emotional state. That approach would get everybody killed. Joe trusted his boss and knew that he would find a way to tip the odds in his favour.

"Let me phone Sam," Ramon said. "I'll get him to come here. Or, better still, you do it, Billy. You dial, and I'll answer."

Joe smiled at Ramon's ingenuity. He'd just tipped the odds by forcing his opponent to consider a small but clear error. Two hands were needed to aim and fire a shotgun of that size. If he were prodding a mobile phone, he wouldn't be holding the gun under Ramon's chin.

A few seconds passed before Billy replied: "Lads, watch these two carefully, while I dial this fuckin' Sam character."

Joe poked his head around again. The two men had moved slightly closer to Ramon and Frank, although they focused their attention on Billy. The small man held the shotgun upright against his left shoulder so that it was pointing at the ceiling, while he scrolled through Ramon's contacts with the other hand.

Joe backed away slightly and glanced over his shoulder at Col. "We take out the black guys."

Both men moved into the doorway and aimed quickly. Joe fixed the iron sight just below his target's Afro and put two in his forehead. Col put his first shot in his target's eye and the second in the throat. Both men stumbled and dropped without firing a shot.

Billy dropped the phone and started bringing the shotgun down, but Ramon ducked low and slammed his fist into his opponent's nuts, grabbed a handful of them and yanked down hard. Billy shrieked and dropped the shotgun, which clattered on the ground, as he crumpled and curled into a foetal ball and cradled his crotch.

Ramon scooped up the weapon and pointed the business end in his direction. Then he turned his attention to Joe and gave him the briefest of nods and a small smile, which he returned with interest.

As soon as Billy had dropped in volume from agonised screams to stuttering sobs, Ramon prodded him with the barrel. "Where's me drugs, Billy?"

The man curled into an even tighter ball and hissed. "I already fuckin' told you."

He prodded again. "You expect me to believe that?"

Billy wafted it away with one of his hands. "Don't give a fuck what you believe."

Ramon pressed the barrel into his side. "Hows about I unload this thing point-blank into your ribcage?"

Billy finally turned his furious gaze towards his aggressor. "Answer will still be the same, dickhead. Plus, you'd be doing me a favour. I've got HIV and fuckin' Hep – I count me time in fuckin' months, not years – so do your worst."

Ramon snorted with amusement. "Actually, you should start counting your time in seconds."

"Then quit wasting it."

Taking a few steps back, Ramon gestured Joe forward with a flick of the shotgun. "If he's infected, might be better not to get his blood everywhere."

Joe came forward, aimed at the man's temple and pulled the trigger. The impact thumped his head against the ground. His body twitched once and went loose. A small wisp of smoke swirled lazily from the hole in Billy's skull. Piss and blood seeped from his crotch, forming lagoons in the dimpled concrete. There was also the meaty smell of shit in the air.

Ramon stared at the corpse for a few moments, before moving in the direction of the suitcases. He opened one, looked inside the industrial waste bag, and curled his lip in disgust. "Fuckin' savages."

"Whadda we gonna do about Harry?" Frank asked. "About these Stanton characters?"

Ramon closed the case. "Nothing right now. Our priority is to get rid of this lot. The rest will keep."

Frank eyeballed Jonno's corpse, then turned his attention to Billy. "There's a lot to dispose of, boss."

"Tell me summat I don't know."

Joe noticed a tattered plastic shopping bag on a wooden workbench. Instinct said it was out of place among the corpses. He walked over and looked inside. His impassive expression cracked, and he allowed himself a small smile.

"Here's summat you don't know," he said, lifting the big in the air. "There's a lotta money in this bag. I'm guessing about the same as Jonno were planning on paying you."

Ramon's eyebrows arched. "Mebbe Harry weren't lying, after all?"

Joe handed him the bag and started walking around the garage, trying to get the measure of the place. It was dusty and old and smelled more like blood than oil. He walked to a broken pile of papier-mâché on the ground beside the office unit. On closer inspection, it was a concrete block cast painted the same colour as the wall. He angled his gaze upwards. About twelve feet off the ground was a scooped out section of brickwork. It didn't take a genius to work out the cast would match the missing brick correctly. He turned away and went back to mingling with the group.

Ramon dropped the money on the ground. "We're gonna scour this place from top to bottom. We clean it thoroughly. Knives, guns, shell casings, if there's owt incriminating we throw it in the cases. We take *everything*. Then we're gonna fold these bastards into the cases, even if we hafta break every fuckin' bone in their bodies to do it. Nowt gets left behind."

"Where we gonna dump 'em?" Frank asked.

"You let *me* worry about that. I know a bloke with a farm out on the Moors. We pay him summa this cash and he'll make them all disappear."

He clapped his hands to get their attention.

"Now let's crack on."

56.

Eric pulled himself over the gate and landed feet first in the Trinity Tavern's small deserted courtyard. He moved around a few empty beer barrels and boxes strewn across the concrete towards a black metal staircase that led up to a door on the first floor.

Eric went up the steps and tried the handle. It turned, but the door didn't budge. He studied the mortise lock, took a 2-in-1 pick from his jacket and adjusted the screws until the picks were in line. Inserting the device into the lock, he twisted the screws until the makeshift key turned smoothly. He turned the handle again, but the door still didn't move. It was bolted from the inside.

Eric back went down the stairs, to where his brother and Darren were waiting. "Can't get in that way." Then he pointed at a pair of long metal doors set in the concrete beneath the stairs. "Can we get in through the beer cellar?"

Darren shook his head. "It's on a deadbolt."

Eric fixed his attention on a door to the left of the stairs with a fire exit sign nailed to it. "Then how about that one?"

Darren pulled a face. "It's alarmed. Sorry."

Eric let out a long sigh. "Then I guess we're going in through the front."

Derek grinned and slammed a massive fist into the palm of his hand. "About fuckin' time we did summat straight up. I'm sick of all this sneaking around."

Derek jumped the gate, with his brother and Darren following close behind. They cut through an unlit alley that reeked of stale piss and turned right on the main street. A fat doorman dressed all in black leant against the front door frame. He took a deep drag on a roll-up and exhaled. He paid no attention as they approached.

Derek pulled the cigarette from the doorman's mouth, which dropped open in shock at the sheer nerve of what had occurred. He took a flailing swipe at Derek in an attempt to retrieve his cigarette, but the big man pushed him against the door and stubbed out the hot end of the roll-up on his left eyeball.

The doorman screamed as he brought his hands up to his face, leaving his stomach exposed. Derek folded him forward with a left to the abdomen and then put him on his back with a right to the chin. He stamped on the man's face twice to ensure that he didn't get up again.

Responding to the screams, another bouncer charged out of the building. Tall and lean, with a broken boxer's face, he swung his hands in Derek's direction, trying to get him in a chokehold. Derek ducked beneath the flapping arms and landed a right in the bouncer's gut. He groaned and fell forward. Derek lifted the bouncer with his shoulder and slammed him against the door. Then he worked the bouncer's ribs and stomach with a flurry of blows as the man thrashed weakly against his back and shoulders. Finally, Derek pulled away, bounced on the spot, and beckoned his opponent forward before settling back into a fighter's stance.

Despite being a bit dazed and wobbly on his feet, the bouncer came forward again and let fly with a right hook. Derek sidestepped left and caught the bouncer in the throat with an open-handed blow. Panicking, gasping for air, the man slid down the wall until he was on his backside. Sensing opportunity, Derek slammed his heel down on the man's shinbone, which cracked under the weight. He ignored the bouncer's squeals and pushed into the bar.

Shouldering and elbowing through crowds of people who bellowed abuse as he passed, Derek moved towards Joey's booth. When the fat man realised what was happening his face contorted in a grotesque expression of terror. He waved his hands at a couple of bouncers standing beside him and pointed at Derek. A stocky black man with thick dreads turned his head and followed the finger. He grabbed a beer bottle and smashed it against the tabletop.

"Fuck him up, Ronnie," Joey roared, pushing the bouncer forward.

Flailing and yelling, drinkers parted left and right to avoid Ronnie's full-speed charge and the jagged bottle he was waving like a knife. Waiting until the very last moment, Derek stepped to one side and kicked out at the bouncer's knee as he put weight on it. It was enough to knock Ronnie off balance.

Landing on his stomach, Ronnie tightened his grip on the bottle but was still dazed from the fall. Sensing hesitation, Derek stamped on the bouncer's hand repeatedly, shattering bone and bottle, and ground his heel down until glass and bone shards protruded through the flesh. Then

Derek silenced Ronnie's screams with a kick to the chin.

He spun on his heels and rushed towards the booth. The second bouncer looked at his boss, who wafted his hands like he was fanning away an unpleasant smell.

"Fuckin' kill him, Chaz," he screamed.

Chaz clenched his fists and sprinted in Derek's direction. He swung a right from the hip. Derek pulled back his head and let the punch breeze past harmlessly.

Realising that things weren't going his way, Joey squeezed out of the booth and crept past horrified onlookers in the direction of the staff door. Eric watched Joey's progress and decided to cut him off. He told Darren to follow him and forced his way through the crowd, elbowing and kicking people out of his way. Eric caught up with Joey just as the big man was turning the handle. He jabbed a silencer barrel into his armpit.

"Going somewhere?"

Joey seemed shocked that this was happening. "Are you fuckin' insane?"

"Not insane, just angry."

"You're gonna regret this."

"Not as much as you will."

Joey's eyes widened. "Whassat supposed to mean?"

Eric pushed closer. "It means you shouldn't have threatened Darren's girlfriend. That kind of shit's outta order."

"That's between Thrombo and me."

Darren dashed forward, grabbed Joey by the throat, and pinned him against the door. The fat man struggled and pushed back, but Darren was too strong: he squeezed Joey's windpipe until his face was the colour of beetroot and he fought for every breath.

"Me name's not Thrombo," he replied. "Call me Darren, or I'll crush your fuckin' throat."

Joey fixed his eyes on Eric. "Gerrim off us, mate," he croaked.

"We're not mates, you piece of shit."

"Gerrim off us, or you'll have the law breathing down your necks."

Eric nodded, and Darren let him go. Joey rubbed his throat, coughed a few times, and turned his attention to what was happening elsewhere.

Teeth gritted, forehead veins throbbing, Derek held Chaz by the hair and slammed his face into the corner of a table. The bouncer was missing most of his front teeth and blood flowed from multiple gashes to his cheeks and chin, but Derek seemed intent on doing more damage and slammed him into the table again, opening a fresh cut beneath his right eye.

One of the barmen was dialling a number. Eric knew what that number was. He nudged Joey with the gun barrel. "You don't want the police involved in this," he said, waving the disc in front of his face. "What's on here's gonna be embarrassing for you on the Internet."

"Then call off your wrecking machine," Joey replied, standing his ground.

Eric pierced the din with a whistle. Derek stopped what he was doing, looked down at the bloodied bouncer with disinterest, and let go of his hair. He dropped out of sight behind the table and stayed down.

Joey shouted at the barman, pointed at the phone, and drew a finger across his throat. The man nodded but then waved his hands at the drinkers, many of who seemed to have the same idea. People were rummaging in pockets and bags for their phones and others appeared to be debating whether or not it was in their best interests to make the call.

Joey made it easy for them.

"If youse put your phones away and forget what you've seen tonight, the next three rounds are on the house," he yelled.

The crowd forgot about their phone calls for a moment and started murmuring. Bracing themselves for the rush, the two men behind the bar positioned themselves near the popular drinks. Although Joey hadn't quite finished his point:

"But I fuckin' swear down, if I see any fuckin' pigs here, I'll find out who made the call and burn down your fuckin' houses with you and your loved ones still in 'em. We fuckin' clear?"

Those in the crowd still debating the decision quickly decided there was no discussion worth having and put their phones away. A tsunami of people collided against the bar, clamouring for attention, waving their hands. The barmen pulled pints and poured shots at a frantic rate and thrust the drinks back into the sea of flailing arms.

Eric pushed Joey through the staff door, in the direction of the stairs. He stopped and tapped Darren on the shoulder and said, "Take him upstairs."

Darren pulled out his gun and prodded Joey up the steps, muttering obscenities in his direction. Eric took the wrapper of Heroin from his pocket and wiped it carefully. He placed it on the bannister and searched for a suitable hiding place that didn't seem too much like a plant.

Derek emerged through the staff door and closed it behind him. Panting for breath, he rested his frame against the wood and wiped his bloodied fingers on his jeans as Eric rooted through the cupboard under the stairs. "What are you doing?" he asked.

"What does it look like I'm doing?"

"Looks like you're sniffing through Joey's dirty laundry."

"Give the man a point for observation."

"Yeah, but what are you really doing?"

"Putting dirty laundry in Joey's basket."

Eric picked up the Heroin with a found rag and waved it in front of his brother's face. Derek realised what was going on and smiled. Eric wiped the Heroin again with the cloth and placed it inside a box filled with packets of peanuts. Then he rubbed the cupboard door and the handle and pocketed the rag. He pointed at the ceiling. Derek nodded and bounded up the steps with Eric hot on his heels. They opened the office door and entered the room.

Joey sat behind a desk; his fingers tapped out a rhythm across its ink-stained surface to pass the time. There was a fresh bruise beneath his right eye. Darren watched the fat man from the comfort of a tattered sofa.

Eric pointed at Joey's face. "Why'd you hit him?"

"He tried to struggle," Darren replied.

Derek crouched beside a heavy filing cabinet situated near Joey's desk, wrapped his arms around the unit, and let out a loud groan as he heaved it off the floor. Huffing and grunting, he took short, staggering steps forward, dropped the unit on its side and wedged it against the foot of the door. It wasn't perfect, but it would slow down anybody attempting to rush in.

Eric approached a media unit near the door. He picked up a remote control and turned on the big flatscreen television that was on top of the cabinet. Then Eric placed the disc in a Blu-ray player, picked up another remote, and positioned himself on the arm of the sofa. He turned his attention to Joey.

The big man stopped drumming his fingers on the desk. "So what's on this disc that you can't wait to show me?"

57.

Harry told the driver to pull over a few streets from his house. He pulled a twenty from one of the wads of cash in the holdall and told him to keep the change. Harry made his way along Meadowgate, but a severe attack of paranoia slowed his progress to a crawl. Every time he glimpsed car lights or heard the oncoming whirr of an engine he moved off the pavement and onto the grass. Harry hid behind the trees that bordered the verge and waited for the cars to pass.

Eventually, Harry cut left. He walked slowly down a long, T-shaped cul-de-sac of red brick semis and studied the vehicles for anything out of the ordinary. He stopped beside a car he recognised without even having to read the licence plate. It was an immaculate black and silver Sierra Cosworth with a sleek body kit and gleaming metal rims. It was the car Charlie Wallace drove when the Ford Focus wasn't available. Harry was thankful that Jonno had sent idiots to do a professional's job.

He moved further down the road until he reached a transit van. He peered at his house from behind the back of the vehicle. The living room was well lit, and the shadow of a figure darkened the drawn curtains before moving out of view. The silhouette was too tall to be his wife.

Harry delved through his pockets for a weapon and cursed his luck when he remembered that he'd left his knife buried in Billy Chin's face. This put him at a disadvantage. Charlie and whoever was with him would no doubt be carrying something more potent than fists. He needed a solid plan if he was going to get back into his house.

His unwelcome visitors were no doubt listening to strange sounds and distant voices. If they weren't rooting through drawers and cupboards for money, they would most likely be sat on chairs, smoking cigarettes, waiting for the scrape of hesitant feet on pavements.

So he intended to make some noises they couldn't ignore.

Harry crept back to the Cosworth. A red LED blinked above the dashboard because this was the kind of vehicle a proud owner would secure with an alarm. He looked around for witnesses. There were no people on the street. Then Harry looked at the houses. Lights blazed from behind closed drapes. The area was awash with ambients sounds from televisions and music systems.

Most people ignored car and house alarms at the best of times. Even if they did poke their noses through the curtains, he wasn't too concerned about anybody calling the police.

Harry grabbed a large jagged stone from a rock feature that bordered a neighbouring lawn and went back to the Cosworth. He drew back his arm and propelled the rock at the window with all his strength.

Glass shattered. The alarm let out a long wavering scream that followed Harry as he sprinted back to the shadow of the van. He gulped down breaths as he watched his house for signs of movement.

Noises from televisions and stereo units increased in volume to compensate for the sound of the alarm and curtains twitched in a few nearby houses, but Harry wasn't interested in them; he was too busy watching his house with fingers crossed, muttering *come on, come on, come on* under his breath.

The front curtains moved. Charlie pushed his bony face through the gap and pressed it up against the window. His breath fogged the glass until he eventually rubbed the condensation away with a sleeve. Charlie's mouth constantly moved as he gesticulated at the outside world. The curtains closed, and Charlie's loud voice drifted out into the street. Harry couldn't make out the words, but he knew for certain that he was angry.

The front door opened, and Charlie sprinted outside. Harry crouched near the rear of the van, waiting for the right moment to make his move. Wailing and cursing, Charlie ran up the street and stopped beside the Cosworth. When he saw the window his hands went to his face, and he pulled at the flesh.

Sucking in his gut, Harry edged through the gap between the rear of the van and the garage door. Bonnie, the tall, barrel-chested man he'd hurt earlier in the day, emerged in the street and laughed at his colleague's feet-stamping tantrum.

The sound of the alarm ended with a single beep. Harry's ears whistled loudly. Arms windmilling and flailing, Charlie yelled at his partner: "Fuckin' savages broke me window. Ow, Bonnie, come an' have a look at this fuckin' shite."

A few more curtains twitched. A couple of folks pressed their noses against windows. Charlie's antics were drawing attention.

Bonnie walked up the road. He didn't notice Harry wedged between the van and the garage because he was too busy chuckling at Charlie's bad fortune. Despite this, Harry attempted to make himself smaller and narrower. It wasn't easy.

Charlie turned to Bonnie: "What's so fuckin' funny? Oh, you think me broken window's good for a chuckle like?"

Bonnie stopped laughing. "Shurrup, you daft bastard, you're making a scene."

Charlie unlocked the driver's door. "Aw, man, there's fuckin' glass everywhere. Swear down; somebody should fuckin' firebomb Eston. This place is a right fuckin' shithole."

"Ow, you cheeky doyle, *I'm* from Eston," Bonnie said, stepping up close with tightened fists. "You say owt like that again, and I'll fuckin' lay you out."

Harry squeezed through the gap and then removed his shoes because he wanted to keep the noise to a minimum. He wasn't fast on his feet so he needed all the head start he could get. Harry studied the road between the van and his front door for broken glass and jagged objects that might slow his progress. It was clear.

He crept forward slowly, flicking constant glances over the shoulder looks for signs of trouble.

"I'll say whatever the fuck I wanna say," Charlie replied. "And if you don't like it you can piss right off."

Harry took another couple of steps.

"I'm proper telling you," Bonnie replied angrily. "Say another word and I'm gonna put you on the deck."

Harry took several diagonal steps so that he stayed behind the van and remained out of view until the very last moment. He hoped that they were too busy bickering to notice him sneak into the house.

"Well, here's four more words for you: go fuck yourself."

Bonnie snorted in derision. "Them's three words; you thick cunt."

"How's that three fuckin' words? Go, fuck, your and self: that's *four* fuckin' words. Where'd you learn English?"

"The same place that you *didn't* learn it: school. Yourself is one word. You're a right fuckin' dunce, you."

Harry took a deep breath and sprinted for home. Loud shouts followed him to the driveway. As he reached the door, Harry heard the fast slap of rubber soles on the tarmac. He got through the door, closed it, and slammed the brass bolt into place. Then he pushed the chain into the sliding mechanism. Somebody slammed against the door and loosened the strike plate. The entire house seemed to shake.

It would only take two or three more heavy blows to tear it off the doorframe.

He needed to work fast if he was going to survive.

58.

Joey slouched behind his desk and pointed at the big screen. "Whatever you're about to show us is gonna hafta be pretty fuckin' mind-blowing to stop me from having youse all killed."

"Oh, it is," replied Eric, pressing play.

Joey stared at the television without expression, hardly blinking, as a shot of an empty bed came on screen. A cute, slim, and petite woman with a beautiful smile staggered into the frame, jumped on the bed, and began a drunken striptease. She flicked her long brunette hair and hummed an off-key rendition of *The Stripper* as she stumbled across the mattress with all the grace of a falling racehorse. She yanked at the buttons of her tight white blouse. Turning in an awkward circle, she nearly fell over while kicking off her high heels.

Alan Piper and a young, well-muscled man in T-shirt and jeans approached the bed. They called out her name several times and goaded her into removing her blouse. She tore off the top, swung it in a wide circle over her head and propelled it out of frame. Enjoying the attention, she giggled as the men fought each other to unhook her bra. They each took turns fondling her breasts and sucking on her nipples. When she yanked up her skirt, Alan and his friend took turns stroking her legs while the other rubbed the gusset of her black panties with all the eroticism of Aladdin rubbing his lamp. Then she ordered both men to strip and performed a slow clap as the clothes came off.

She applauded loudly as the pair kicked their underwear across the room and shouted, "Yay, big dicks," in broad Dublin brogue, "I've not seen one of those in a while, never mind two of them."

She pulled off her skirt and panties quickly, dropped on the bed with her legs parted, and beckoned them forward with a wave of the finger.

Alan approached and thrust his erection towards her face. "Always thought Joey were packing? He's a big lad."

"Is he bollocks," she replied, stroking his cock. "The only thing big about him is his gut. It's the size of my little finger when he can actually get it up."

Joey's face twitched for the first time. Beads of sweat dotted his forehead. His cheeks drained of colour.

She gave Alan a long gaze, brought her head forward, and took him in her mouth. She worked her head back and forth, never breaking eye contact. After a few seconds, she stopped sucking, kissed the tip, and said: "I've seen the way you look at me."

Alan brushed his fingers up and down her cheek. "Surprised you noticed. You never seemed to gimme a second glance?"

"*Ooh*, did that piss you off?"

"Mebbe."

She giggled. "Unlike you, I know how to look without being caught."

"I never expected you to be so willing."

"Are you kidding? Joey couldn't make me do summing I don't wanna do," she said. "He's not that fecking smart. I get to have youse all weekend; then I get to go home and make him feel like shit afterwards. Joey will be so guilty I'll probably get a lotta new jewellery outta him. I'll tell him some sob story about how horrible youse were, flutter my eyelids, then point him in the direction of a pink gold Cartier watch I've had my eyes on for a while."

Sweat beads rolled down Joey's forehead and into his eyes. He blinked them away, and they moved down his cheeks like tears. His hands pressed against the desk, fingers scraping the surface, as he struggled to keep his anger in check.

Eric pressed fast-forward, increasing the speed of the action until it resembled a pornographic version of a Benny Hill sketch, as the sexual positions altered at an increasingly frantic rate. Finally, he chuckled, announcing, "Now this here's my favourite bit," and let go of the fast-forward button.

All three people were naked on the bed. The stranger was on his back at the bottom of the pile, with Aisling on top of him, wrapping her fists around the duvet, pushing her face into the sheets, while Alan thrust into her from behind. She screamed *fuck me harder* into the mattress. Alan picked up speed until the sweat dripped off his chin and down the gulley of her spine. He kept going until Aisling raised her flushed face from the tangle of sheets, screeched *I'm coming*, and wailed loudly as both men pounded her to a climax.

Eric paused the video and stepped in front of the screen. "You really wanna see any more of this? It only gets worse. Your wife and Alan get pretty intimate when they're on their own. They're both into some kinky shit."

Suppressed rage darkened Joey's complexion, and he pursed his lips tightly. His fingernails scraped across the desk and left shallow indents in the wood. He trembled so violently that he seemed ready to explode at a moment's notice. Then he finally opened his mouth and said: "Whaddaya want to make this disappear?"

Eric considered pressing Joey for money, especially as the disc was a particularly juicy blackmail tool, but realised that his primary goal was to protect Darren. Although he had come close to ruining the job on several occasions with his stupidity, for better or worse they were partners.

"Darren gets to walk with his cash, and you leave his girlfriend alone," Eric said. "And you'd better not put out a sneaky contract on any of us several months down the line."

The tension left Joey's face, and his expression softened. "That's it?"

"That's it."

"And you leave the disc?"

Eric wagged his finger "I'll give you points for cheek. The DVD goes with us. Besides, we have copies. *Alan* has copies. Should you try and take the disc by force, Alan will make sure your wife's multiple orgasms become an Internet sensation."

"And if I go back on me word later?"

Eric laughed. "If you go back on your word, I'll put this shit online and email the link to everybody you know. The world gets to see your wife paying off your debts, talking behind your back, laughing at you, fuckin' other men and *enjoying* it. You'll become the local fuckin' joke."

Joey nodded, and his lips went tight again. "You wanna know summat? She made me feel so fuckin' bad that I bought her that watch."

"The Cartier?"

"Aye. Ten grand, even though I couldn't fuckin' afford it," Joey replied. "The Funny thing is, I only got in so much debt 'cause she were spending me money faster than I could make it. There were nowt I wouldn't have given her if she asked. All I wanted in return were a little respect… She couldn't even give me that much."

Eric almost felt sorry for Joey. As ruthless and vicious as he was, this was a show of genuine emotion. It wasn't done for sympathy because he was playing to an indifferent audience. For better or worse, this was Joey with all the bravado and bullshit stripped away. The man at his most human.

Joey rubbed his beard. "It weren't worth it, you know."

"What wasn't?"

"Getting Ash to pay off me debt like that. I knew it were a mistake before I even asked her. I knew it would change things between us, but I convinced meself it would be okay.

"She kicked off summat rotten when I first suggested it. She even cried in my arms when I told her it were the only way to pay it off. She said she'd never forgive me. I remember telling her I'd never forgive meself. And now I realise that she enjoyed being given a free pass to fuck around. And here I am, in even worse debt than before trying to buy back the affection of somebody who never really cared for me in the first place."

Joey laughed bitterly and slapped the desk. "Jesus, what a fuckin' chump. I shoulda found some other way to pay Piper."

"There wasn't another way," Eric reminded him. "The other way involved extreme physical pain."

"There's always another way," Joey replied. "And I'd take extreme physical pain over what I'm feeling right now."

Eric ejected the disc. "Maybe you can still fix things with the wife."

Joey gazed into the distance as if running some future scenario through his head. "Oh, I'll fix things alright," he said.

Rage twinkled behind the green surface of his eyes. Aisling Judd was in a lot of trouble, and Eric needed to warn her as soon as possible.

He placed the disc back in the envelope and approached the desk.

"Are we good?" he asked.

Joey turned his angry gaze on Eric and thought about it.

"I want an answer – yes or no?" Eric added. "Darren walks with the money, and you leave his girlfriend alone – yes or no?"

Joey nodded. "Okay, but I wanna guarantee from youse that Ash's film debut isn't gonna end up as jizz of the week on some fuckin' bongo site."

"You keep your word, and we'll keep ours."

Joey extended his hand. "Then we have a deal."

Eric shook it and stepped back.

Joey focused on Darren, still watching proceedings from the sofa.

"Don't *ever* set foot in this place again," he said. "And you better prepare yourself for a *long* fuckin' period outta the ring. Like forever. You'll have no fuckin' reputation left by the time I've finished badmouthing you."

Darren grumbled momentarily but fell silent after a couple sharp glares from his companions.

"Now get up, Joey," Eric said.

A fleeting expression of confusion slackened the fat man's face. "What?"

"I'm gonna go out on a limb here and say you've probably got men with guns lurking in the courtyard."

Joey huffed but didn't deny it.

"Get up, now. Don't make me ask again."

Joey came around the desk. Eric pushed and prodded him until he was beside Derek, who pulled back the deadbolt on the courtyard door. He removed the gun from beneath his waistband, crouched beside the door and pushed with his free hand. It creaked open, letting cold air flood into the windowless room. Derek edged around the doorframe and sneaked a peak.

A couple of tall heavies in hooded tracksuits waited at the bottom of the stairs. Their hands tightened around gun handles when they noticed Derek. They ascended the steps slowly. The metal clanged and shuddered with every footstep.

Derek chuckled. "This day keeps on getting better and better."

59.

Harry stumbled as he rushed up the stairs. He drew air into his burning lungs, pushed himself back to his feet, staggered to the top and then closed all the doors on his way to the master bedroom to buy himself a few more precious seconds.

Harry shut the door and slammed in the bolt that stopped Terry from entering the room whenever he made love to Babs. He tossed the holdall aside and made his way to the wardrobe and yanked open a small, hinged door at the top of the unit. He tore through the towels and sheets, scattering them across the room, and pulled out a locked wooden box.

Downstairs the door burst open with a thud. Heavy feet stomped around in the entrance hall. "Where the fuck is he?" Charlie hissed.

Harry slammed the box against the wall repeatedly until the wood split and broke apart. A small revolver and several bullets spilt out and bounced across the carpet.

"Fucker's upstairs," Bonnie replied.

Harry dropped to his knees and grabbed the gun. Panicking, he scooped up as many bullets as he could find, opened the empty cylinder and slid the rounds into the chambers.

Charlie and Bonnie ran up the stairs and opened each of the doors one-by-one.

"Front bedroom," Charlie said.

The door handle turned but didn't open. Somebody cursed loudly.

Harry snapped the cylinder into place with only four bullets inside and drew back the hammer. Then he put the gun on the bed within easy reach as the last resort and opened the main wardrobe doors. Reaching down, he found a dusty dumbbell beneath a pile of old clothes.

Somebody slammed against the door.

Harry felt the impact in his bones.

The bolt held. Just.

Harry hefted the dumbbell and shifted his body into position. He bent his right arm and focused all his attention on a point just in front of the door. If Harry timed his throw right, the weight would put somebody down and keep them there, but if his timing was wrong… he just hoped there were enough bullets in the gun.

The door shook on its hinges again. One of the nails holding the strike plate in place went flying across the room.

Harry ground his heels into the carpet and braced himself.

The door flew open. Bonnie rushed in and staggered to a stop a few feet in front of Harry, who threw the weight with everything he had. The dumbbell smashed into Bonnie's face and sent him reeling back into Charlie's path. Both men collided and went to ground.

Harry rushed to the bed and grabbed the gun.

Charlie clawed his way over Bonnie and stumbled towards Harry, who jammed the revolver barrel in his face.

"Don't even think it," he said. "Now lemme see your hands go high."

Charlie lifted his hands over his head.

"Now move back."

As Charlie stepped towards the door, his heel brushed the sole of Bonnie's shoe. The big man stirred, mumbled something unintelligible, and attempted to sit upright, but his movements were uncoordinated, and he stumbled on his side. His nose was crushed almost flat, and his left cheekbone was concave despite the swelling.

"He needs the hospital," Charlie said. "He's proper fucked."

"So take him. I'm not stopping you."

"When this is all sorted I'm gonna come back for you, you fat fuck."

Harry smiled. "I won't be here when you get back," he said. "And just remember your manners, *Charles*. Otherwise, I'll scratch my itchy finger with this trigger."

Charlie recoiled slightly but maintained his bravery. "I'll find you."

"You're welcome to waste your time trying," Harry replied. As soon as he had his family's passports and his rainy day stash, he would be out the door. The job could be done-and-dusted in under half an hour, if only he could get rid of these idiots first.

"Now empty your pockets," he said, thrusting the gun at Charlie, "and be careful about it. Throw that shit on the bed."

Charlie delved through his jeans pockets and threw a switchblade, wallet, car keys, lock picks, and mobile phone on the bed and then lifted his hands again. Harry crouched down and took everything but the car keys as Charlie watched, waiting for the chance to make his move.

"I'll need help carrying him."

Harry shook his head. "You *want* help carrying him. But you won't be getting any."

Charlie shrugged. "So now what?"

Harry jabbed the gun into his chest. "Now we go get your car."

60.

The heavies in hoodies stopped moving halfway up the steps. They waited silently and watched the doorway for movement. Derek sneaked a peek and pulled back his head. He looked over his shoulder at Joey.

"Get ridda the muscle."

Joey sneered. "Or what?"

One-handed, Derek grabbed him by the back of the neck and slammed him face first into the wall. Joey went *oof* and blinked with shock as Derek manhandled him towards the doorway. "Or I'll use you as a battering ram and roll you down those fuckin' stairs."

Eric removed the disc envelope from his pocket and waved it in the air. "Or, if you prefer, we can disarm your boys and force them to watch what's on this disc. *Every* filthy fuckin' second of it."

Joey wiped away the blood that trickled from his nostrils. He studied the smear on the back of his hand. Then he shouted:

"Oz, Muzzy? Is that youse?"

"You okay, boss man?" asked a deep rumble of a voice.

Joey rubbed at another blood trickle. "Yeah, I'm alright, lads."

"You sure, boss man? 'Cause it's like a fuckin' bloodbath in the bar."

"Swear down, I'm all right, Muzz."

"Are these the bastards what smashed shit up downstairs?"

"Aye, but it was just a misunderstanding."

Muzz snorted loudly and spat. "Hard to misunderstand some cunt stubbing out a fag on Jezza's eyeball."

Joey glowered at Derek. "You stubbed out a cigarette on Jerry's eye?"

Derek shrugged. "He was in the way."

"Fuckin' animal."

Eric coughed for Joey's attention. "Let's not forget what you had planned for Darren's girlfriend. We wouldn't even be here if it wasn't for your bullshit. Get talking or else."

Joey nodded. "It's all right, Muzz. Fuckin' swear down it is. We sorted out our problems all amicable like."

"You don't sound okay, boss man. We're coming in."

Derek jammed the gun into his back and pushed him into the doorway. Joey stared down at the men. "Well, if youse are coming in, you'd better put them guns away."

Muzzy said something low-pitched and indecipherable. Joey shook his head in response. Derek yanked him back into the room by his collar and pushed the gun deep into a roll of back flab. "You wouldn't be trying summat sneaky, would you?" he said.

Joey looked over his shoulder. "Muzz asked if I wanted them to come in blasting," he replied. "You saw me shaking me fuckin' head."

Derek crouched behind Joey and shouted: "Come on in. But if either of youse come through the door firing off caps, be warned that it's your fuckin' boss who'll be taking most of 'em."

Darren kneeled behind the arm of the chair and aimed at the doorway. Eric pulled his weapon and moved in close to Joey, whispering: "Unless they're excellent shots most of these bullets are gonna hit you."

Joey gulped and shivered.

A tall, muscular black man filled the doorway. His hands were in the air and in his right he held a semi-automatic by the barrel. "Easy now, fellas. Just wanna make sure JJ's okay."

Eric beckoned him in with a small wave of his gun. "Come in nice and slow. Then put the semi on the floor and kick it towards me."

"What's going on?" Muzzy asked. "What happened to his nose?"

"Joey had a disagreement with a wall and came off second best."

Muzzy hesitated. He let the gun barrel slide slowly in his hand so that his fingers were closer to the handle.

Eric turned and placed the silencer barrel against Joey's temple. "Pull that little trick with the gun again and I'll put one in his skull," he said. "If you wanna come in you play by *our* rules."

Muzzy turned to Joey. "Boss man?"

Joey's body stiffened. An irritated huff escaped him. "Do as you're fuckin' told, Muzz, and toss the gun."

Muzzy stooped and placed the gun on the floor; then he kicked it towards Eric, who scooped up the weapon and pointed it at its previous owner.

Muzzy pulled back his hood, revealing a shaven head and a thick neck festooned with elaborate tattoos, and walked into the middle of the room with his hands high.

Oz came next. Like his partner, he filled the doorway with sheer physical bulk. He also held his gun by the barrel, but instead of placing it down carefully, he let it drop. Then he kicked it beneath the media unit and joined Muzzy in a two-man huddle.

Eric prodded Joey forward. The fat man took a few slow, uncertain steps, licking his lips nervously. Both brothers jabbed him with gun barrels and told him to pick up the pace. "Now we're gonna take a trip downstairs."

"But…"

"These lads gave up just a little too easy for my liking," Eric said and glanced at the two heavies. "You two, on the floor now."

Muzzy nodded. "We don't want no bloodshed, fella. There's nobody with us. Take it easy." He got on his stomach and placed his hands behind his head.

Oz remained on his feet.

Eric gave him a glance. "English not your first language, sweetie?"

Oz smiled without teeth. "Jus' remembering your face is all."

"Well, while you're busy putting my details in the wank bank, try multitasking and get on your fuckin' stomach."

The man folded his arms in defiance.

Eric looked at Darren and jerked his chin at Oz's direction. Darren pocketed the gun and moved closer. "Let's play nice," he said. "I don't wanna hafta drop you."

The bouncer grinned. "Fuck you, Thrombo, you fuckin' no-mark. You'll be on the floor before me."

Darren shrugged. "Then take the first crack."

Oz swung a powerful standing right that Darren ducked beneath easily. Darren responded with a hard blow to Oz's gut, which bent him forward and left him gasping for air. As the bouncer lifted back his head and tried to draw breath, Darren caught him with a savage left to the jaw.

Oz's eyes lost their focus, and he drooled blood and tooth shards down his chin. He came forward on unsteady legs, flailed a right hook, and walked into a flurry of punches that shattered his jaw and put him on his stomach beside Muzzy.

Darren removed the gun from his pocket, stepped towards Muzzy, and slammed the butt against the back of his neck. The man groaned once and went limp. Darren quickly moved behind Joey's desk and began rummaging through the drawers.

"Forget about tying them up," Eric said. "We'll be gone by the time they come around."

Derek jabbed Joey with his gun and manoeuvred him into the doorway and out onto the stairs. As if awaiting a fusillade of bullets, Joey threw his hands in front of his face and grimaced. When he realised how much of a coward he looked, Joey lowered his hands and coughed with embarrassment.

Derek sniggered and glanced at his brother. "If anybody was out there they woulda already shot him," he said, before adding, "but I guarantee they'll be on their way."

"Then let's not hang around."

Pushing Joey down the steps, the three men checked the shadows of the courtyard for signs of trouble. When they knew they were alone, they opened the back door and emerged onto Kings Mews.

The sweet funk of potent weed filled their nostrils. Eric looked left and saw the brief glow of a joint tip in the shadows of the parking recess. He pushed his gun deeper into Joey's side. The big man winced and whispered: "They're not mine."

Studying the gloom, Eric noticed two small skinny figures in hoodies passing a spliff back and forth. The youths stared back for a few moments, deciding on whether they were a threat, and then returned to the pleasures of their joint.

Derek shoved the fat man in the direction of the car. Joey dragged his feet. Derek pushed him harder. When they reached the vehicle, Eric glanced up and down the street for signs of trouble. It was clear.

Derek unlocked the driver's side door and pulled the seat forward. "Get in," he said.

Joey looked at the car and shivered. "And if I don't?"

"I'm not asking. Get in the back now or I'll break your spine and stuff your crippled arse in the boot."

Joey studied Derek's angry expression for a moment and got in the back seat without further complaint. Darren slid in beside him and jammed a gun against his gut. When the two brothers were sitting in the front seats, Joey said: "Where are you taking me?"

"Not too far," Eric replied. "Just gonna make sure nobody's following us. Then you're on your own."

Derek started the vehicle and took a couple of turns onto Kings Road. He saw the distant blue flicker of police lights in his rearview mirror, heading in the direction of the Trinity Tavern.

"Looks like somebody made that phone call after all," he said.

Joey turned in his seat and stared through the rear window. Another police car whizzed across the junction.

"For fuck's sake," he hissed. "At least nobody will talk."

61.

Charlie used his sleeve to wipe the biggest slivers of broken glass off the driver's seat and into the footwell. He sat down and shifted uncomfortably. Then he frowned at Harry in the rearview mirror. "You know how much one of these windows costs?"

Harry pressed the gun against his shoulder. "No. And I don't much care, either. Stop fuckin' shuffling."

"I'm sitting on pieces of broken glass. It's uncomfortable."

"So's a bullet in the collarbone," Harry replied, pressing harder. "Now get a shift on."

Charlie muttered under his breath and turned the key. He let the car roll down the road, mounted the kerb, and stopped on Harry's drive. The two men got out of the car and Harry pushed Charlie back into the house.

Bonnie was sitting upright on the entrance hall carpet with his broad back against the wall. One-half of his face was swollen and shapeless, and the other bruised and bloody. He blinked uncontrollably and mumbled gibberish that neither Harry nor Charlie understood.

Charlie crouched beside him. "I'm gonna get you to a hospital now, mate. Just hang in there." Then he looked up a Harry. "I need me wallet and phone."

Harry shook his head. "Forget it. There's more than enough petrol in your car to make it to the hospital. If you wanna make some calls, you'll hafta make them there."

Charlie muttered again. He grabbed Bonnie beneath the armpits, hooked an arm up and around his shoulder, and groaned as he lifted him. He wedged his body against Bonnie's and pressed him to the wall.

Charlie bent his knees slightly, wrapped his right arm around the man's thick torso and stepped towards the door. They tottered and swayed but managed to remain on their feet. Charlie shifted his position a couple of times to stop his friend from falling, but they finally made it to the car.

Charlie pressed a hand against Bonnie's chest and kept him upright as he fumbled with the passenger door. After bundling him into the seat, Charlie pulled the belt across and fixed him in place. Then he looked over his shoulder at Harry.

"I'm coming back with guns," he said.

"You'll be wasting your time," Harry replied.

Charlie smiled. "Mebbe I'll find your wife and son instead. Bury them out on the moors."

Harry stepped forward and grabbed him by the throat. He dragged the man back into the house, slammed the door shut, and kicked his feet from under him. Charlie landed on his knees and flapped his fists around but couldn't land a decent punch. Harry hit him in the face several times with the revolver barrel, opening small gashes, and told him to open his mouth.

This time, Charlie flailed more defensively. Harry swatted away his hands and pushed the barrel against his face. Charlie kept his lips together, resisting all attempts to insert the gun.

Harry slammed the gun barrel against Charlie's lips repeatedly until he'd split the top and bottom lips in half and knocked out all his front teeth. He slipped the barrel between gums slick with blood and came in close. Charlie regarded him with wide, blinking eyes.

"Listen to me, you skeletal fuck. You ever threaten my wife and son again, and that'll be the fuckin' end of you. And you know I'm telling the truth, Charlie, 'cause I'm a man of my word.

"If owt ever happens to them, I'll come back here for you and tear down your family tree by its fuckin' roots. You hearing me down there, *cunt?*"

Charlie nodded and mumbled a bloody apology.

"If you come for me and mine then you do it like a fuckin' man. But guess what? I'll be waiting."

The revolver made a popping sound when Harry yanked it from Charlie's mouth. He waved the bloodied gun barrel at the door. "Now go take your friend to the hospital."

Charlie gazed down at the wet patch spreading out from his crotch and down his legs. He spat blood on the carpet as he got to his feet and wobbled out into the night. The door closed behind him.

The engine growled into life, and the car reversed off the drive with a screech. Then it screamed up the street and skidded into the turn.

Harry rushed upstairs and into the master bedroom. He pulled open his bedside table drawer, grabbed three passports and a wad of loose money. He took another fold of notes from his wife's underwear drawer.

Harry went to the bed, picked up Charlie's blade, and pulled the wardrobe forward on its casters. Then he squeezed behind the unit and dropped to his knees. Harry pulled up the carpet in the far corner, exposing the floorboards, poked the blade between the last two boards and gouged up a twelve-inch chunk of wood.

Harry pushed his hand into the hole until he snagged his forearm on a nail. Another push was enough for him to reach a cotton bag that was dangling from it. He wrapped his fingers around the bag and removed it from the hole. Then he replaced the boards, flattened the carpet, and put the wardrobe back as he'd found it.

Harry emptied the bag onto the mattress and stared at it. Here were years of broken laws, broken bones, and the gradual breakdown of his marriage condensed into ten fat rolls of twenties: approximately twenty grand of running money. It wasn't much to show for his endeavour. He picked up the money and dumped it in the holdall on top of the cash he'd received from Alan Piper.

Then he stripped off and jumped in the shower. He washed carefully and cleaned the area around the shredded flesh wound. It opened again, and a trickle of blood flowed down his legs. Grabbing a couple of fresh towels, he pressed one against the wound and wrapped the second around his torso tightly to hold it in place. He put on a loose polo shirt and jeans, pressing down on the makeshift dressing frequently to ensure it stayed in place, and threw some more clothes into the holdall.

He picked up the house phone and dialled a number. It rang for a long time before somebody finally answered.

"This had better be good?"

"Frenchy, it's Harry Sparks."

Albert 'Frenchy' Allen paused for a moment. "Bit late for a social call."

"Because I'm not being sociable."

"That's a pity. I don't like working late."

"Sorry. Can't be helped."

"That'll cost you extra."

"Fair enough."

"What are you after?"

"Just a stitch-up, I think."

"You think, or know?"

"I think. Can't be certain."

"Then you better get over here ASAP," Frenchy replied. "Can you walk? Or do I need to send someone to collect you?"

"I can make it on my own."

"Good. That'll save me time and save you money. How long will you be?"

"Half an hour."

Harry ended the call and phoned for a cab.

62.

Derek pulled into a layby beside a used car lot on Old Station Road and got out of the vehicle. The area was dark and quiet apart from the occasional headlight glare and drone of a passing automobile. There were no residences, just lots of closed commercial units. At this time of night, it wasn't kind of area that people walked through voluntarily without a good reason. Despite this, Derek looked around out of habit and waved Joey out of the car.

"Come on, fat boy. Chop chop."

Joey stomped around the pavement and shook the feeling back into his legs. Then he wrapped his arms around his chest and patted his upper arms to keep warm.

"Now what?"

Derek hitched a thumb over his shoulder. "Now it's time to get some exercise. Back the way we came."

Joey turned in the direction of the roundabout to the A66. "It's a good couple of miles back to the Trinity," he said.

Derek shrugged. "Remind me why I should give a fuck?"

"At least gimme some coins so's I can make a call?"

Derek shook his head. "You're getting nowt from me. Besides, the walk'll do you good, burn some calories."

Joey crouched down and looked through the car window.

"Come on, Eric," he said. "Gimme some dosh, so's I can get back."

Eric didn't bother with eye contact. "You heard the man," he replied. "The sooner you start walking, the better it'll be for you."

Derek climbed back in the car and started the engine. They left Joey shivering in the fading glare of their rear lights, turned right on Imperial, and made their way towards South Bank.

Derek pulled up beside a telephone booth on Normanby Road. Eric entered the cubicle and adjusted his nose to the stench of piss. Then he dialled a number off a scrap of paper that Alan had pushed in his hand.

A lilting Irish voice said: "Hello, Judd residence. Aisling speaking."

"You don't know me, but I know you."

Her voice lost the musical cadence. "Listen, fella; I'm gonna hang up now."

"You wanna know how well I know you?"

"Not really… Goodbye."

"I've seen you in a film."

There was an uncertain pause. "Good for you… Bye now, freak."

"A very naughty film starring you, Alan Piper, and some young bloke with muscles and a hefty cock. It's a very well made amateur production. Lots of angles."

"Ah, Jaysus, did Alan…"

"Yes, Alan recorded your session."

"All… all of it?"

"Every sec."

"That bastard. He promised he wouldn't."

"When it comes to getting women, Alan's promises mean almost nothing."

"Ah, no. And why're you telling me? Is this blackmail?"

"It's not blackmail," Eric replied. "It's a friendly warning."

"Warning? I dunno…"

"Joey's seen the video."

She gasped, tried to speak, but made only consonant sounds.

"He saw everything. He heard all the stuff you said about him."

"Ah, God."

"God won't save you from Joey."

"He's… he's angry?"

"Take a wild fuckin' guess. By the expression on Joey's face, I'd say he's gonna put a serious hurt on you."

"Ah, Jaysus."

"He's not gonna be much help to you either," Eric said. "Look, you've got maybe a couple of hours or so before he gets home. You might have more time than that if I can pull summat off."

"Why're you helping me?"

"Because it's my fault Joey saw the video."

Aisling let out a small sob and sniffled down the line.

"You need to stop crying," Eric said. " What's done is done. Deal with it. Grab whatever money you can and do it now. Pick up that expensive Cartier watch he bought you and put it in a bag along with some clothes. Do you know Joey's safe combo? Then I suggest you use it. Got somewhere you can stay that Joey doesn't know? Get on the phone and arrange it. Then grab your passport, take whatever you can carry and run before he gets home. I'm sorry."

She sobbed again before he hung up. A twinge of guilt tightened his guts. Eric knew that he'd just left Aisling Judd to an uncertain fate, but he also knew he had to side with Darren. It was amazing how one stupid mistake had caused all this damage, how one moment of greed had changed so many lives forever. It should have been fifty grand of easy money. But today had been anything but easy. Next time would be easier. He'd plan more thoroughly. He'd choose his partners with a lot more care. No more stupid mistakes.

He dialled another number. The operator asked what service he wanted. He kept the call short and sweet. He told them about the bag of heroin he'd hidden at Joey's (although he neglected to mention his part in hiding it), and where it was hidden. To speed up the process he also told them he'd seen men with guns, and that another fight had broken out, and he was worried about people's welfare. When they asked him for his name and location, he told them he was a concerned passer-by and hung up.

Eric got back in the car. His brother started the engine.

"Where to now?" he asked.

Eric hooked a thumb over his shoulder towards Darren. "We drop him off," he replied. "And then we should think about laying low for a while."

Harry sat on a makeshift medical table in a makeshift operating theatre in Albert 'Frenchy' Allen's spare bedroom. He wondered just how clean this pokey room with cheap floral wallpaper was. There was an unpleasant smell behind the overpowering stench of disinfectant and medical alcohol. The carpets had disturbing discolorations and stains. He wondered how many were blood.

Harry winced as Frenchy stitched his stomach with a skin stapler. Despite the local anaesthetic, Harry flinched with every stapler click. Frenchy snorted with amusement behind his surgical mask.

"Stop being a baby. You've been anaesthetised."

Frenchy laid the stapler beside some bloodstained surgical tweezers that rested in a kidney tray. He picked up a single shotgun pellet fragment between his fingers. It wasn't much to behold.

"You got lucky."

"I know."

Frenchy shook his head. "I don't think you do. This fragment looks like it came from a large piece of shot. A few more inches toward you and your guts would resemble an explosion in a sausage factory."

Frenchy dropped the fragment back in the dish and removed his latex gloves. He pulled down his mask, took a couple of steps back, and studied the work he'd just finished. His fat, florid face was expressionless for a few moments, although his thick salt-and-pepper moustache occasionally twitched, then his mouth curved up in a small smile. "That should hold you for a while."

"Will they tear?"

Frenchy shrugged. "Depends. If you start running and jumping around, then they will tear. But if you're careful, and rest up for a few days, you shouldn't have any problems."

Frenchy removed his blood-stained surgical smock and placed it in a black plastic bag that he dropped on the floor. Then he dabbed antiseptic on a clean surgical pad and wiped it around the wound area before taping a fresh bandage over the stitches.

Frenchy crouched down and pulled a package of bandages and a small carton of surgical tape from a cardboard box on the floor. He placed them on the table beside Harry. "The main thing is preventing infection. Change the dressing regularly and keep the wound clean."

He left the room and came back with a small pill bottle that he placed beside the dressings. "Some antibiotics to help fight any infection. Two a day should last you a fortnight. After that, if you maintain good hygiene I expect you'll heal without complications. You might need a Tetanus injection if you haven't already had one."

"I'm covered."

Harry eased off the table and reached into his holdall. He peeled seven hundred and fifty off one of the rolls and pressed the money into Frenchy's hand. Harry tried to explain his wound, and warned the surgeon not to say anything. Frenchy pinched his thumb and forefinger together and shook his head.

"The less you tell, the less I can say under duress."

Harry put on a grey polo shirt and let it hang over his jeans. He slipped into his trainers and jacket and picked up the holdall. Frenchy led him down the stairs and into his dusty entrance hall. "If you're getting a cab, you might want to walk up the road a while. Cabbies sometimes have a tendency to talk."

Harry walked until he reached James Cook Hospital and phoned a cab to pick him up from there. He told the cabbie to drop him at the end of Eileen's street.

He was looking forward to reuniting his family.

There were a lot of apologies to make.

64.

Sebastian James ran electric shears roughly over Jonno's severed head. The motor screamed several times when it ran into tough patches that were thick with product. Clumps of waxed hair fell into a cotton bag that also contained his teeth.

When he'd finished, Seb tossed the hairless head into a drove of large pigs that fought over it aggressively. He sheared hair from other body parts and tossed them into other pens. The pigs went wild for their share of the flesh. The sound of their frenzy reverberated off the unit's ceilings and walls.

Seb turned away and back towards Ramon. His broad face was ruddy from a combination of the cold weather and anger. Goosebumps dotted his bare forearms. He wiped his gloved hands on a dirty apron.

"This is gonna cost you, lad."

"You owe me a favour."

He nodded his curly blonde head. "Aye, one body for free. I know I might be a lowly farmer, with only a few GCSEs to my name, but my arithmetic skills are good enough to count to eight."

"So you want seven grand?"

"I charge a grand a corpse under normal circumstances. What you've brought me is anything but normal."

Ramon sighed. "Okay. Then what are you after?"

Seb lifted three plush cases from his apron pocket and opened them. "I want these."

Ramon craned forward and inspected the watches. He noted the Patek Phillipe and the Rolex – they didn't come cheap.

"I found these hidden in the Chinese fella's pockets."

"How much are they worth?"

Seb gave him a faint smile. "A lot more than seven grand."

"How much more?"

"Somewhere in the region of thirty."

"That's a lotta bread."

"These are a lot of corpses."

"If I say no?"

"Then you can take the rest of the bodies and be on your merry."

"But…"

"Look, I usually have to starve these pigs for twenty-four hours just to fully dispose of a couple of bodies. You've brought me *eight* of the things with no bloody warning, lad. I'm gonna need to chop them up, refrigerate the pieces, shear their heads and pubes, remove their teeth, and then dump them discretely along with the clothes. Then I need to keep starving the pigs. That's a lot of work.

"What if there's a random inspection? They do happen, you know. How do I explain the curious case of the fridge full of corpses? You've given me a good four days worth of work here, and a lot of potential trouble."

Ramon shrugged. "Fair point. Keep 'em."

He saw no point in arguing. He hadn't known about the watches when he'd folded Billy into the same suitcase as Jonno, and Seb could have kept their existence to himself. Losing them was a price worth paying for the permanent disposal of eight inconvenient problems.

"Will you phone me when you dispose of the last one?" he added.

Seb nodded again. "Bear in mind it'll take a few days. I'll send you a text from a burner whatever the outcome," he replied. "I'll write: 'All's golden, amigo,' if things are good. Or I'll text: 'A bad case of indigestion, brother,' if there's a problem."

"I've dumped my burner," Ramon replied. "The less that links me with this mess, the better. I've got your number at home. When I get the new handset, I'll send you a text with four hashtags. That way you've got the new number."

"Cool."

Ramon nodded. "Thanks, Seb."

"You're welcome. Tell your lads to put the rest of the cases near the shed."

Ramon left the unit and wandered back to the people carrier where his men were waiting. They looked bored. Frank stared at the first glimmers of dawn light creeping over the uneven horizon. The sound of crunching gravel made him turn and look.

"Are we okay, boss."

Ramon smiled ruefully. "Not quite. It cost me."

"How much?"

"Billy had some very expensive watches."

"But you get to keep the cash, right?"

"Aye."

"Well, that's summat, at least."

"True. But them watches were worth thirty grand."

"You did kinda drop this on him."

"True."

"So whadda we gonna now? We gonna put a contract out on Harry?"

Ramon shook his head. "I don't want owt linking us with this shit. I'm pretty sure nobody will give a fuck about Billy and his lot. They all looked like junkies – and it's in their nature to disappear. So I think we're clear on that front.

"Jonno didn't have a family, and I'm pretty sure most of the others didn't either. Jonno frowned on wives and kids, which were why he always moaned about Harry. If there's a missing person's report, then mebbe the Filth will look into it for about ten minutes. But Jonno's people are smart enough to keep their fuckin' mouths shut, and pretty soon these bodies are gonna be nowt but pig shit, so there won't be owt to find.

"Now that we've wiped and dumped all the burners too there's nowt concrete linking us with this shit."

"Except Harry and ToJo."

Ramon grinned. "Harry's gone by now. Like Lord Lucan were what he said. And ToJo's gone forever, too. By Monday he'll be Toby Jones again, working admin at his Dad's brewery, with nice neat hair and trousers that actually fuckin' fit him. We'll visit the prick, lean on him, warn him that his time with us were just a bad fuckin' dream. That should be enough to scare him into permanent silence."

"And the Stanton brothers? Are you gonna give 'em a free pass?"

Ramon lifted both arms and let them drop to his sides. "At the end of the day, we got paid. I don't really care much about the how and the why."

Frank eyed him. "Which leaves Bobby, dunnit? He's the only other one who can link us with all this, right?"

The mention of Bobby's name made Ramon frown. He rubbed his chin until it was red and then he pulled at bottom lip nervously. It was obvious when he thought about it.

"It were Bobby," he said. "He planned it."

Frank's mouth formed an O of surprise. "You think?"

"Had to be. It would explain Billy's presence. Junky talk and all that shite. Bobby knew the routine, he's a junky, so always needs the money, and he's smart enough to plan summat like this. After all, he set up this fuckin' deal in the first place."

"Then he's gotta go."

"Right, he's gotta go."

Frank rubbed his hands together. "I'll find him and make him disappear."

Ramon smiled. "Fuck it. There's an easier way. And if it works it might even act as a warning for the Stantons."

The cab parked beside a neat row of bungalows. Harry paid the driver and waited until he pulled away and turned the corner. When he was certain the coast was clear, he walked until he reached a junction and turned into Eileen's street. When he arrived at her front door, he knocked a couple of times and waited.

There was commotion coming from inside. It sounded like Barbara and Eileen arguing. Their voices were too low for Harry to recognise the words, but he didn't need words to realise that his wife was angry. It was at that point that he knew this reunion was only going to go the one way.

The door snapped open. Harry pasted on his best smile and tried to appear casual.

Barbara didn't bother with a smile. Her face was red and puffy with anger and other emotions. There were old tear tracks in her make-up, and some of her mascara had run. Eileen hung back in the hallway with a sheepish expression on her face. She shook her head and mouthed the word sorry. Barbara noticed the direction of her husband's gaze and turned towards her mother. "I want a conversation with Harry. *Alone*."

"I'll be inside if you nee…"

"Go away. *Now*."

Eileen backed into the living and closed the door.

Barbara scowled at him. "You hit our son."

"Babe, I didn…"

"Don't even bother making excuses. I don't wanna hear them."

"Listen, I'm…"

"I'm *done* listening to you, Harry. I've heard all the excuses, all the bullshit, and I'm sick of them. You took our boy to a bloody Heroin deal, and then you exposed him to armed robbery. And when everything went wrong, you took out your anger on a five-year-old boy who had no idea what was going on."

"Listen, it's…"

"Shut up. I'm not done talking. That's just one of your many flaws,

Harry; you don't know when to let me speak. You think because I'm a woman, that my little female brain can't process all the intricacies of your job – if I can call it that."

"Can I speak now?"

"Don't you *dare* get the hump with me. Who the bloody hell d'you think you are? That bruise under Terry's eye is so black and blue I'm gonna have to keep him off school for the rest of the week. He's terrified. It took me hours to get him to sleep. Christ, he's probably awake now, sobbing his heart out."

"Can I talk to him?"

"No you bloody well can't. You've done enough damage."

Harry bristled. "Don't tell me what I can and can't do."

A nasty smile appeared on Barbara's face. "Oh, are you gonna push me out the way, maybe slap me around a bit? Maybe get in a two-for-one? Smack both of us around on the same day? What a big man you are. My hero."

"I didn't mean…"

"Keep your excuses," she said, shaking her head sadly. Leaning against the doorframe, she gazed at her husband of eight years without a trace of love in her eyes. "I don't care anymore. Just go away."

"Maybe I should come back tomorrow, like. Give you a chance to calm down a bit."

"Did I *say* come back tomorrow? Did I?"

"But…"

"You just don't get it, do you? D'you think I want a *Heroin* dealer for a husband? D'you think I'll just put up with you using Terry as some kind of front for your bullshit?"

"Listen, I'm not…"

"Not what?"

"I'm not doing that anymore, sweets. I'm out."

She fluttered her eyelashes theatrically and clasped her hands to her bosom. "Oh, you're not doing it anymore? Well, that's all right then, come on in, sweetheart, and make yourself right at home."

Harry backed away slightly, horrified by the anger on her face.

"You think just because you're out *now* that I'm just gonna let the last several months slide then you're sorely mistaken. I'm done, Harry. *We're* done. I want a divorce. And if you're as smart as you like to think you are you'll gimme what I want on the quiet."

"If I don't?"

Her eyes glittered. Her jaw flexed. "Don't go there. Seriously, don't test me."

Harry backed into the driveway. Barbara followed him

"I've been unhappy for a while. Only you've been too deluded to see it. Oh, I knew you were a villain when we married, but not Heroin, not *serious* stuff. I told myself it's just stolen electronics, weed, pills, roughing up the occasional villain. So maybe *I'm* the delusional one? I heard stories, of course, often wondered why we had so much money, but I put them at the back of my mind. I told myself that deep down you're a decent bloke."

Harry noticed that he was standing on the pavement and stopped moving. Barbara came forward and jabbed his chest with a forefinger. So Harry began stepping back again.

"I'm the deluded one," she added. "I must be. A decent bloke wouldn't sell *that* filth, and he certainly wouldn't use a child to cover his tracks. And any self-respecting wife and mother wouldn't put up with it, either. And, you know what? I'm gonna show some self-respect for once in my miserable life and send you packing."

"Sweets…"

"Don't. Just don't, Harry. At least show some decency and leave us alone."

Her anger had faded into pain, and new tears rolled down her face. She wiped them away and sniffled. "Don't expect me to forgive you just because you're out from under Jonno. I can't forgive you for this. I *won't* forgive you for this."

She turned her back on him and walked back towards the house.

"Babs…"

"Don't Babs me. I always hated that nickname."

"Since when?"

"Since forever." She stopped on the doorstep and looked over her shoulder. "Only you were too selfish to notice, and I was too in love to let you know. But now – it feels like the right time to say how I feel. So long, Harry."

She closed the door. Harry called her name a few times. The door remained shut. The living room curtains didn't twitch.

It felt like somebody had scooped Harry's heart from his chest and left behind an aching cavity. Tears bubbled up to the surface, but he fought the sensation and swallowed them back. Harry walked to the end of the street, turned the corner, and sat on the nearest garden wall. Staring at the pavement for what seemed like forever, he counted the ways in which he had failed his family. He was still totting up the number when he decided to do the right thing for once in his life.

He texted Eileen: *Sneak out the house when u have the chance. Got ur Xmas hamper money plus a little xtra as interest. Don't tell Barbara.*

Eileen made him wait quite some time.

Harry was still tallying his failures when she turned the corner in her blue fleece dressing gown and matching slippers. Shivering and huffing, she wrapped her arms around her chest to keep warm. He stepped away from the wall and waved her over.

She came in close. "What the hell are you doing, Harry? If Barbara finds out I'm here she'll have a fit."

Harry reached into the bag and removed a roll. He peeled off five hundred and pressed it into her hand. "For your troubles."

She blinked at the money.

"I told you you'd get it back with interest."

Eileen quickly dropped the cash inside one of her gown pockets.

Harry pointed at them. "How deep are they?"

Eileen frowned for a moment and pushed both hands inside the dressing gown. "Up to my wrist. Why?"

"Do you still play bingo?"

"Every fortnight."

"What's the monthly full house jackpot?"

"Fifteen grand."

"You think you can fit it in that gown?"

Eileen's jaw dropped a touch. "Are you joking?"

"Does it look like I am?"

She shook her head slowly. "No. It really doesn't."

"Then that answers your question."

One–by-one Harry handed Eileen rolls of money that she stuffed into her pockets. By the time she'd finished, the dressing gown bulged with cash. She grinned in disbelief.

"Now listen to me."

Eileen eventually managed to divert her attention from the cash. She was still smiling.

"Can you hide this money?" Harry asked.

Eileen thought about it and nodded.

"I mean somewhere safe from everyone – Len included."

"I have places. Various cigarette hiding spots that Len doesn't know about."

"Good. Make sure you hide it well. Wait a month or two, to avoid suspicion, then announce that you've won the jackpot."

"I take it none of this money's for Len and me?"

"Keep some aside, for your troubles, but use the rest to send Babs back to university," he said. "Tell her that you want to do summat for her with the winnings. She'll try and turn it down. Be insistent and tell her she can pay you back when she's in a high-paid job. You might need to insist a few times.

"If there's owt left over, use it to support Babs and Terry a while. If you need more cash then get in touch and I'll send it over. They can't go home yet, maybe not ever. I dunno for sure."

Eileen smiled. "I'll look after her. I'll put a little aside for Len and me. Maybe enough for a week in Spain, but I promise the rest goes on her education and looking after Terry. They'll want for nowt."

Harry nodded. "Then I guess this is it."

Eileen paused for a moment. She put her hand on Harry's shoulder and squeezed gently. "She might forgive you eventually."

"I can't wait that long. And I'm not sure I deserve it."

"Did you put things right? You know, with the, ahem, trouble?"

"In a fashion."

Her hand dropped from his shoulder. "I tried not to say owt. But that bruise on Terry's face just went darker and darker. I couldn't lie to her. I'm sorry."

Harry shook his head. "You've got nowt to be sorry for. This is all my fault."

Eileen fixed her eyes on his. "Look after yourself."

"You too. And take care of Babs and Terry."

"With my life," she replied.

"If you ever have to risk your life, I want you to call me. I'll deal with it."

She began to turn away. "Where'll you go?"

"Far away from here," Harry replied. He thought about Thailand, Vietnam, Cambodia, India, and other hot places where he could sweat himself clean and start afresh. Places where his money would stretch while he decided what it was he wanted to do with the rest of his life. He had a lot of options.

"Goodbye, Harry."

She placed her hands in the pockets, to prevent the cash from falling out, and walked away quickly. Once she turned the corner and disappeared from view, Harry stood for a while and resumed count of his failings and regrets. Once he'd finished, he realised the only things he didn't regret in his life were his wife and son.

Then he sat back on the wall and wept quietly.

Joey couldn't stop sweating. What little hair he had was matted to his scalp. His drenched shirt clung to the folds and bulges of his body. Occasionally he checked his reflection in parked car windows and each time it disgusted him. His legs ached in ways he never knew possible, and the inside of his thighs had been rubbed raw. It had been years since he'd walked any further than the distance from the front door to the car and from the car to the Trinity. His body wasn't used to this level of exercise. Now, all he wanted was a hot shower and a fresh change of clothes.

What he got was the police.

Joey noticed the ruckus at the corner of Conyers Way. Police cars and vans blocked the road. Flashing blue lights bounced off nearby buildings. Uniformed pigs of all ranks ran around frantically. Some pointed fingers and gesticulated. A few plainclothes types watched from the edges and attempted to blend in with the mob of gawkers surrounding the place.

Joey couldn't believe that the police were still here. Somebody in the Trinity must have kicked off and caused a scene. Once he knew their identity he'd have them kneecapped.

He walked down the road at pace. By the time he reached the Trinity, he was short of breath and glistening with fresh sweat. He recognised one of the officers and tipped him a nod and a wink.

Constable Ryan Douglas – rake-thin, baby-faced, and with a penchant for spilling his guts in exchange for drinks and the occasional fifty-pound note – looked straight through him as if he didn't exist and blocked his path to the front door.

Joey raised his hands to shoulder height. "Would some fucker mind telling me what's going on?"

Ryan ignored the familiarity. "Please watch your language, sir."

"Oh, that's fuckin' canny, that is. Nice to see me tax money hard at work messing with a law-abiding businessman."

Ryan backed away and found a senior officer. The constable whispered in the hawkish man's ear and pointed at Joey. The officer looked Joey up and down a few times and nodded. He approached Joey with a confident, stiff-backed gait and stood ramrod straight before him with a couple of grinning helpers on each side.

"Are you Joseph Judd?"

"Only me Mam calls me Joseph," he added and grinned. "Can I go inside now?"

He was surprised to find the officer reading him his rights. He was even more surprised to be charged with drugs and firearms offences.

He didn't let people deal or take drugs in his establishment and firearms were only distributed to a select few. Anybody carrying weapons always went out the back door on the rare occasions the police came in through the front. Either somebody had been carrying serious weight when things had kicked off earlier in the evening, or the whole situation was a frame-up – with local pigs looking for help with their pension funds.

Somebody was going to pay all right, but it wouldn't be him.

As Joey was being cuffed, an officer wearing latex gloves went past carrying a box of salted peanuts. He opened it for the senior officer, who inspected the contents carefully.

"Oh, is it against the law to be in possession of fuckin' peanuts now?" Joey snapped. "I know there's an allergy risk, and all that, but last time I checked they weren't considered an offensive fuckin' weapon. Besides, they're entirely legitimate and paid for, I might add."

Both men smiled and turned their gazes on him. There was a malevolent glint in the hawkish officer's eye, an arrogance that made Joey feel very alone and vulnerable. Another officer exited the building with Oz's gun in an evidence bag. A cold chill that had more to do with the situation than damp clothes and cold night air settled in Joey's bones. That gun had been used to injure people and was probably on more than one set of ballistics reports.

Joey demanded his lawyer as a couple of grinning policemen cuffed and loaded him into the back of a car. As the car pulled away, he thought about the amount of time Eric had taken downstairs while he sat upstairs with Darren watching him. It was more than enough time to hide something he might want easily found, which got him thinking about Darren's earlier phone call about the heroin. Maybe Eric had grabbed the merchandise, after all? And maybe he was a much smarter operator than Joey had realised.

The fat man threw back his head and guffawed. The two officers escorting him to the station didn't like this and asked what was so funny?

Joey shook his head and told them they wouldn't understand.

He knew that his expensive solicitor would argue that he hadn't been in the Trinity that evening and knew nothing about drugs or guns. He would strong-arm and bribe enough willing witnesses to corroborate his version of events. He already knew who the fall guy would be. Joey would make Oz take the hit for both offences in exchange for cash and the promise that he would help smuggle him out of the country before it went to trial. The fact that he was going to have to go to some trouble to extricate himself from this unpleasant situation irritated him immensely. Still, Joey couldn't help but admire the way he'd been stitched up. Grinning like a fool, he stared at his feet and muttered under his breath:

"Eric, you clever cunt."

67.

A week later, while Harry Sparks was waiting in a Heathrow departure lounge for his flight to Bangkok, while Eric and Derek Stanton were smoking weed and discussing who they should raid next, and while Joey Judd was convincing Owen 'Oz' Osman to accept ten grand cash and a place in the back of a Hollis Haulage truck to the Costa del Sol in exchange for taking the blame for the gun and the heroin, Bobby Manning hobbled on crutches across a road of crumbling, pitted tarmac and over a patch of dogshit strewn grass so that he could enter a Southbank junky hovel through the back door.

He performed a rhythmic sequence of knocks and waited for the gate to open. A slim effeminate man with sallow skin and shoulder length hair let Bobby into a high-walled courtyard littered with rubbish. The man stepped back and wiped his hands on his tight white t-shirt and butt-hugging blue jeans, curling his lip as though he'd just touched something disgusting. He stared at the cast, the crutches, and the poorly bandaged ears with barely disguised amusement.

"Upset somebody, did we?"

Bobby glowered back. "You've got some fella's pubes between your front teeth, Fran."

Francis Clarke picked at his teeth with his fingernails until he realised it was a wind-up. "Oh, you're fuckin' hilarious."

Bobby grinned. "It's not even ten in the fuckin' morning, and you've already gobbed a punter off?"

Francis held up two fingers. "Couple of punters, actually."

"Filthy bastard."

"I'm not the one who sticks that muck in me veins."

"No, you just take yours up the shitter."

"Nobody puts *anything* up there," he said, drawing close. "I'm strictly all mouth." He slowly brought up his right hand to his lips and simulated smoking, but then raised his left and mimicked cupping and stroking an imaginary set of balls as he opened his mouth and performed fake fellatio.

He kept his eyes locked on Bobby and smiled as the junky began to look uncomfortable and slowly edged away.

"Is Sami in?"

Francis stopped performing his mimicry. "Mebbe he is and mebbe he isn't," he replied. "Besides, I thought you was Billy Chin's bitch?"

Shifting his body weight, Bobby gripped his clutches tightly and prepared to move past the rent boy. "Step out of me way."

Folding his arms and cocking his hip, Francis remained in front of Bobby. "You ever thought that mebbe Sami don't wanna sell to you?"

Bobby shook one of the crutches near Francis' face. "If you don't step out me way, I'm gonna fuckin' clobber you with this."

Francis sighed and pulled back the black metal shutter to allow Bobby to open the door and shuffle into the house.

A candle lamp swung back-and-forth from a hook in the kitchen ceiling, sending his shadow sliding around the room. The light danced across boxes and cartons littering the lino and for a moment it seemed as if the entire floor was moving. Even the pipes and loose wires jutting from graffiti-covered walls appeared to have a life of their own. For a few seconds, Bobby thought he was reliving an old acid trip. He blinked his eyes and took a few deep of breaths of piss-infused air until the feeling passed. He readjusted his crutches, which were squeaking unpleasantly against the sticky vinyl floor.

"Ow! What fucker's causing all that palaver in there?" shouted a voice from the next room. "Gerrin here now, you squeaky piece of shit."

Bobby clomped into the candlelit living room. An Asian man in a black sweater and jeans sneered at him from the comfort of a tattered sofa. Beside him, a skinny blonde teen in tight hotpants ran her hands through his messy black hair and stared blankly into the distance. The man lifted his slippered feet off the ground and rested them on a coffee table that consisted of a plank of veneered MDF nailed to a couple of plastic storage boxes. His gaze angled towards the crutches.

"If it in't Long John Silver," he said with a smirk. "Where's the parrot?"

Bobby gave him a weak smile. "Hello, Sami."

"What happened to you?"

"Long story."

Sami clicked his fingers a couple of times. "Edited highlights."

Bobby shuffled. "Don't wanna go into it right now."

Sami turned to the girl. "Oooh, look at him, all sensitive and shit."

The impassive teen continued stroking his hair and nodded a couple of times. When Sami realised she was ignoring him, he rolled his eyes and focused his attention back on Bobby. "Then what are you here for, like?"

"Whaddaya think?"

"I don't think owt. It's been a while since you've knocked on me door, so I dunno whatcha into nowadays."

"Aitch."

Sami nodded. "Ow much you after?"

"What can I get for two hundred?"

Sami got off the sofa and brushed himself down. He clicked his fingers once and told the girl to get lost. She vacated the room slowly and stomped up the stairs at an even more ponderous pace. When he heard the loud slam of a bedroom door, Sami retrieved an electric scale from behind the sofa and placed it on the coffee table. He put a small piece of paper on the scale and compensated for the weight by setting the display back to zero. Then Sami pushed his hand inside the sofa and removed a small dented cocoa container. He spooned powder from the container and dropped it on the paper, occasionally pausing to check the measurement.

His eyes drifted up to the ceiling and narrowed. He stopped scooping heroin and pointed the spoon upwards.

"You hear summat?"

"Like what?"

"Footsteps."

"What footsteps. I don't hear owt."

"That silly bitch is doing summat up there," Sami said. "Go check it out for us."

Bobby coughed. "I'm on crutches."

Sami shrugged. "And I'm measuring your medication. Look, fella, if you really wanna buy from me, then you better go and find out what she's up to."

Bobby groaned and said okay. He struggled out of the living room and his crutches thumped against the steps. When Sami realised Bobby wasn't coming back in a hurry, he removed a small sachet from his trouser pocket, opened it, and poured the white powdery contents into the Heroin. He stirred them together carefully with the spoon, so that it was perfectly combined, put the paper back in his trousers and waited.

Bobby came back into the living room. His face was red with effort, and he panted for breath. "Right waste of me fuckin' time that were. She were just laying on the bed."

"She weren't doing nowt filthy like fingering herself, were she?"

"You think I'da come straight back down if she were sinking the pink?"

Sami wafted his hand at the paper. "There's your shit. Check it."

Bobby stepped forward and studied the display. "Bit light, innit?"

"Me going rate's changed since you've been buying from Billy."

"Not for the better."

"Ey, you wanna quibble over the price then piss off and leave me in peace," Sami replied, wafting his hand at the door. "That's right, fella. Off you fuck."

"Fine, fine, I'll take it."

"Mighty fuckin' big of you," Sami said, holding out his hand. "Payment please."

Bobby rested on his left crutch and hunted through his jacket pockets with his right. He pulled out a wad of crumpled twenties and pushed them into the dealer's hand. He counted the notes carefully and held them up in the candle light.

"It's all there," Bobby said. "It's all real."

Sami regarded Bobby coldly. "The day I take a junky at his word is the day I retire penniless from this fuckin' business." When he finished counting, Sami flapped his hand at the powder. "It's all yours."

Bobby folded the paper carefully around the Heroin and lifted it off the scales. "You mind if I do some here?"

Sami nodded. "Yeah, I do mind."

"Billy always lets me shoot up on-site."

"I know I'm Asian," Sami replied. "But do I look like Billy?"

Bobby shook his head.

"That's right, fella, because I'm a different kinda Asian. And d'you see any bagheads cluttering up me place?"

Bobby shook his head again.

"Because there's a no junky policy," Sami added, pointing in the direction of the kitchen. "All that fuckin' filth out there's from the days when I *did* allow you lot to get all leisurely at me expense."

Bobby put the sachet in his pocket. "Well, I'll be seeing you then."

Sami waved him away. As soon as the junky had shambled out of the room, Sami cocked his head and waited, first for the slam of the back door closing and then for the clack of crutches in the courtyard. When he was certain that Bobby wasn't coming back, he picked up a mobile phone and dialled a number.

"Yeah? Whosis?"

"It's Sami."

"Yeah?"

"It's done."

"Bobby?"

"Who the fuck else would I be referring to?"

"You sure it'll put him down?"

"I gave him enough fentanyl to wipe out an entire fuckin' football team. You have me guarantee that the moment he uses he's a goner."

"Then I'll pay you later today."

Ramon had contacted most of the dealers in the Teesside area and offered them all the same deal: the first person to give Bobby Manning a hot dose would get a two grand bonus. Sami didn't ask why, because he didn't care; it wasn't his business, he just wanted the money.

He ended the call, sat back, and smiled.

After a few seconds, he began to laugh.

68.

The next day, Eric parked his car in a street near Marianne's flat block and exited the vehicle. As he turned the corner and approached the building, Eric thought about a proposition he had for Bobby: did he want to make their temporary arrangement into something more permanent?

Maybe Bobby knew other dealers who were susceptible to quick strikes and random attacks? Maybe he could trade what he knew for an equal share of the take? The right information was worth paying for.

Eric stopped for a moment when he saw something that disturbed him out of his thoughts. A crowd of onlookers were being shepherded away from a barrier by a couple of uniformed police officers. Several other officers and a couple of paramedics milled around behind two diagonally parked police cars and a coroner's van. The crowd craned their necks to get a good look at the proceedings.

Eric joined the crowd and lingered at its edge. He caught the eye of the nearest gawker and asked: "What's going on?"

A bald, stocky man in blue overalls pointed at the building. "Couple of smackheads OD'd."

"Who?" Eric asked, despite already knowing the answer.

"Some little blonde lass and her fella. Her Dad came round this morning, while we was working on the electrics a couple of floors below. The old fella must've let hisself in, coz he let out a right yell and started shouting for help. The door were already open when we arrived upstairs, and the poor old bugger were bawling his eyes out on the living room floor."

"D'you see the bodies?"

The man nodded. "Couldn't miss the poor sods. The lass were on the bed in her undies, and her fella were on the sofa. Both was white as sheets with needles poking out their arms. The place stank summat awful. They must've been dead all night, I reckons."

"Where's her Dad?"

The man shrugged. "Got taken away about fifteen minutes ago. He were proper broken up about it. Not that I blames the poor bugger, what with his daughter the way she was."

Eric cast another glance at the building as he backed away. Although he couldn't be certain, the situation reeked of a hot dose. Bobby was smart enough to know his measurements and bright enough to buy them from trusted suppliers. The problem for him was that it was easy for somebody else to learn the names of those providers, too. A smart individual could offer a dealer an incentive to look out for a particular junky and poison his dose. Creatures of habit like drug users couldn't stay hidden for long; sooner or later they had to surface and buy more dope. If enough dealers had the same incentive, then the junky wouldn't last long.

In the days following the Forum job, Eric had called in a couple of favours and asked around discreetly about certain people. Billy hadn't shown up at any of his squats, and none of his junkies had heard from him, either. Jonno had disappeared, and several of his people were also nowhere to be seen. Ramon, on the other hand, was alive and well and partying hard in Chapeltown.

So this had to be Ramon's handiwork.

Eric wasn't sure if Bobby's death was revenge or a warning, but he knew that his days of swanning around in public without a care in the world were over, and his comfortable life had ended. New enemies like Ramon and Joey could easily find out where he lived and send professionals over to take care of him. He intended not to be there when they arrived.

He went back to the car and phoned his brother.

"Whaddayou want?"

"Nice manners."

"Get fucked."

"Spoken like a true English gentleman."

"You're starting to fuckin' irritate me."

"Only *starting* to?"

"I'm gonna hang up now."

Eric sighed. "Hang on a sec. Are you at home?"

Derek paused. "Yeah, why?"

"'Cause I think you should leave. Like now."

"Why?"

"Bobby's dead."

"That's no fuckin' surprise. Junkies die all the time."

"I think it was a hot dose."

Derek paused again. "You think it were Ramon?"

"With a little help from some dealer."

"You think we're next?"

"I dunno. But better safe than sorry."

"You wanna leave town for awhile?"

"Fifteen grand's not gonna last long."

"Better than nowt."

"But not by much."

"Then we *are* gonna keep doing this?"

Eric turned the ignition. The engine coughed and sputtered. "Definitely."

"Well, I guess I'm leaving."

"Go to Toby's for now."

"He's not gonna be happy we're crashing at his again."

"He'll cope for a few days. Then we'll arrange summat else."

Derek sniffed. "You going back to yours?"

"Why bother?"

There were no family photos, no possessions that he couldn't afford to lose, and the clothes on his back and his wallet were pretty much the only things he owned. His deposit was a pittance; the landlord could keep it. He had no reason to return.

"Then I'll see you at Toby's."

"Yeah, see you."

Eric put the car in gear and hit the accelerator. He spared a quick thought for Bobby and his girlfriend and then pushed it away to the back of mind.

He had people to see and money to steal.

THANK YOU!

Thank you for buying the latest Stanton brothers' novel. I hope you enjoyed it. If you did, and if you have the time, then please leave me an Amazon review.

Your reviews are very important. Firstly, they let me know I did something right (or wrong); secondly, they let other readers know that my work is worth buying (or not, as the case may be); and lastly, your reviews help boost the novel's profile on Amazon. Independent authors, like me, need all the help we can get in this regard. We lack the advertising budgets of the big publishers, so reader reviews play a big part in advertising our work.

I aim to provide readers with the best possible ebook and paperback experience, so if the quality of this work falls short then please let me know and I'll do my best to correct it. I hate reading badly edited and formatted books as much as you do. It's even worse when I'm the one responsible for a badly put together piece of crap. So if there are issues that I can correct, please do let me know.

The Stantons will be back in 2017 in the novella *Sexy Lexy*, and the short story *Get Santa*. They also have a cameo role in the Mark Kandinsky novel *The Amsterdamned* (also scheduled for next year).

And don't forget, you can get *The Greatest Show in Town (and other shorts)* (including several Stanton Brothers' short stories) for FREE when you sign up for my mailing list at *www.martinstanleyauthor.com*, along with future access to other exclusive, never-before-published Stanton brothers' short stories.

Printed in Great Britain
by Amazon